for Kayla and Bella, the belly rub queens

Ω

Copyright © 2013 by Kenneth Finkelstein
First Edition – August 2013

ISBN
978-1-4602-1968-3 (Hardcover)
978-1-4602-1969-0 (Paperback)
978-1-4602-1970-6 (eBook)

All rights reserved.
Copyright © 2013 Kenneth Finkelstein
www.kennethfinkelstein.com

Cover image:photographer: Leigh Prather purchased on Shutterstock.com

This book is a work of fiction. Names, characters, places and incidents are either the product of the author's imagination or are used fictitiously. Any resemblance to actual persons, living or dead, events or locales is entirely coincidental.

Produced by:

FriesenPress
Suite 300 – 852 Fort Street
Victoria, BC, Canada V8W 1H8

www.friesenpress.com

Distributed to the trade by The Ingram Book Company

KENNETH FINKELSTEIN

searching for
SHACKLETON

"I know from my own painful searching,
with its many blind alleys,
how hard it is to take a reliable step,
be it ever so small,
towards the understanding of that
which is truly significant."
-Albert Einstein

Chapter 1
Poof!

In the middle of this road we call our life
I found myself in a dark wood
With no clear path through
-Dante Alighieri

The ground trembled.

"I don't understand. What are you saying? You're leaving me? This is what you want? Is it? Life without me? Are you serious? You've thought about this? How could you? How?! The thought of me being without you has never, ever, entered my head. No, I won't let it happen. We took vows. You can't break us up, break our bond, get up and go just like that. No, absolutely not. Do you hear what I'm saying? You're not looking at me when I'm talking to you. Look at me! The answer is no. Do you hear me? No!

"We have issues. I know. You've told me. Maybe I didn't listen to you before. Maybe I didn't want to listen, hoping that whatever problems we have would go away on their own. It's not like I was ignoring you. I heard you but I didn't want to fight, that's all. You know I don't like confrontation. It scares me. But I'm listening now. I am. I'll talk about anything you want. Whatever the problem is, whatever's bothering you, let's talk about it, work it out. We can do this. I know we can. You have to try. Both of us have to try. It takes two, right? It's not like I'm the only one at fault. You're making it sound as if only I'm to blame for our difficulties and that's not fair. You're not being fair and you know it! You're rushing away before giving us a chance to fix what needs fixing. How can we heal if you won't take responsibility too? We can do this, if only you'll give us a chance. You have to give us a chance. You just have to because … because … because this is not your decision to make alone, damn it! Who says you're allowed to decide for us? If you do this, if you destroy who we are, what happens next? Have you thought one step ahead? I have and I'll tell you what happens; we'll suffer, both of us will suffer, and we'll be hurt like never before and neither of us will ever recover. Ever! Is this what you want, to cause me horrible pain? We share too much, we're too connected, we need each other! You can't cut short our time and decide our ending. You don't have that right!

"Don't you know how much I love you? How could you not know? Oh my goodness! Just because I don't say it you think I don't love you? If I haven't said it often enough then I'm saying it now. I'm shouting with all my heart: Sam, I don't want you to go; I don't want to live my life without you! You're my white knight. I'm your princess. From the moment we met, I've known where I belong and I belong in your arms as much then as I do now. I can't begin to think about who I'd be, what my life would be like, if I hadn't met you. I'm grateful for every moment of every day that you're in my life. I've loved you for so long that I can't remember a time when I existed without you. You know it's not easy for me to say what's on my mind. I wasn't taught to express my emotions. Can I help it if I was brought up to believe that silence is golden? You didn't mention any problems so I thought our relationship was golden too. Still, even if I only told God of my love for you, well, that's just as good isn't it? God is in you too so, really, I've been speaking to you just the same. Besides, actions are more meaningful than words and it's my actions that speak my love for you. I mean, think about what I do for you: keeping our home beautiful, cooking dinner for you most every night and staying up late talking with you though I'm tired and would prefer sleep. Don't you know I do this for you, put you first, to make you happy? Don't you see how I take care of you, how I wash and mend your clothes, making sure you look smart when you're out in the business world, how I arrange our social calendar to fit around your work schedule all so you can spend more time earning money that's put toward building a better life for us? And I don't complain, do I? Because I love you no matter what. Even when you change plans on me at the last minute and decide you'd rather be with one of your friends instead of working or being with me, I'm okay with that. By all means, go, be with your friends. I support you. I've always supported you. I'm not one of those women who discourages their husband from having friends of their own no matter what I think about them. Have I ever opposed your friendships? Have I? And don't count Jack. He's different. He's plain weird. What you see in him I have no idea. How can you even stand next to him? He smells awful! I feel like throwing up whenever he enters our home. Doesn't his wife keep soap in the house? How can she live with someone so disgusting? But Jack's welcome anytime because he's your friend and I love you so I sacrifice for you. That's what married couples do for each other. It's part of our agreement. I've held up my end of the bargain, haven't I? I've done everything that's expected of me! Do you think I'm managing our lives only for my benefit?

"I'm not saying I'm perfect. I know sometimes I get caught up in wanting things my way without considering what you want. I'm big enough to admit that. Like last year when we renovated our home. You said the color scheme was too bland, the furniture too conventional. Really, I didn't pay much attention to you because the fact is style is not one of your strong points. I've even heard you say so yourself. Need I remind you that I'm the one who helps you match your clothes? The thing is, I don't want to live in a clown's house and that's what would happen if I were to let you make the decisions. Our home would be an embarrassment. What would my friends say? But if you recall, I did compromise. I said you could decorate your office anyway you like and I said nothing, not a word, when you covered the walls with odd sized black framed pictures of colored doors and windows. I don't get it; who wants drawings and photos of doors on the wall? Never mind the strangeness of the pictures, you put up so many that you could barely see the color of the walls although that may have been a good thing since you painted the walls a hideous aqua blue. But it didn't matter if I understood or not and up until now I kept my opinion to myself. Why should I say anything that might hurt you? I would never try to hurt you. You're so wonderful. Our life is wonderful.

"Look at your ring. Look at the inscription. I know you know what it says but I want you to read it out loud. Go on, take it off and read it to me: Together, Amy & Sam. Together. You said that all we needed was one word, together. That's what you told the jeweler to inscribe. That's all you wanted the ring to say, nothing else. And you told him you didn't want gold or silver, you wanted to splurge for platinum because only platinum was good enough for me, your wife. Do you remember why you told him that? I do. I remember your exact words. You said that platinum is a scarce, noble metal, extraordinarily resistant to corrosion and this fits us because the love we have for each other is extraordinary and our love will always be and never will it waste away. Don't you remember? Those were your words to me. Have you forgotten? How could you forget?! I'll always remember. You're so much a part of me. How can I live without you? I can't. If you leave, I'll die. Is this what you want, for me to be dead?! Do you want to murder me? Are you so callous? Do I mean nothing to you? Have I always been nothing?

"You bastard! How many other women are you sleeping with? You're screwing Malak aren't you? I know you are. Why? Is it because you know I've never liked her? But what I think about her doesn't matter to you, does it? I know women better than you. I see how she looks at you, how she dresses like a tramp whenever she visits. Do you think it's a coincidence when her cleavage is spilling out? She may as well splay herself out on a silver platter for you. It's pathetic, it's sickening how she pretends to laugh at your juvenile stories and then goes out of her way to minimize anything I contribute to conversation, making me look like a dolt. And you never come to my defense! Do you know how that makes me feel? Watching you getting sucked into her act, listening to her every word like a puppy dog waiting for a pat on the head. Don't you think this bothers me?

"Is she a better lay? Is she? Her breasts are bigger. You like that don't you. Does it get you hot, thinking of slobbering over her breasts? What is it exactly that you can do with large breasts that you can't do with smaller ones? Is that why you ejaculate prematurely when we're in bed? Because you're fantasizing about Malak and you get so excited that you can't hold back long enough for me to get any satisfaction? I use to chalk up our sputtering sex life to your getting older and being tired from working so much. I was fooling myself wasn't I? Is Malak the only one or are there others? Well? How many? Who are they? What are their names? Does Malak know you're sleeping with women other than me? Does she care? Probably not. She's so disease ridden that she'll take one more bout of chlamydia in stride. As long as she gets her fill, right? Sluts are like that.

"You know, I would have been better off never meeting you. I was in the wrong place at the wrong time wasn't I? I always thought that destiny brought us together but now I see that our meeting was more like the other shoe dropping. At least I don't have to wait any longer for the thud. It all makes sense now, why you stayed with me. From the day we met you wouldn't let me go because you were weak, you didn't believe you could succeed on your own, and you needed someone to lean on, to prop you up, to help transform your dreams into reality, turn your cubicle into a corner window office, your nobody status to top of the social heap and now that you have what you want and you think you're strong, you don't need me anymore. It's true isn't it? Isn't it! I was your happenstance support system, there to guide you during your delayed onset teenage growth spurt. Well, look at you now. All puffed up, feeling invincible, a full fledged adult laying claim to prestige and a fat bank account, no longer afraid to fly away from the nest and leave me here alone. You don't need me anymore. Why would you? Your new bimbo is waiting, the one who drops her powdered panties on cue when you chalk up your pole. Isn't that what I read in your email? Are those the games you two kids like to play? Gee, isn't that cute.

"You're smitten. You send her handwritten poems. You're so cruel that you leave them on your desktop for me to see, not even bothering to hide the files. You wanted me to find the poems didn't you because you've fallen in love with her! I remember when you fell in love with me, when I was the one who treasured your gifts, reveled in your attention, listened to your goofy jokes, filed your nails, and endured your tedious work stories. You stopped writing poetry for me a long time ago didn't you? I never questioned why. Maybe I should have. Maybe I should have done a lot of things differently. Oh, I hate myself for loving you!

"I'm sorry. Truly, I'm sorry. That was terrible of me to say. None of it's true. I know it's not true no matter what you wrote in your emails. You're scaring me, that's all. My thoughts are so dark, causing me to think the worst. I know, in my heart of hearts, that you love me; that you've always loved me and always will. How could you not? Damn you! How could you not! Then why do you tell me you're leaving, your voice hollow, as if you don't care, as if destroying my life is a sensible task on your to do list, one more item to check off, one more achievement to accomplish. I know your arrogance, your smugness, your inflated self-regard. I've seen you dismiss those whom you call the little people, but never have you behaved this way toward me, held me in such contempt, and I will not stand for it! Let me tell you something you thoughtless asshole: despite your cocksure veneer and never ending streams of condescending verbiage, you don't have the right to change us. Do you hear me? You have no right! No entitlement! You're not God! We belong to each other, you and I, Samuel Shackleton, and don't for a second think that you can unilaterally shut us down. What you're proposing is out of the question, especially now, given that your head is such a mess.

"I'm not about to stand by and let you harm yourself. What kind of wife would I be? Your irrationality is temporary, a symptom of something else, I'm sure. But until you feel better, until we figure out the real source of your problem, I have to look after you. It's my responsibility. And to do that I need to get through to you, to make you understand that I'm not the cause of your juvenile behavior, and that your wanting someone new in your life is not a sign of dissatisfaction with me or our relationship but a sign of your own troubles. I have to make you understand that you won't escape your problems, you can't escape, by running away from me and into another woman's bed; you'll only make things worse for yourself, much worse.

"You have to believe me when I say that you do have problems and they're quite serious I'm afraid. Starting with depression. You've been depressed for some time. I haven't said anything up until now because I thought you were improving. But then I broke into your email account and read your letters to her and I knew that you needed my help more than ever. I mean, look at what's happened to you; look at what you've done. Depression has led you to this, to being on the verge of making a decision that will change your life forever, that will hurt you in who knows how many ways. I'm telling you I had no choice but to take action.

"You're scheduled to see Dr. Knapp next week. You'll go see her won't you? You know I wouldn't have gone to the trouble if I didn't think it was absolutely necessary. Please trust me on this; if anyone can help you it's Dr. Knapp. She has medical degrees from both McGill and Oxford, operates her own private psychiatry practice and is on staff at Sunnybrook Hospital. She's the best there is. I spoke to her receptionist who said that she's willing to start with talk therapy and move on to medication with your consent. Although she did imply that, in the near term, at least until you regain your balance, medication is preferred since real progress from talk therapy can take years! Will you at least think about it? For me? We want our relationship back as soon as possible, don't we? Wouldn't it be wonderful to go back to the way we were? I'm not saying you have to take medication but at least consider what the doctor has to say. If you like, I'll stay with you during your sessions. If you don't want my support that's fine but I think it would be a good idea for me to be in the room with you, to be your advocate, don't you? Whatever you want. It's up to you. I'm just happy you're hearing me out on this. Asking for help takes courage, believe me, and if we can't solve your problem by ourselves then it's best we rely on a professional. You will go see Dr. Knapp, won't you, before you make any hasty decisions? Please, do this for me. I'm so concerned for you. You're not thinking right. If you don't get help, you could devastate your life, forget about mine. Despite what you've done to me, I still love you, I'll always love you, and I forgive you for what you did. But let's not dwell on the past. What's done is done. Tell me you'll stay with me and that you'll go to the appointment. Tell me you'll do what needs to be done to get better and make our relationship better. Okay? You're all I have Sam. I need you. You have to stay with our story; you have to! It's in the book, our book, the book of Amy and Sam, which was written long before we met. You have to listen to the words in the book, written words are sacred; you can't edit our book! No one gave you permission! You can't let go of me just like that. You're not allowed to let go at all!"

Heaving sobs poured forth. Amy clutched her mid-section, groping for air. I sat there, oddly detached, observing.

"The pain is excruciating! WHY are you doing this to me? WHY are you hurting me? You have to stop, stop it already! It's too much, I can't go on like this, I just can't. If you care for me in even the smallest way, you'll end my pain. Go on, take the lamp cord over there and strangle me. Kill me. I'm already dead inside. Ten seconds, no mess to clean up, and you're free. This is what you want, right? Go on then, don't be a coward. I'm begging you, put me out of my misery, do it already! You don't want me, that's what you're telling me, that I'm no longer part of you, that you can't wait to get rid of me. Maybe I was never part of you but you're inside of me, damn it, and there's nothing I can do about that! If you leave, if you walk out that door, if you tell me this is goodbye then my life is over. Who will I be without you? After all our time together, all I've given to you, the love I've showered on you, my devotion, loyalty, sacrifice, MY LIFE, I deserve better. I deserve you. Oh Sam, where did I go wrong?!"

Frantically tearing off her wedding ring, face colored crimson with rage, Amy hurled the innocent jewel at me. Frozen by the peculiar sight of her angular, twisted face, the diamond's edge struck my right temple, grazing taut skin, leaving a conspicuous jagged cut from which droplets of blood dribbled out. I would feel the pain next morning.

"You pompous asshole! I don't need you; take your stupid ring! It never meant anything to you. I never meant anything, did I? Did I?! For all these years I pretended you let me in but you didn't because you don't know how to open yourself to anyone. You're so alone and dead inside; how could you know what love means? For you, it's all about the adrenaline rush. You think once the rush is gone that love disappears? You're wrong. That's not how it works! The passion, the sensations, these are only the beginning. If you would have been patient, you would have learned that love is deeper, it's about quietly sharing space, it's not about banging up a storm. If you needed a kick-start, why not take up car racing or sky diving instead of sticking your penis in whatever orifice opens your way? Go ahead, dress up your girlfriend in whorish costumes to satisfy your whims, savor the excitement you so obviously crave. We may not have fireworks every night but who does? That's not what love is. My goodness, we're best friends! I'm your wife; I'm not your source of entertainment. Are you so simple that you could be satisfied with a mouth breathing sex toy who counts on her fingers?!

"You're bored? You want a new plaything? A new and improved model? If it's excitement you think you're missing then I swear to you we'll recapture our passion. Our roots are so deep we can withstand whatever storm comes our way and that's exactly what this is, a storm that will pass by. This too shall pass, just like Dickinson wrote. Isn't that the way life works; in time, everything passes by. Hold on Sam; don't let go. You've got a whirlwind of crazy emotions swirling around inside of you. Let it settle; wait until you're on solid ground before making any decisions. It's not too late. You haven't really done anything yet. You're still here, right? We're still talking, right? Our bond is too strong; our love is too strong. Sex is only one part, a small part of what we share. It's not that important.

"But it's not only sex with her, is it? You've formed an emotional attachment to her, haven't you? How could you?! How screwed up are you?! Is your need for approval so desperate that you're willing to bury seven years of our lives and ruin our future in exchange for humping an anorexic tart with a pretty smile? This is all it takes to reel you in? Under cover of your savvy is nothing but a scared little boy wanting to prove his manliness. I'm the one who lights your fire, damn it! What do I have to do, don my birthday present red latex bodysuit and thigh high black boots you bought for me last year, coo about how big and strong you are, ego stroke with tales of your potency, or how about a boob job, will that do it, will bigger boobs provide you with a visual feast enough to keep us afloat? Will that add more spice to our sex life?

"I'm spiraling, losing my mind! But what do you care; you sit there, say nothing and shred my life. You're a grown man, Sam! Look in the mirror: you have wrinkles, a receding hairline, expanding waist; you're not a nineteen-year old kid worshipping your mushroom head. At your age, the big head runs the show. How about this: I'll take you to my favorite lingerie store on Danforth Avenue and if you can keep it in your pants long enough for me to buy fishnet stockings, silk underwear and adhesive gold stars to paste on my nipples, we'll rush home and I'll put on the best show you ever had. I'll be whoever you want me to be. You could even pretend that I'm her if you want. Won't that be exciting? And if the same old me doesn't do it for you, then I'll give you a one month free pass to sleep with whoever you like and do whatever it is you want to do that apparently my body doesn't allow for. Go ahead, do it, I won't mind, well, yes, I will but I don't need to know any details; I don't want to know. All I need from you is your word that after thirty days, you'll come back to me, and only me, and we'll resume living our life together just like before, just like none of this happened and we'll never talk about it again. If that's what you want, I'll do it because I love you, but what I can't and won't do is allow you to emotionally withdraw from me like you're doing now. I'm looking at you and you're not there, you've disconnected and that frightens me, and you're just sitting there, saying nothing. Say something!"

Tears streaming from bloodshot eyes, smudged mascara running down her cheeks, compact fists clenched, Amy lunged at me, pounding my chest in uncoiled fury. I moved to hug her but was pushed away.

"YOU DISGUST ME! Don't you dare touch me, don't you dare pretend that you care. You send another woman chocolates, flowers, sleep in her bed, show HER that you care and now act as if I matter to you? You think you can have both of us? Get away from me. I can smell her vile scent on you and it's making me sick! How thick are you? We're not on the same side anymore. We're not friends; we're enemies and that's how it will be from here on in. Oh, Sam. My sweet Sammy, you're so confused, you have no idea how much you'll regret leaving me. I give it two months before the novelty fades and you come to realize how you've wrecked your life, but it will be too late by then."

"Amy," was all I could get out before she interrupted.

"No! There is nothing you can say! I know what I want and what I need and I want you and I need you and I've never ever doubted us or my feelings for you or my wish to live my life with you and that's why I'm forcing myself to be more emotionally vulnerable than I've ever let myself be and it terrifies me to be wide open like this but I'm doing it because I have no choice because I love you and you love me and one day, when it's too late, when you're missing me, when you're lonely and depressed, when you crave my touch and want me to listen to you, I won't be there and only then will you finally get it. And when that day arrives, I'll feel sad for you and for me because I'll be reminded of the time we were together and the years we've been apart knowing that we were meant to stay together but we didn't because of you. But we don't get a second chance at life, there is no dress rehearsal is there? So we'll grow old and we won't talk and we won't see each other and we won't know each other and our memories will fade and we'll both find someone else but never will we replace our love because that's not possible. THAT could never be possible! And years will pass by and every minute of every hour of every day of all those years both of us will carry a locket of emptiness and sorrow wherever we go, wherever we are, and we'll both know that it didn't have to be this way, that you could have chosen to continue but you chose to quit. And when your life is almost over, you'll shake your head and reflect on what could have, should have, been but wasn't because somewhere along the way you got lost. But I'll be fine. When I'm ready, I'll meet some second-rate material and make him my friend and let him sleep with me because I need a friend by my side, someone whose loyalty I can count on, who wants me more than I want him. I don't want to age alone, in darkness, devolving into bitterness, draped in ratty wool blankets, desperately trying to stay warm during hot summer nights because I'll be so thin from not eating that even the slightest draft will chill my bones.

I'm not so proud or foolish that I won't enter old age without taking a companion who will at least ease my pain.

"You're so oddly charming, so peculiar and comforting, so strange and familiar. I'll never find another loveable screwball like you, will I? Take my hand. Don't let go. It's too much for me; the thought of never again hearing your laughter, feeling tingles from your touch or watching you sleep. You're my anchor, Sam. I'm safe with you. Don't do this to me. Please be gentle. Please don't hurt me."

"Amy!" I started again, "I think ..."

"You don't think! That's the problem. You and that laudable brain of yours have seized up. You're running as fast as you can but to where? Where are you going? There's no one saying you have to listen to the inner adrenaline junkie demanding action for the sake of action regardless of consequences. Try Sam, try to slow that mind of yours. There's no rush to decision; you've got to step on the brakes, reflect on the side of the road instead of driving round in circles desperate to go somewhere, anywhere, for no reason except that you're unsure of what to do with the idyllic stillness that is our relationship. Lulls are okay, really they are. You used to feed your habit through work; routing your manic energy into new projects before you had time to sour on old ones. That was okay. It really was. You were constructively satisfying your needs. But this, what you're doing now, is totally destructive to you and the people who love you. Oh, sure, it's exciting isn't it? A gold digging tart who jump starts your engine. New body to explore. New mind to manipulate. Think of the challenges and don't forget those delightful rewards. What happens though after the body bores you and you realize that the mind in question is as shrewd as a mule, one that can't read without moving her lips? Am I getting through to you? Is anything sinking in? Sam, it's time to come to your senses and snap out of it. Do you hear me? Snap out of it!

"You're abandoning me for a blockhead; the girl's a high school drop out! What could you possibly have in common? Cartoons? You, with your dry wit, unbridled curiosity, thirst for knowledge, the sensitive intellectual spouting off about Bellow, Matisse and Watts, suddenly hanker for the home shopping network and Academy Awards? Or is it an empty container that's the attraction, drawing you like a proverbial moth to flame? That's it! You think you need to save her, to shelter and protect, this makes you feel like a man doing his ancestral duty. Amazing! In ten thousand years of supposed evolution toward civilization, everything changes and nothing changes. It could have been any woman radiating battered self-esteem and comely curves seeking a savior. Sure, her lights may not burn bright but she knows exactly what she's doing. She knows her feminine power, she knows the art of seduction and she knows that her prime asset, the only asset, she has to offer a man like you is her body, to be defiled at your whim and pleasure, hoping that this will be enough to let her skimpy brain fly under your radar. I'll bet she goes to bed with makeup on. She does, doesn't she? What a surprise. Until she wraps you up, she can't take the chance of revealing wear and tear. And what about vaginoplasty? Older women like her know that they loosen up. Has she made herself nice and tight for you? Is that what keeps you going back for more: a painted face and snug vagina? What more could you want? You know, just because I'm smart and independent doesn't mean I don't need you. I can take care of myself but I still need you! I'll always need you. Are you listening to me? Does anything I say register? Anything at all? Damn you! Damn you! Damn you!"

"I'm leaving Amy. We can talk when you calm down."

"I'm warning you, Sam, don't do what I think you're about to do. If you walk out that door, I'll change the locks and hire security to keep you out. You'll never set foot in this house again. I swear, you'll leave here with the clothes on your back and nothing more. I'll hire the best lawyers to strip you bare. The silver tea set that was a wedding gift from your grandmother, I'll melt it before letting you get your hands on it. The ring from your father inscribed with his name that you keep in your sock drawer and planned to give to the son you claimed to want to have with me one day, I'll sell it to a pawn shop or throw it in the sewer where it belongs, where you belong. Your clothes go to charity. Your computer I'll throw out the window but not before copying the hard drive and making a backup copy. You never know when I'll need to blackmail you. Any photos of you, I'll burn. I'll disinfect the house three times over to rid all trace of you. All reminders of you will be erased. That's what you're doing to me, isn't it? Erasing me? Acting as if I never existed? Forcing me to rebuild my life? Maybe you're smarter than me; maybe you can reinvent yourself overnight but I don't know how to do that and I don't want to change my life. I can't change my life, you son of a bitch! Even if you leave, I'll never be rid of you no matter what I do. Oh Lord, what am I going to do? Am I such a bad person that I deserve this?!

"I'm so distressed. I even called your mother to talk. In all the time we've known each other, I've never called your mother. Why would I? She hates me. The woman who has not so much as given me eye contact since the day we met. You're her favorite and I'm the woman who stole her little boy as far as she's concerned. And it doesn't help that I was born outside the tribe. That's one more reason for your mother to reject me. No matter what I did or how hard I tried, I was never good enough. Who could be good enough for her beloved son? Is this why you're leaving me, because you finally caved to your mother? I know for a fact that she's the reason for your delaying having our own children. Given the choice of no grandchildren or grandchildren with *goyim* infected blood, I'm sure she encouraged you not to have kids with me, to wait until you found a Jewish woman who would be mother to your children. I've always known that you would leave me one day for a Rivka or a Rachel but I didn't want to believe it. You always said you couldn't care less about the religion I was born into but now I see you were lying and this was only wishful thinking on my part.

"I remember how you reacted two years ago when I said I wanted to convert. You pounced on me, over and over asking me why, in that bulldog way of yours. And I told you that I wanted our children to arrive into this world as Jews. Then you said that's impossible because I'm not a Jew. But that's why I wanted to convert; I thought this would make you happy and bring us closer together. I was even willing to go so far as to change my name. I would have felt left out if I didn't share the same last name as you and our children. But you opposed that too, questioning how an educated woman could be so subservient and volunteer to give up part of her identity. Even when I showed you I was serious and registered for conversion classes at Temple Kol Tikvah, and you questioned why I wanted to convert and tried to persuade me not to go through with it, I assumed this was because you resented having to attend weekly classes with me. A waste of your time, you said. And I asked you, but what about me and us and our future children, but you didn't answer. Only after I completed twelve months of conversion classes, learned to read and write Hebrew, attended Friday night *Shabbat* services at the synagogue week after week, countless *Bar* and *Bat Mitzvahs* and weddings, danced the *hora* with too many old Jewish men who wouldn't stop groping the *shiksa*, the forbidden fruit, learned to speak

English with that upturned inflection at the end of sentences and speak Hebrew words as if I were coughing up phlegm, nailed a *mezuzah* to our front door and even attached a velcro one to our car interior, voyaged to Israel to experience Jewish history in a Jewish country (why we couldn't have visited Manhattan, I don't know), perfected cooking *matzoh* ball soup, preparing *gefilte* fish and making *charoset* for the High Holidays, held my nose and ate chopped liver to please your family, tolerated *lox* as a diet staple, got used to frightening emotional outpourings, barbed sarcasm, and arguments as a normal mode of communication for you people that didn't require police or medical intervention and, after all this, done in good faith on my part to strengthen feelings of connection to Judaism, to mold myself into a 'good Jew' and, most importantly, to bring myself closer to you and to convince you that we should have children, have a family, it's clear that my efforts were in vain. Once a *shiksa*, always a *shiksa*, right? You'll never accept me as a Jew. Despite the Temple's blessings upon my conversion, you would never allow a child of yours to vacate my uterus.

"Misgivings aside, I called your mother. Who else could I talk to? My mother? Please, she would blame me for your leaving, saying that somehow it was my fault, that I had it coming, that I wasn't good enough, didn't work hard enough, and maybe now I would learn to stay quiet, to stay in my place, to stay in my true community and stop fooling around with 'those people' and thumbing my nose at our Savior. But your mother listened to me. I was shocked! She was kind, empathetic and on my side. She was compassionate and stood by me in female solidarity as I told her what happened. I told her everything you did to me, everything. I was so happy that she listened and that she believed me, I cried, and before I knew it she was crying too. We were crying together and now we've become friends and we call each other all the time and she gives me advice about how to handle you. You don't mind if your mother and I are friends do you? Isn't it ironic; you're sticking a knife in my back was the catalyst for friendship between your mother and I. Maybe we have more in common than I thought. But don't worry; I'm sure she loves you all the same and your relationship with her will stay strong no matter what I tell her.

"Let's stop talking. I'm exhausted. I'm cold. Brrr. I'm shivering. Are you cold? How about you make a fire and I'll fetch a few warm blankets from the linen closet and we can snuggle. I love the crackling sounds and smells of a wood burning fire. You do too. I know you do. I know everything about you. Come. It's been so long since we've done this. Let's take our clothes off, okay? The fire will warm us up. Come closer. There, isn't this nice? Look at me. Look at my belly. I lost five pounds this week thanks to you. I couldn't eat anything since I found out. I'm skinny now, just like her."

Chapter 2
Freedom Tastes of Reality

*Just 'cause you got the monkey off your back
doesn't mean the circus has left town*
– George Carlin

Ouch! Where did this gut pain come from? Ouch! There it goes again. What's going on?

A steady voice inside of me answers.

'Man. You're feeling the pain of expansion.'

Expansion? I'm expanding? Why am I expanding? I didn't sign up for expansion. Even if I did, what does expansion have to do with gut pain? There shouldn't be any pain. I'm out, I tell you. Free. I should be feeling good all over. It's supposed to be easy now.

Psyche goes on. 'Severing bonds of intimacy? Dissolving attachment? This is easy?'

Yes! It's done! The hard part is behind me.

'Is it?'

Isn't it?

'You say you're out, you're free. Does freedom know mental bedlam, fitful anxiety, haze concealing tangerine arrows pointing the way forward?'

Bedlam and anxiety, those are a given; they've been riding shotgun for sometime. As for tangerine arrows, I'm at a loss. Anyway, what does it matter? And why are you badgering me like this? Can't we stop the questioning for once? You're confusing me.

'No, man, you're mistaken. Your confusion precedes my emergence.'

What are you saying? I wasn't in my right mind? Didn't know what I was doing? Made a mistake? No, I couldn't have, that's not possible. I'm sure there was no mistake. I had good reason. I did. It's not like I left on a whim. The end was years in the making. There was nothing left but arguments, counter-arguments, resentment, frustration and distrust; that's what remained of the emotional crux of our bond. And don't think she didn't know it too. I mean, once a week or more, we would take turns boiling over, threatening to leave, but neither of us did. The threats were empty, more like shotgun flares briefly blinding onlookers before dimming amid resumption of routine, acceptance of dysfunction, and eventual return to status quo. What was status quo? Clinging to each other. No matter what, we clinged. Until, that is, status quo buckled under the rotting burden of animosity. Should I tell you what gave rise to mutual hostilities? Should I? Should I?

'Man, don't go there. It won't do any good. You've launched a new course, one designed to activate core opening imperative to achieving corrective restructuring of a kind unrelated to orthopedic rehabilitation. That's why I'm here: to guide you along your new course.'

No, no, it's better that I tell you, that I get it out. It's important for me to explain, and for you to understand, that I didn't set out to do harm. That definitely wasn't the purpose. No, never. In fact, at this point, I'm using pretty much all my strength to keep my distance from her since a large part of me wants to go back. You know me, I'm a man, I'm weak when it comes to fending off women. Picturing her as a fully clothed horned elf helps to resist hypnotic pull.

'What's done is done. There's no need to demonize her. That would only damage your self; prolong your healing process. Other than acknowledging love lost, nothing more need be said for or against either of you.'

You don't think I needed a reason for leaving? A good, solid reason explaining my actions? Shouldn't I at least be convinced of the validity of my behavior? When people ask why I did it, I should have an answer, I should be able to sum it up nicely, shouldn't I, elevator pitch style? I do have reasons you know. Starting with deception. Doesn't that register as legitimate cause? As far as I'm concerned, that's all I needed. It's not like she hadn't deceived me before but the latest episode was a doozy. What was I supposed to do? Let it go? I couldn't. I was too tired of letting it go! What kind of lunatic pokes pin holes in packaged condoms? Nine weeks later, she breaks the news and I break more of a sweat than I do when eating *chana masala* at her favorite restaurant, that stinking hole in the wall on Gerrard Street in Little India. So I ask her, how did you get pregnant? I say to her, we took precautions, what's going on here?

And she replies in that thick way of hers, 'Sweetheart, no form of contraception is one hundred percent. I'm so excited! Aren't you excited?! I've already thought about names. If the baby's a girl, we'll name her Georgia. And if it's a boy, Noah. Aren't those darling names? Oh, what if I have one of each? Twins! Then we could use both names! What color should we paint their rooms? What about beds? Will they sleep with us or should we buy a crib? One crib or two? There's so many decisions to make, so much to do!'

Are you kidding? I'm not ready for kids and you're not exactly mother material.

'That's awful! Why are you being so mean? We're going to have a baby! Maybe two babies! You're going to be a father. This is the most exciting time of my life!'

I'm sorry. I'm nervous that's all. It's unexpected. We didn't plan this. I'm not ready for a child. This will change everything. I'm not looking for change. Later. We'll have time for children later. We're young. I'll call around and find out where to get an abortion. The Morgentaler Clinic is probably best.

'No, it's too late, the baby's heart is already beating so a doctor can't perform an abortion. I know we didn't plan on me getting pregnant but can't you be happy for us? Can't you be happy for me? Sometimes the best things in life are unplanned, you know.'

This isn't one of those things. Why did you wait so long to tell me?

'I didn't know until I went for an ultrasound. My periods are inconsistent, I've been telling you that for years.'

You went for an ultrasound? When?

'I'm sure I mentioned my appointment to you. You're so busy with work all the time you must have forgotten.'

I can't forget something I'm not told about. It's not too late. I've heard of abortions done up to twenty-four weeks. I'll find someone. We'll go to Amsterdam if we have to.

'I am not murdering my child!'

All of a sudden abortion is murder? Since when? You're the one who shouts from the rooftops about primacy of women's reproductive rights. How no one can tell you what to do with your body.

'That's right. You can't tell me what to do and it's my right to keep my baby!'

Shortly before week thirteen, I cancelled our flight on KLM Royal Dutch Airlines after spontaneous miscarriage befell Amy. The night it happened, nursing sorrow with a bottle of chardonnay into early morning hours, she let slip the details of how the dam broke and fertilization came to be. At first I dismissed the truth of her story, attributing narrative to the ramblings of a heartbroken, inebriated woman. But then, after she passed out, I filled up my remaining condom supply with water to check for leaks. Sure enough, I got all wet.

It's not like it was the first time I got tangled in her sticky web. Oh no, variations of her gamesmanship happened too many times to recount. But no matter what she said or did, she knew there was nothing to fear from me, that I wasn't going anywhere as long as she could prick an Achilles heel that, contrary to Gray's Anatomy, isn't in my foot. Whenever jumping offside, all she had to do was turn up the heat by activating that body of hers. Comforting me like a Japanese *Oiran*, persuading me to forgive if not forget, what could I do but surrender?

This last time though, after sexual fever broke, I resolved to break the cycle. Not that I hadn't made resolutions before, each of which reliably broke down in the face of her undulating groin. But this time, THIS TIME, would be different. I would call upon self-control. I would curb wanton enthusiasm. And I would do so by retaining cerebral cortex. Yes, a deliberate internal investigation was needed to get to the bottom of my behavior.

The next morning, an answer was delivered. Seems that, hidden in cerebral cortex's temporal lobe was an historical blueprint sketch of a mother-son relationship to which I've been party since birth. Within this sketch were drawn underpinnings of unconditional love and trust. Apparently, not unlike other men subconsciously seeking maternal traits in their mate, I sought the same dynamic in my relations with Amy.

Ah, but therein lay the problem. You see, she wasn't receptive. She couldn't be. It wasn't possible. Her cortex, hastily assembled under generations of familial duress, was averse to trusting her own self never mind me. Without trust, her notion of love was primitive, political, contaminated by ...

'Man, listen,' said Psyche, brushing aside my explanations, discrediting investigative results, 'Who she is, how she behaved, what she did or did not do or say, that's all behind you. You're on your path now, a new path, and there's no one else in sight but you.'

But I need a reason! If you ask me why I did it, all I can say is I pinned personal salvation to the tail of a spindly rope called a feeling. The thing is, I'm not entirely sure what that means, a feeling?

'Be patient. In time, you will learn. For now, please step forward.'

What's with the doors?

'They are here for you. Choose one, anyone you like.'

How do I know which one to choose?

'Choose.'

Maybe I'll try door number four?

'Go on then, take a stroll inside.'

Automatic double doors open wide into a darkened room save for cinema sized screen on which appears a version of myself, decades from now. Encircled by an iron gated retirement villa in plastic Boca Raton, I watch octogenarians in weathered bathrobes aimlessly wander astride clear-cut edges of pesticide showered manicured lawns bordering my very own non-descript, two-bedroom hurricane shuttered condo. Inside, rising from antiseptic laminate flooring, are rose painted walls blending into a sparsely furnished interior dominated by one appallingly tepid flesh tone velour sectional sofa and matching Victorian chair sheathed in plastic in case inadvertent spills cause discomforting stains and foul the entire ensemble, the reaction to which would be, to a tee, exasperated hands hastily rising to flushed cheeks mutely expressing the ruin that has become the furniture, that has, symbolically, become the inhabitant, me.

Out! I want out! Hit the lights!

'Man, don't stop now. This is a dry run. See it through.'

I return to my seat only to watch my unbending body drop into a large automobile, a white, four-door, leather clad, wood paneled, immaculate Fleetwood Cadillac programmed to putter along Interstate 95 to the Chicken Nest. I arrive ahead of the rush, twenty minutes before five o'clock opening. Hundreds of years of Prussian cultural behavior swimming in my genetic pool demand being on time. Impatient, irritable, I wait to be escorted to my table, knowing that, once seated, Sadie the waitress will bring a bowl of warm chicken soup, with four saltine crackers on the side. The soup arrives. But it's too hot. Seeing my distress, Sadie pacifies me with ice cubes. As the soup cools, I slurp in haste because I know no other way and because a meaty slice of dry, unsalted brisket will be delivered any moment and I want to finish my soup before it arrives. But I can't enjoy the meal because I'm worrying about whether or not I turned down the air conditioning in the condo and what kind of energy bill I'll have on my hands next month. But worry doesn't stop me from gorging as if this were my last supper. I leave Sadie a buck tip and warily drive back to paradise where an unavoidably fitful sleep awaits in my temperature controlled box.

Credits roll. Stupefied, I exit. A different door, I plead, let me choose a different door.

Psyche responds, lighter now.

'As the monkey has been removed from your back, I am pleased to report that the number of available doors is limited only by your imagination.'

My back may be monkey free but what about my head? Mental processes loop, elation races, consternation drags and there's no off ramp in sight. If I can't escape the circle, then how about a rest stop, a couch? I'll settle for a couch. Tradition commands a couch! More than one; a slew of couches beside which aged, bearded, bespectacled men smoking pipes get down to the sober business of observing tics and shudders, noting jumbled histrionics in which lay deceptively connected subconscious streams wherein answers decidedly lurk. Surely, the learned men will explain how I've morphed not into a Kafkaesque bug but a pathetic pedestrian tribal caricature.

'What's to explain? Part and parcel of the collective, you are doomed to replicate. Free will is a rube's game,' roars Psyche before taking leave.

Hemmed in by neurological fog, rendered helpless against high anxiety's rickety spokes, internal alarm bells ring out as gut pain worsens. Alone, I blindly rummage within for a way out.

$$\Omega$$

The weekend before we fell apart, I took a road trip, driving east six hours on highway 401 from Toronto to Montreal then northward upon winding concrete roads hugging the craggy Laurentian mountains. Navigating ascending altitude, speeding around narrow corridors scarcely wide enough for two cars traveling in opposite directions to safely pass each other, reading ominous signs and symbols warning of falling boulders, I stole glances at magnificent vistas overlooking humungous fishbowl shaped basins of pristine pools of Canadian lake water. Heavenly.

Then I looked down. And off the water's gleaming surface bounced a reflection, a vision, of two childlike flute playing blue angels. Floating in midair, these not so innocent cherubs teasingly flashed the cover of a manuscript titled, Guide for the Perplexed.

Reading this sparked a brief interlude of transient insanity. Perception altered, time ceased to be a unit of measurement, the merry go round that is life ground to a halt, and I was flooded by an overwhelming impulse to ram straight through steel safety blockades and soar into the fourth dimension. But before I could steer the wheel skyward, as suddenly as they arrived, the winged toddlers disappeared and in their place arose a round window. Subbing for the face of lucidity, the window stayed opened long enough for me to question its presence. And this simple act of questioning, of inquiry, was all it took to dispel perilous musings.

My knuckles turned from white back to red. Headlights illuminated the road ahead. To no one in particular, I wondered aloud who or what was responsible for saving myself from myself? Was there anybody out there?

Dusk approached. Casually, I descended the mountain road, settling in for a monotonous drive home. Tuned to AM radio, the British Broadcasting Corporation kept me company.

"Sir, may I help you?"

"Clarity".

"Pardon me?"

"I'd like to order clarity, please."

"Sir, I'm afraid that clarity is not on the menu."

"But, I'd like to order clarity. It says right here that you serve happiness, joy, contentment, balance, poise, stability, equilibrium, delight, and general feelings of well being. I don't see why there would be a problem for your establishment to whip up a shot of clarity."

"I'm terribly sorry, sir, it's not that simple."

"Of course it's not that simple! If it were, I wouldn't have to order it from you. But it's not. That's why I'm here. One large serving of clarity. That's my order and that's what I want. Be a kind gent will you, run along to the back and bring me my clarity. Chop, chop."

"Sir, there was a time when indeed clarity was offered on our menu but, as I've said, the menu has changed and, I'm sorry to say, we no longer have the wherewithal to fill your order."

"Now you listen to me: I demand clarity!"

"Sir, with the ingredient list subject to frequent change, our establishment is not in a position to assure patrons such as yourself that they will receive the quality or depth of clarity that meets our standards. We truly regret the inherent unreliability of our sources. May I suggest you return next week at which time we may be able to help although I'm not in a position to offer guarantees. Please accept my sincerest apologies."

"Balls!"

"Balls we have. How many would you like?"

Chapter 3
Swedish Meat Girls

Doubt is not a pleasant condition
but certainty is absurd
– Voltaire

Circumstances had escalated beyond comprehension. I needed to consult the big thinkers. They knew more than me about the game of life. They would help me figure out questions leading to answers.

Staring down my bookshelves, where the thinkers are housed, a newspaper clipping poking out from an otherwise orderly (others might say obsessive) arrangement caught my eye. Odd, I couldn't recall seeing the stray paper there before. Pulling it out, unfolding it like an origami puzzle, the clipping revealed itself as the front page of the Humansville Register, a daily rag purporting to be published in Humansville, Missouri.

In big bold type a headline shouted, Hippocampus Vital to Establishing Sensory Integration. Seemingly as good a place to start as any, I scanned below the headline to an interview excerpt with a group described as the Perennial Spring Time Nominees for the Missouri Medal of Science & Lore.

"What's a hippocampus?" read the opening lob.

The Nominees answered, "The hippocampus is a smooth functioning seahorse shaped sheet of neurons located inside the medial temporal lobe, beneath the cortical surface."

"Uh huh. And the big deal is what?" the journalist volleyed back.

"The big deal," scoffed the pasty men of science, "is the alarming growth rate of society's sensory disconnection from nature at large."

"Ya? What do you suppose is causing this growing disconnect?"

"It's obvious! The catastrophic increase of damaged hippocampi!"

"I don't get it."

"A damaged hippocampus prevents adequate processing of stimuli. An inability to process and make sense of stimuli, be it visual, auditory or olfactory, disconnects one from one's surroundings."

"Really. And what are you saying is the reason for the increasing prevalence of a screwy hippo whatever?"

"Sensory integration dysfunction – write that down as your reason! Our senses are out of whack because we're out of whack. Too many folks operating as separate parts, not as a unified whole working together. When parts run independently of each other, confusion reigns; disorder becomes the individual's modus operandi."

"Oh, the M.O.! Cool. How many people would you say are whacked out? Could you give me a number? Our readers like numbers."

"Twenty-three per cent of the population, with males predominantly afflicted."

"What about a pill? Couldn't confusion be avoided by popping a pill?"

"There is only one manner of achieving integration. The infant child must attach to mother's breast immediately after uterine evacuation. Ideally, the child remains upon the breast for its first twenty-four months.

"If the breast is withdrawn early, the child experiences abandonment issues, fundamental nourishment is compromised, aberrant mapping of the pre-frontal cortex results and from then on the child exists off balance.

"The male in particular suffers notable consequences. Owing to insufficient breast milk consumption, the male experiences insatiable craving for semen ejection upon reaching reproductive age. Symbolically, you see, semen represents breast milk and it is breast milk that the male subconscious craves. Temporarily, semen ejaculation alleviates desire."

"Whoa! If you boys haven't already crossed the line, you're darn sure bordering on blasphemy. In fact, statements like that make me think your message is paid for by the mother's milk movement. Is it? Are you anti-corporate baby food manufacturers too? Anti-capitalist? Commies, reds, socialists? Are you French? What's that you're hiding behind your back? A beret? You are French, aren't you? Admit it!"

What they were drinking in Humansville, Missouri, I didn't know but it probably wasn't mother's milk. My knee jerk reaction was to judge the Nominees nuts. Then again, I reasoned, genius has been known to straddle, if not cross, the sanity line. Take Pythagoras, the Greek mathematician. He was frightened of edible beans, believing them to be inherently evil. And what about Edgar Allen Poe who said "men have called me mad; but the question is not yet settled, whether much that is glorious, whether all that is profound, does not spring from disease of thought, from moods of mind exalted at the expense of the general intellect."

Sitting on a small straight back metal chair, hands clasped together behind my head, I threw my hat in the ring with the Nominee's and went about testing their theory. Wanting to know whether I was sensorially integrated or not, I probed memory, back to a time and space shortly after birth.

There I was, eyes shut tight like a newborn kitten, my eight pound rag doll body latched on to a nipple on a breast on a woman lying in bed. The breast and I were one. If I peeped, hungry or not, the nipple's owner nestled me into a wondrously nourishing collection of glandular fibrous tissues. I was balanced. I was fulfilled. According to the Midwestern scientists, presuming union of the breast and I for the next two years, I was a prime candidate for a fully functional hippocampus, one wired for ideal sensory cohesion. If this were so, I had nothing to worry about; my present state of confusion, my search for questions leading to answers, was a temporary glitch soon to be righted.

Or not. Returning to the newspaper, I read the next headline announcing the names of the medal winners. Underneath the headline was their photo. In ten gallon Stetsons, sporting grins wider than the Colorado river, the lone star men drawled:

"Bless our Missouri friends but they've got it wrong. When y'all restrict an infant's exposure to the breast, the child is deprived of other sensory experiences. And it's a known fact that when you deprive the child then the child is, uh, uh, sensorially deprived. Then two things happen: one, y'all wind up with what we call a subdued stimulus response. This means you need to blow the doors off the henhouse to get a feel for excitement so you're prone to taking crazy risks that most folk would shy away from. Second, like we said in our paper published in the prestigious Chronicle of Confederate Truth, when a child is subjected to excessive breast attachment, later in life, that child will compensate for loss of breast by sublimating sensory disturbance into abnormal sexual activity."

How this newspaper clipping found its way onto my bookshelf I hadn't the faintest. Nonsense? Sure. Intriguing? Of course. Wanting to learn more, I researched scores of peer reviewed studies published in meaningful textbooks and impressively titled journals headed by three letter acronyms only to find near unanimous support for the Southerners ballyhooed conclusions.

This was a problem. If the Southerners were right then my state of bewilderment could be traced to fallout from excessive breast attachment. But that was a big if and, regardless the consensus view, I wasn't ready to concede just yet. More research was required. Rooting for the Nominees, trusting in their madness, again I reached back into memory to review and compare other seminal events of my formative years.

Twenty-six months of age. A hungry toddler doing what I was trained to do: lift the lady's nursing flap to gorge from the nipple. But the flap wouldn't lift. Someone had changed the cup covering. Stymied, furious, I alternated between screaming and holding my breath. I wanted the breast. I needed the breast. I was hooked. Addicted. The breast. My savior. I had to have the breast! The lady, however, wouldn't budge. 'Check it out,' she said, 'these bent out of shape deflated wind sockets are your doing and I've had enough.' From that day forward, I dined on infant formula transmitted through a stout latex nipple leaving a sour, and faintly leather, aftertaste. 'Suck it up,' said the lady.

It wasn't looking good for the Nominees. Despite breast attachment duration exceeding minimum prescription by two months, discombobulation remained my waking state during the next seven years. My step (once I could walk) lacked bounce. Something was missing. But I couldn't put my finger, or my mouth, on it. Until spring of grade four when I, a hormonally precocious nine year old, was reacquainted with the female.

Michelle, my elementary school chum, kick the can pal and four-square teammate invited me to her home during lunch hour. A standard issue latchkey kid of a divorced mom working long days to make ends meet, Michelle knew how to take care of herself. She had no other choice. After the school bell rang, we would run to her home (not because we were in a hurry but because running was fun), located less than a long block from school. Every day, we'd debate the menu all of ten seconds: macaroni and cheese or peanut butter sandwiches on white bread and a glass of cold milk. Peanut butter, hands down, usually won out. We liked how it stuck to the roof of our mouth, and we could eat it fast, leaving more make out time.

That's right. Michelle was that rare breed of girl who was as curious as me about touching, feeling and squeezing. With crumbs on our lips, smidgens of peanut butter on our cheeks, and kid sized wonder in our pants, we fumbled onto a worn, green shag rug in the family room where Michelle would take over, instructing me to lay on top, press my lips against hers.

'This is how they do it on T.V.,' she'd tell me. What did I know? A *pisher* pitched an easy walk to first base and within striking distance of second, I wasn't about to cross a five-foot tall tetherball champion who could run faster than me and snort milk out her nostrils at will. Our pint sized bodies rubbed denim and locked smeared lips for as long as we could coordinate the kissing thing or until one of us sneezed. Our record was twenty-two minutes. I knew because I timed us on my Seiko watch.

For what seemed like forever, maybe two weeks, our lunch time rendevous' continued. And each school day before lunch, I'd mentally check out of class and map out schemes designed to unfasten the passcode to her training bra. National Geographic taught me everything I needed know: girls had nipples so that meant Michelle had nipples because she was a girl and where there are nipples, breasts are sure to grow so it was possible she had breasts too.

But Michelle was no slouch. Two inches taller, ten pounds heavier and gifted with intelligence unburdened by trickling testosterone, she greeted roaming hands with polite but steadfast denial.

Then, to make clear who was in charge, and to penalize me for committing uninvited transgressions, she would turn up lip sucking pressure, not backing off until I started turning blue (she knew when to stop because we kissed with our eyes open). Being an adenoid sufferer, inhaling through my nose wasn't an option.

Our noon hour trysts came to a premature end when her mother asked about peanut butter stains on the sofa pillows. That led to a phone call to my mother and, ultimately, to banishment from Michelle's home. Though I never was made privy to her silken (in my dreams) chest, I was sure that a hint of a bounce in my step had returned and, as grade four drew to a close, the bounce grew and grew.

The teen years. Mobile phones had just entered the mainstream. I got myself one. It was bulky but I kept it in my front pants pocket anyway. Because after the first time it rang, I had no choice. With the ringer set to vibrate, it tickled my genitals. Boy, it felt good. From then on, the phone and I were inseparable. Others said they were concerned for me, said I was ignoring the important things in life. I didn't care. I had to do something to alleviate libidinal pressure and this seemed preferable to my friend Darron's suggestion that I scotch tape my penis to my thigh (radiation may kill sperm but at least I would avoid chafing and rawness). Inevitably, incoming vibrations set off throbbing sensations triggering mental wandering taking me to a fantasyland populated by juicy Sicilian nurses with fiery dispositions and meaty buttocks. For much of the day, it was the only place I wanted to be. Nighttime too. If this were abnormal sexual activity then the Texans had me pegged.

Then came one sunny June morning. A classroom presentation by latter day hippies. They started by talking about rhesus monkeys who, so I learned, belong to an advanced primate social hierarchy similar to humans. And though they strive for group inclusion, we were told, 'males in particular are unable to subjugate individual desires, this being most apparent when observing their fast and frequent public masturbation.' You can imagine the snickering that followed a line like that in a classroom full of teenagers, me included.

But I straightened up pretty quick when I heard what the hippies said next. First, humans share ninety-eight per cent of the rhesus monkey's DNA. Second, like masturbating monkeys, humans, in their role as consumer, are driven to satisfy the same contradictory needs: to belong and to individuate. Knowing this, the telecommunications industry believes that penetration of new commercial markets is dependent on corralling these paradoxical urges. To underscore telecom's intrinsic evil, they put on a skit.

'Welcome to your family! Two billion strong and growing! Choose a phone, any phone. Color, size, features, applications, whatever you want, we will find it today. Why delay gratification, why forsake desire, when it may be yours! And if tomorrow you change, then change you must! Whatever is your wish, we will satisfy. We are here to serve you. Charting course for the new you; reinvigorate, reinvent, revitalize your self! Out with the old in with the new, isn't that right kids?! You are your phone, your phone is you, isn't that right too? So, tell us, who do you wish to be today?'

Mars, the lead presenter, closed the show with an imitation of Marshall McLuhan complete with foaming at the mouth, ranting and head shaking.

'Vile is the relentless pace at which personal identity recedes into the crowd. The self-governing individual eradicated through perpetuation of mindless veneration of insensate objects. The independent thinker, his expansive, eclectic web of influences dwindling, run out of town by uniformly dim witted homogeneous herds blindly pursuing meaning in their otherwise fruitless existence through resolute commitment to dehumanizing devices screeching for urgency and efficiency. Consumption, consumption, consumption, what the fuck is your function?! Great swaths of humanity plugged into evil, radiating power that is the discorded telephone. Seeds of dis-connection and consequent destruction planted and fertilized by corporate keepers dead set on power and fortune, and the muttonhead crowds plead for their share of this sinister crop!'

The skit over, my reminiscing ended. And I asked myself, had the telecommunications industry planted malignant cable in my brain? Had radioactive transmissions mutated, now controlling activation of base urges other than craving a phone?

If so, and if my sensory circuits weren't blackened like an overdone fried chicken steak, then the Texas yahoos were wrong, I'm not a poster child for breast separation anxiety, and I can stand tall next to the Midwest Nominees.

But if early life breast exposure was adequate, and my hippocampus isn't damaged, what accounts for present day confusion? Is it me that's mad, not the scientists? I don't know. I don't know what to think anymore. Where do these thoughts come from anyway? Should I even listen to my thoughts? Why? Do I even know whether thoughts that I think are my thoughts are my thoughts? If not, then how may I possibly know what I think and if I do not know what I think, how do I know who I am for I am what I think, am I not?

$$\Omega$$

The phone rang. Startled, I fell off my chair.

"How are you?" asked Malak.

For others, a perfunctory phrase, a trite greeting awaiting pithy reply. Not Malak. For her, words were measured before spoken.

"How many species of olive trees exist?"

"Sam."

"One. Can you believe it? *Olea Europaea*. The one and only olive tree. Who would have thought? So many olives and all originating from the same tree."

"Amy was part of your life for seven years. You can't remove your left arm and not feel anything."

"I never thought of that. You mean I'm suffering from phantom Amy syndrome?"

"Let yourself grieve, Sam. Make friends with pain, let it work its way through your system."

"Let's not do this over the phone. Can you meet with me?"

"Where?"

"Amelios."

"I'll be there in fifteen minutes."

I arrived at the café before Malak. It was late morning. The usual assortment of characters were hanging about. Procrastinating college student, books piled on table, yellow hi-liters, pens, pencils, Ipod, earbuds, laptop and caffeine supply carried in stainless steel, environmentally friendly reusable container; two high school aged girls, hair tugged into ponytails, braces gleaming through broad smiles, excitedly engaged in conversation punctuated by chronic giggling, blissfully unaware of their emerging flower power; a gaggle of grey men beyond their working years longing for a rush of social interaction sunk into oversized leather chairs eating butter croissants in silence and reading, as if their life depended on it, about business; Estee Lauder painted divorcee softly sipping tea, taking care not to disturb lines temporarily smoothed by botoxed brows, twirling long hair between fingers as a mating call signal to buff young buck on red alert for withering blossoms holding fast to last few petals; bag eyed, bald nine to five office worker decked out in slacks, belt, loafers and crisp dress shirt adorned by blue papermate pen clipped onto shirt pocket ordering one half dozen extra large coffees for himself and co-workers. And then there was me. Unhinged thirty-nine year old man sitting and watching.

"Hey! You almost skewered me with that fork!" Four evenly spaced circular indentations marked my arm courtesy of a shuffling fat man wielding a stray fork. A checkered grey scarf was wrapped around his neck. Lint lingered on his coat collar and the corners of his mouth were turned down.

"My sincere apologies. If you're bleeding, may I suggest you call for medical assistance," came his gravelly tone.

The tables were arranged close together like in a Bronx deli. The man proceeded to sit at a table next to mine. Wary of another stabbing, I watched him out of the corner of my eye. Purposefully, he spread a napkin across his lap. Next, he organized cutlery; one spoon, one knife, and one fork, evenly lined up in a row set atop a second napkin laid adjacent to a saucer sized plate on which lay an apricot scone and steaming cup of lemon tea. I inhaled the citrus scent. Surveying the arrangement, he let go a confident harumph, indicating satisfaction and readiness to move on. Reaching inside his herringbone coat pocket, the man removed a hard shell eyeglass case. Cautiously, as if fearing revelation of contents, he opened the case and took out a compact audio recorder. Hunched forward, he began whispering into the microphone.

"This past December, when winter winds were bitter, I lost Elizabeth. I've looked, I've asked others for help, but no one is up to the task. Her whereabouts remain uncertain. They tell me she's not gone, that I carry her with me. What are they talking about? I know I'll find her. I have to find her. Presently, I need rest. I'm tired. Elizabeth would be happy knowing I'm warm and resting. She would insist on it. I miss her. Where is she? Where did she go? I need to find Elizabeth. I need to help her, to care for her. She needs me. Why can't I find my love, my Elizabeth?"

The man stopped talking. His head hung low, shoulders slumped. The tea had cooled; steam no longer rising. I looked at the fork marks and rubbed my arm. I hadn't felt much else in the last while.

My flagging energy gauge angled hard to the right at the sight of Malak entering. She greeted me with customary full body hug and dual cheek kiss. The fat man took notice, benignly lifting his head. Indulgently, Malak returned his smile as she would to a child. Then she placed her hand on his shoulder and wished him well. The man turned away, teary eyed.

"What's with the expression? You look constipated," she said to me.

"Hah! That's what life is all about, isn't it? And I'm not talking about carburetors, man. It comes down to whether or not we're carrying shit, how much shit and are we able to let it go. Smoothly operating digestive processes permit mountain climbing without breaking a sweat. But when blockage materializes and our small intestine isn't absorbing food or convincingly propelling it to and through the gastrointestinal tract, when enzyme performance fails to support facilitation of chemical digestion, then the whole system breaks down. Would Kadinsky have been able to share his gift of abstraction, Le Corbusier the integrity of the architectural form, if persistently preoccupied with removing fecal blockage, with suffering from indigestible food solubles unable to thrust through the large intestine via peristaltic waves, mass movements and haustral churning thereby engaging the reflex action elicited by rectal distension. When …"

"Dear, please, that's enough. I'm all too familiar with your shit dissertation. Talk to me. Tell me what's been going on since you left Amy."

"Poseidon spoke to me."

"Hmmm."

"No matter how rough the waters, you've got to ride the waves."

"Koan?"

"Back of a cereal box. Could have been Cap'n Crunch."

"Uh huh."

"You know the precept, let there be space in togetherness? Well, that was all dandy when heavenly winds foxtrotted but when the boy and girl lost their groove, infernal breezes altered the two-step to the goosestep."

"And how are you feeling now?"

"Like a guy wearing a sandwich board for Pink Lobster Palace. I'm flat. The air has been let out of my oomph. Unlike Costello, I'm at a loss as to how to pump it up. Yes, I slipped out from under the burden of a knotted relationship. But now where am I? Am I having a breakdown? I've read about breakdowns. I've seen people fall into sinkholes. I recall the mother of a childhood friend. She'd had enough; was screaming to be let out. Not too many knew the real story. Friends and neighbors were told that the woman had been suffering from a nervous breakdown that finally came to a head. On hearing these two ominous words, adults would nod their head, murmur 'oooh' and 'ahhh' as if mumblings alone convey comprehension of torment underlying a suicide attempt, as if the words 'nervous' and 'breakdown' strung together made plain this woman's story, as if all would be well with them now knowing that a layman's label had been affixed to the clinical depressive succumbing to unknowable demons and they could all contentedly return to the absorption of their daily grind under the deluded notion that a label allows one to make sense of the inconceivable, the tragic, the horrifying. But what the label did was allow perception to alter, the neighbors believing that she wasn't normal, and therefore something like this could not happen to them because they were normal because, as far as they knew, they didn't have a label. But my friend's mother did. After gulping sleeping pills washed down by a mickey of whiskey, ambulance sirens interrupted dinner hour and my friend's final image of his mother was that of a limp body gurney strapped and loaded into the back of a white van by two men doing their job. So here I am, wondering if we all have labels, wondering what mine says."

"What should it say?"

"The reason. The label should explain the reason."

"For?"

"What I'm doing."

"What are you doing?"

"Trying to figure out my place in the universal order. Better yet, determining whether there even exists universal order. And if it doesn't exist, then does that mean we're rolling on this giant gravity weighted orb in a state of perpetual chaos, coincidences popping forth every now and then fooling us into believing we have some measure of control over our lives, feeding fleeting illusions of purpose and meaning when in fact there is none?!"

"Do you know what Mies van der Rohe said?"

"What?"

"God is in the details."

"Details? What isn't a detail?"

"Precisely."

"Care to expand?"

"All that *is* matters and has meaning in and of itself."

"Everything matters? What about a hierarchy? Surely there must be a hierarchy clarifying what matters more or less. Without a hierarchy establishing relative value then, objectively speaking, all that *is* matters equally. And if that's what you're saying, if everything is inherently equal, then we randomly ascribe meaning based on selfish and entirely subjective motives."

"Correct."

"How can that be? If there's no hierarchy, how am I to prioritize, to plan? How will I know what to do first, where to focus my attention? How will I get anything done if I don't know where to start?"

"Be like others."

"What do others do?"

"They don't think. They stay busy. Someone asks, what did you do today? They say, oh, I was busy. Awfully busy. So busy, I don't know where the time went. Is it Friday already? How about that! Where did the week go? Before you know it, Monday will be here again and then we can repeat this inane conversation."

"Why stay busy?"

"Why else? When you're busy, you're attending to IMPORTANT THINGS. What is more important than keeping the wheel spinning, being gainfully employed, rising in status, filling your plate and being counted as a productive member of society. Bury yourself in busyness! Yes, busyness, the good ole' reliable hedge against emptiness that stirs the crock of agitation and self-preoccupation. And whatever you do, don't pull the cover off the mirror. The mirror is scary. No sane person would look inside. Is that what you're considering? Looking in the mirror, peering inside your self? Do you really want to risk upending knowledge and prejudices you've strived so hard to attain?"

"Bringing out the sarcastic edge are we?"

"Let me tell you a story. Once upon a time a smattering of young folk, warmed to the stimulus of electric kool aid, adopted a mantra reeking of insubordination. Spreading the good word, their generation was counseled to turn on, tune in, drop out, fornicate in the woods and boycott Woolworths. Informed leaders, wise to the plot, doggedly sniffed out and apprehended the guiding minds whose sinister MANIFESTO SUPPORTING DOING NOTHING threatened to cause civil unrest by destabilizing established economic order. Fingered perpetrators, be they red or blue, were painted as societal pariahs, or worse, for the heinous crime of promoting inner peace and thereby thwarting outward striving.

"And the people in charge said, WE CANNOT LET THIS BE! Without the stick encouraging earning and the carrot inducing spending, there is no mixing, churning and moving the earth for that most noble purpose of increasing our standard of living. THIS IS OUR PURPOSE! For if we do not maximize efficiencies and grow bigger then surely we will suffer catastrophic contraction not unlike that experienced by late twentieth century Japan, a once formidable economic powerhouse become failed capitalist experiment and now land of descending sun, twilight binding a nations' waning pride and puny manhood.

"The moral of the story? Fear is your purpose. Fear is your friend. Fear instills a constant state of economic insecurity impelling you to chase higher investment returns thus spurring you on to glory. Imagine what would happen if THE PEOPLE repudiated Disney perpetuated dreams, stopped spending, thereby threatening our very existence, our *raison d'etre*. Think about it: a consumer society that doesn't spend and consume? Indeed, this is our one and only purpose without which we would be set adrift, rudderless, lost like an atheist. If you're to continue on your fixed course, distractions must never abate; immersion in mundane, soul crunching activity must continue! The mirror must remain covered! For it is DENIAL that offers control over your life, that offers the one true path to salvation. Peace and happiness be damned!"

"Are you done?"

"I presume I've made my point."

"I should get away from it all. Isn't that the saying? Tomorrow, I'm leaving on a jet plane. Find myself a cave. Don't know if I'll be back again."

"Running away is not an answer."

"I like to think of it as running toward."

"What?"

"Meaning."

"In?"

"Existence."

"You're existence has lost meaning?"

"Did it ever have meaning? Brushing up against forty, reviewing personal history, noting achievements and accolades, what does any of it matter? Am I doing anything other than enabling the existential drama that is life? If not, and if the promise of bikini clad Swedish models goes unfulfilled, what's the point of continuing?"

"Swedish models?"

"Well, if someone did dangle leggy Nordic blondes my way then maybe the outlook wouldn't be so bleak now would it?"

"Let's put that one to the side."

"Fine. What do I care."

"You do care. That's why I'm so happy for you."

"You've got your aphorisms mixed up. Misery loves company not happiness."

"You've only just stepped out of the cage. Be patient. Your wings will grow back."

"Wings? Cage? What, was I an imprisoned blue-belied parrot and Amy was my keeper?"

"No one is responsible for keeping you but yourself. You needed to be with Amy to get to where you are today. Amy was no accident. She was integral to your growth."

"I'm not following. Can we go back to the Swedish meat girls?"

Malak reached across the round table, taking hold my hands.

"Dear," she said in a raspy voice, "You've entered the promised land."

"Israel? Are you kidding?! Temple makes me nervous enough what with all that mumbling in tongues. And the desert heat! Oh no, too hot for this fair skinned lad."

"The promised land is a space inside of you. It is a space of love and harmony. As we speak, your energy is realigning to a higher plane."

"Well, if I'm traveling, I'll need refreshments. I'm getting a peppermint hot chocolate. You want one?"

I excused myself to order, returning minutes later with two tall mugs.

"Blech! Warm! If it's not steaming hot, why bother? Have you tried yours? Is it warm too? Go ahead, have a sip. I'm taking mine back. Give me your cup. I'll have new drinks made. And I'll get different mugs. White is so plain. No, white will not do. I feel like orange today. I want orange mugs. Do you want an orange mug too? I'll get you one. Orange is good. Orange dances and flirts, teases and grins. Orange brings laughter to children. The number one color of popsicles? Orange. Brightest crayon on the crayola giant box of sixty-four with built-in pencil sharpener? Orange. If anyone knows anything about colors, it's kids. What other color has a fruit for its namesake? Can you rhyme any words with orange? No, you can't. So what, you say? I say, additional support for the singular uniqueness and superiority of orange. What boggles the mind is that, somehow, on the totem pole of color preference, orange places in the middle, behind red, blue, green, even yellow for goodness sake. Ask someone, anyone, their favorite color. Odds are that orange will not be their first answer. Why? What happened? Is it too common? Does ubiquity spell death? Orange, orange is everywhere but instead of hosting center stage, orange is shunned, picked from time to time but mostly neglected until winter storms damage Floridian harvests, denting supply, undermining stability of futures markets and consequently jacking up prices until outpourings of outrage, and outrageous outpourings, swamp Consumer Complaints Bureaus nationwide because America's favorite morning juice skyrocketed in price. While this is all well and good for proponents of fifteen minutes of fame and wider distribution channels, in the long run we can't rely on Jack Frost to hoist orange into the spotlight! Stand up for orange; the king of colors must be given its due!"

"Sam, you've opened the door to sweet spirits, letting them cross into every fiber of your being, every molecule, every atom. They're telling you to let go, sit back, let your self evolve and, for now, forget about making yourself comfortable. Instead, know that pain, chaos, confusion and angst are part and parcel of the process of mind, body and spirit uniting; accept the process, see it as an adventure in learning about yourself, about who you are."

"Ah ha! I knew it! They were holding out on me. Look over there. Those people have orange mugs. Well then, we'll have orange too!"

"Sam."

"Look, you're my friend. I trust you. But as far as me running on up the rungs of a transcendental ladder, the supernatural act doesn't play well. Let's talk concrete. I walked out on her. Now she's suicidal. Aren't I responsible? What am I supposed to do? But if I go back, what will happen to me? Are you still teaching nude pilates to the butch lesbian crowd?"

"Don't do that, Sam. Don't hang yourself on a cross. You don't need to justify your leaving. You don't need to convince yourself or anyone else that you intended no harm. The clock stopped ticking. You gathered up the strength to say goodbye. End of story. Done. Over. Stop hitting rewind. The production has closed down. The two of you lasted this long. Bravo. But both of you were bound to go your separate ways. Not only because of her but because of you too. While others strive for stability, you suffocate under its crushing weight. You get bored."

"So I get bored. Who doesn't get bored? I still loved her, no?"

"You did and still do."

"Then why am I here with you instead of with Amy?"

"Walt Whitman said, 'yes, I contradict myself! I contain infinities!' You're no Whitman but you too contain conflicting infinities. She never read Whitman and she never knew anyone like you. Her love for you is deep, pure. Be that as it may, she's equally as frightened of you. You're disruptive, obstinate, intense, you're unable to walk a straight line and this she didn't understand, this unnerved her, disturbed her, kept her off balance. So, as a matter of self-preservation, not strategic calculation as you may be thinking, Amy did what she could to hold fast to illusions of control, to prevent stability from wavering.

"To breed consistency, to shape you, Amy resorted to subtle feminine manipulation, nothing extraordinary, nothing that other woman don't do to civilize men, sort them into husbands and fathers. Understanding that repeated behavior habituates and becomes the norm, she involved herself in your life as much as she could believing that the more you were exposed to her thinking, her mannerisms, her actions, the sooner she would ooze into you thereby altering your natural course. And she was right. No surprise there. With men being generally clueless when it comes to intimacy, changing you wasn't terribly difficult. To round out your edges, you were immersed in a world of gentility, force fitted into Osh Kosh overalls and surrounded by trees; your home decorated with floral furniture and barnyard paintings. Determined as she was, she even bought you a toolbox thinking one day you might be able to tell a hammer from a wrench, even put it to use. Ambition she didn't lack.

"Amy knew enough about you. She knew of your vanity and your rescue fantasies. She knew you were a nice boy and a good catch from a decent, middle class family. And she knew you were good for her and even if you weren't entirely good for her then you were okay and okay was good enough. Within this realm of an acceptable, if not perfectly compatible, mate she was well within her rights to feign happiness now and then. For the sake of the relationship, her performance had to go on because you, Linus, were her security blanket, slaying predators, real and imagined, your presence alone making manageable chronic fear of not being good enough, fear that manifested as perfectionism, achievement and the need to please others. And like others who've yet to grow to see solitude as an ally rather than an enemy, her fears were misplaced. Of course they were; she's strong as an ox but doesn't know it.

"But she did know about your dalliances, every one of them. And she was hurt, devastated, each fresh betrayal magnifying her pain and animosity but also her resolve to continue. Because exposing you for exposing yourself was not an option; no transgression, no matter how damning, was reason enough for her to say goodbye. To the contrary, she was convinced that your pain was greater than hers, that your prancing libido was a blatant cry for help from a wounded soul.

"So she tried, she did what she could to help, but you shut her out and, as unsure of yourself as you were, as you still are, you walked out. That was your solution. But it wasn't a solution at all. Far from it. You can abandon others but not your self. When you left, the pain followed and now its become worse. That's why you're here talking to me. Because you're looking not for a way out but a way in, a path to understanding your self, your life. Oh, don't give me that look! The one that says I'm a harebrained sorcerer."

"You're not? That's what I love about you."

"Okay, let me put it in your language. Remember the recurring dream you've been telling me about, the one where you're wiping your ass but no matter how many times you wipe, the shit doesn't go away? Your subconscious is giving you two choices: one, be tormented by colon and rectum fallout in the form of anal fissure, perianal abscesses and hemorrhoids the size of a ten pin bowling ball or, two, make friends with the struggle, surrender to the unknown, the uncertainty, the freedom to fly without knowing if or where you'll land, step off the brown path and gravitate toward purple, red, blue, green and, yes, orange."

"And until that choice is made?"

"What else? Sip."

Chapter 4
Random Seduction

Who looks outside dreams,
who looks inside awakes
— Carl Jung —

I'm looking up at the sky. Rain is falling from a big grey cloud. It's a twenty-minute walk to the yoga studio, thirty if I dawdle. I'm dawdling. Because falling raindrops soothe my head and my head needs soothing. And because yogis don't run. Not that I'm a yogi but I've been known to pretend.

I don't carry an umbrella. I don't cringe, scurry for shelter, wear a hat, coat, gloves, pants or moisture repelling boots. I do, however, just for the heck of it, stand on guard for thee holding a bar of oatmeal soap saluting raindrops of all size and shape, marvel at the sight of cleansing streams spurting forth from billowy masses of condensed water vapor, and prostrate myself in thanks, chanting praise to Mother Nature for showering bountiful life force upon voluptuous planet Earth.

Palpable shouts of shock and dismay rise from a chorus of onlookers.

"Look at you; you're all wet! Get out of the rain, the rain. Good God, get out!"

Panicking, the people are concerned that I'll melt. Or something.

"Look at him standing there like that getting soaked. What's wrong? Help him!"

They bring me in from the wet cold. On a dry landing, they towel me off, buzzing about until assured of my physical comfort.

"Soon you will be dry," they say, consoling me, believing I need consoling, relieved that I'm doing as they want.

"Yes, soon I'll be dry. Then I'll be wet again for as long as it takes before I'm dry. Life is like that, yo-yoing from places of comfort to discomfort and back again. As long as perspective is inflexible, equilibrium remains elusive," I tell them.

They look at me as if I'm out of reach, as if I can't be saved.

I step back into the drizzle. The chorus frowns, feeling sorry for me. I wonder whether they've been saved and what that means. Maybe they're B.J. Thomas fans, he who gave rain a bad rap, equating liquid precipitation with the blues. Word on the street is that, when rain fell, B.J. was plagued by biblical images of amphibians falling from the sky. Turn these images upside down and he would have recognized a gift, not a plague. A present in the form of *Ch'ing Wa-Sheng*, the Chinese frog spirit, ushering in healing and good fortune, a mainstay of historical Chinese culture, a permanent extra-terrestrial guest seated at the pecking order of nations table whose omnipotent powers dispel all reasonable debate about the source of China's exponential expansion. Confucian adherents may practice humility but this doesn't mean they don't have a golden frog or two up their collective sleeve. Ribbit.

Arriving at the studio, I'm greeted by a yellowing photo of a flabby, solemn looking Indian fellow. The accompanying caption reads: '*Breath flows in and out yet never does it pause. To pause is to seize up, to stop living. Find your breath and you find your life.*'

The change room is straight ahead. I swipe aside drab tan curtains hiding unclothed, parading men from indifferent women. I strip naked save for shorts in anticipation of baking in one hundred and ten degree Delhi like heat holding out the promise of fevered exhaustion for the uninitiated or for those who break before they bend.

At my side administering fluids, as need be, will be Nina; she who materialized from a recurring daytime fantasy, revelation, premonition, whatever you want to call it. For eighty-seven consecutive days, her image (nameless at the time) visited me in daydreams, interrupting headspace crammed with deteriorating states of relations between Amy and I. Then, on the eighty-eighth day after the vision first appeared, at the croak of midday, happenstance rolled into motion.

It started with a telephone call from my brother Benji, the dentist, doctor in the family, chess whiz, orchestral flutist, pillar of the community, religiously devoted hypochondriac. The hypochondriac was on the line.

"Sam, is that you?"

"No."

"Sam, this is no time for jokes. Mrs. Albertson was in the chair, I'm drilling into a decaying back molar when pain shoots through my arm, setting off spastic twitching causing me to clasp the drill too tight, push down and bore a hole straight through her gums. Lucky for me the old lady's phobic about needles and, before the procedure started, she sucked back enough gas to anesthetize a rhino. My assistant repaired the mess and gave her a month's supply of painkillers. Why am I talking about this? Enough about Mrs. Albertson! I don't have much time. I need you to come to the office and take me to the hospital. I can't breathe. I'm dizzy.

I'm having a heart attack. I'm going to die! Where are you? I need your help. When can you be here?"

"You had thirty-six good years. Be thankful."

"I should have recognized the signs last night when we were celebrating my in-laws wedding anniversary. But chest tightness is par for the curse, I mean course, when I'm in the same room as them and …"

"Fascinating. Would love to hear more but I have a scalp massage appointment. Dandruff. Oh, will you look at that? Flakes. I'm late. Gotta go."

"Wait, don't hang up! Leave me and it'll be on your conscience! Is that what you want? To be responsible for your one and only brother's death? Is it?"

"Why are you calling me? What can I do? Call 911."

"Don't you think I already did? They're late. They should have been here already. This woman says they can't be trusted."

"What woman?"

"This patient of mine, sitting in the waiting room, watching what's going on."

"Since when do you listen to your patients? Is she a doctor? A nurse? What does she know?"

"That's exactly what I asked her. She says she's seen people have heart attacks and claims I'm not having one. She says I'm fine. Here I am, my heart on the verge of exploding and she says there's no problem. Well, I say, I'M NOT FINE! There's a problem, a real problem. And you know what she does? She smirks. Who does she think she is, challenging me? If she wasn't a patient of mine and if I had the strength and I wasn't about to die, I'd have tossed her out on her rear end."

"And you're listening to this person because …"

"Because she's talking! I'm in my office, she's talking and I can't get away from her jabbering about how I should choose my foods more carefully and that trans fats are probably plugging up my arteries. And as she's talking she blurts out our surname and says, now I know who you are. I roll my eyes and say, that's right you twit, I'm your dentist and I've been your dentist for the past three years! But she ignores me and asks if I have a brother and I didn't know where she was going with this but I was weak so I admitted your existence. Well, then it gets scary. Her fish eyes start bugging out, she's biting her fingernails and her forehead frowns in consternation as if she were one thought away from curing cancer if her head didn't explode first. Finally, she speaks, asking me where I grew up. So I tell her. What a mistake! She moves closer to me and I'm thinking she's going to push me onto the floor and force me into something that could be considered outside acceptable bounds of doctor-patient relationship. Despite my near death condition, I see what's happening and I see that if I don't stop her I could lose my dental license so I tell her to calm down because I'm married and, besides, my heart has all the excitement it can handle just now. She blurts out that the two of you knew each other when you were teenagers. I tell her that's not possible because I knew pretty much all the strumpets you dated and I didn't recall her. Make of it what you will but by then she was twirling like a ballerina. Listen to me; forget about her. I need you to drive me to the hospital. My time's running out!"

"Her name?"

"Nina something or other. Who cares?!"

"Maybe this is my premonition brought to life? Maybe this Nina is the inspiration for my visions? It's possible isn't it? Why else would she get so excited at the mention of my name? Maybe she's been having visions of me? Any physicist worth their Himalayan sea salt knows that science advances through acceptance of absurdities, believing in the heretofore unbelievable, erasing straight lines of ivory tower stilted logic and sensibility. Is it absurd to suggest that *thoughts* traverse deep, middle and shallow space cloaked in energy particles put *out there* to hop, skip and jump about until boomeranging to a predetermined destination, in one form or another, when magnetic pull takes hold?"

"Hey, I'm dying over here and you're rambling on about sea salt!"

"And what if the power of thoughts, ideas and dreams transcend dimensions of time and space, float in this beige field we call THE UNIVERSE, and come together at a deep space grand central station where connections are made, never early nor late but always on time, prayers, petitions, pleadings and man made schedules notwithstanding?"

"Sam, I've got no more than sixty seconds before …"

I hung up. A few minutes later, anxiously, I dialed Benji's office and charmed the receptionist into giving me Nina's number. Then I called her and we spoke, small talk stuff (too soon for big talk). And on the premise of two old friends visiting, we arranged to meet the next day, six o'clock at Cedarvale Park, near the fenced in dog playground.

Arriving early, I saw signs telling walkers to walk on the left, joggers to yield to baby strollers, cyclists to stay right, and teenagers not to gather in packs of more than three. Unfortunately, I didn't spot a sign spelling out the theory of quantum mechanics. A reminder of the theory's two basic precepts could have saved me a heap of future trouble: one, the universe, at its most elemental level, is a random place operating oblivious to man made morality; and two, boomerangs traveling faster than the speed of light contain force fields sufficient to send metaphysical understanding of self into wobbly tailspin.

There was no glass to brake in the event of emergency. So I scoped out park exits for nearby escape routes. If the years had been unkind to Nina, I would sneak out the back without smiling, nodding my head or hand waving to acknowledge her presence, one of three generally accepted continental greeting forms. For extra protection, I milled about with dog owners, silently reserving the option to co-opt a large breed for enhanced cover. That was the plan. And it failed. Miserably. I didn't count on her recognizing me after all these years. But she did. There she was, looking in my direction, amiably calling my name. Do I answer? By my calculation, precisely four ticks remained to admit who I was or bolt. Why was I here? Because of a dream? I'm letting dreams guide my waking life? What next, Scientology? Yikes, it was too late! Frozen in mid-debate, she moved toward me, hugging me, spraying me with her sugary pheromones, bamboozling my decision making and leaving me no choice but to surreptitiously look her up and down before cautiously setting sail down the bumpy stone walkway.

I asked myself, is it she who has been surfing the strata of my subconscious? And my subconscious answered, 'Come on, you know very well that established scientific principles recognize the impossibility of an effect happening before the cause.'

What about parapsychologists? They're scientists aren't they? Maybe even doctors. They say that precognition is a form of extrasensory perception, you know, ESP, that doesn't rely on our commonly known senses. And just because it can't be explained by traditional measures doesn't make it any less valid.

'You're throwing your hat in the ring with clairvoyants now?'

Then how do you explain my dreaming of Nina? It was surreal. How could I dream of someone one day and there they are the next?

I felt dizzy. Really dizzy. Struggling to process Nina's three-dimensional form, reality and dream states battled for supremacy, causing bodily functioning to fall into disarray. Spools of spit clustered on corners of my mouth. One hand glided across my jaw, blotting wayward drool to prop outward appearance of tenuous normalcy. Holding saliva production in check, hearing was next to go awry. At first, I thought she might be wily enough to be mouthing words to me without speaking, as if she were Milli Vanilli pulling wool over the Grammys. But I was mistaken. Craftiness wasn't in her bones. Rather, my auditory processing was on the fritz; sound came through but her words were garbled. Sense of touch was next to shut down. I learned of this only after slipping on a gang of forest tent caterpillars, falling and denting my nose against the sidewalk without so much as an ouch from me but an audible gasp from Nina that, coincidentally, and gratefully, provoked hearing reset. Yet, I didn't rejoice. Too busy tending to my bloody nose, I sprinted to a nearby pond, my jerky movements disturbing floating Mallards causing them to flutter away while dropping turds of alarm. Water cupped in hands, splashing my face and neck, my stupor finally ruptured and I regained some semblance of balance.

Recalling what the Indian man said, I tried to find my breath. In and out, long and deep, again and again, I breathed. And soon, throbbing proboscis pain broke through, my dream state dissolved, and I faced Nina. She was looking at me, quizzically but compassionately, in a way suggestive of familiarity with asylum inmate behavior. Apparently not overly concerned with my outburst, she resumed speaking in words I now comprehended, talking something about the essence of vitalism while cradling nose cartilage wrapped in tissue.

Pleasantly surprised she hadn't concocted an excuse to leave (not that concoctions were needed) I postponed the escape plan. By the end of our prolonged getting to know you, telepathic force fields gyrating on inter-planetary hula hoops concluded that our inimitable indentations fit sublimely. Or so I believed until a purposeful boomerang cozied up in my back pocket suggesting otherwise, suggesting that a soon to be passionate mutual absorption masked fundamental incompatibility.

Ω

By the time I entered the studio Nina was absorbed in a meditative trance, dry heat limbering her mind and body.

Softly, she spoke. "Honey, you're late. You know I like you to be with me before class starts."

"I was with Malak. Lost track of time."

"That's the third time this week you've seen Malak. You spend a lot of time with her, don't you? How is she? You know what, tell me after class. Come lie down. I saved a spot for you. Why are you all wet?"

The studio was full. Nina wore a tube top and black shorts revealing hips known to inspire quivering in dead men, the beginnings of a self-conscious belly roll on an otherwise firm aging body, and unusually small breasts that she adored. I assumed position beside her, physically readying myself for class. Mental preparation, however, wasn't easy. My mind racing, I sought solace in past teachings.

'Concentrate. Let go your thoughts. Empty your mind.'

Concentrate to let go? If I'm concentrating, I'm holding on, not letting go. And how am I supposed to concentrate if my mind is empty?

'To empty your mind means to channel your thoughts toward this very moment, letting go stories, both past and future, so all you have is this porthole in time. Your needs satisfied, your wants suspended, you are complete, here in the moment.'

For the next ninety minutes, I was anywhere but here. Challenged to stand on my feet never mind my head, and thoroughly distracted by scantily clad, panting, glistening, straining, contorting female bodies emitting barrels of dank sweat, benign delirium took hold as I tried to keep up with the class.

"Push!" screamed a lithesome, squinty-eyed instructor named Owl, jolting me out of hallucination and into the studio's four corners. Perching herself front and center upon a short dais, Owl screeched commands into her headset, her itchy voice blaring from six speakers affixed to a low ceiling.

"Everyone, stand up! Hands clasped together, heels and toes touching, hips forward, transfer your weight to your heels, YOUR HEELS, back straight, shoulders relaxed, elbows down, looking at yourself in the mirror, NOW, breathe … in … slowly. OK, TREE POSTURE, EVERYONE, TREE POSTURE!" she snarled. "One hand pressed against the other, index finger and thumb unclasped, reach up, up, UP, elbows straight, parallel to the ears, weight on your heels, hips forward, ankles and toes touching, feet together, reach toward the ceiling, higher, HIGHER, now, gently, move your arms to the right, nothing else moves, NOTHING, bend to the right, arms straight, elbows locked, LOCKED I said, like a branch, hold it there, go deep, deeper, okay, now bend back to center, reach up toward the ceiling, now we're moving to the left, remember to breathe, always remember your breath, be one with your breath …"

Straining to follow Owl's flight path, I endured twenty-six *asanas* ending in *savasana*, corpse pose.

"Good class?" I asked Nina.

"Baby, I'm walking on air."

"You hungry?"

"More thirsty."

"What do you feel like?"

"Hey, hold that thought."

Nina strolled over to a disheveled man, his age hidden by grime covered clothes and blistered skin. He could have been twenty; he could have been fifty. Nina dropped two dollars worth of coins into a soiled cup held in the man's outstretched hand then wished him a pleasant day.

"Fuck off, bitch!" cursed the man after hearing the tinkle.

"Excuse me?" Nina said, taken aback.

"Does that make you feel better? Assuage your fucking conscience? Done your good deed for the day? Do you think your fat ass and dirty money brighten my day? Think again, bitch. Your money doesn't do a thing for me. Not one fucking thing. But your ego feels better doesn't it? Sure it does. You giving me money is all about you, not me. You don't give horseshit about me. You only care about yourself, making yourself feel good. What will two dollars do for me? Tell me, what?! You think you're helping? You think I don't want to be here on the street sleeping on sidewalk grates blowing filthy subway steam, waking to an empty stomach, dumpster diving outside restaurants for stale bread, begging strangers for miserly handouts, being ignored by assholes like you as if I were invisible, wondering whether I'll survive another bitter winter without shelter? Will your two dollars restore my dignity? Is that what you think? You don't know anything. You want to help me, give me five thousand dollars. That would help. But two fucking dollars? Get out of here!"

Sheepishly, Nina listened to the tirade. She was quiet for a time before responding.

"You're right. You're absolutely right. I don't know who you are. I don't know why you're begging on the street. I don't know what choices you've made in life. I overstepped your boundary. I didn't think about you. I didn't respect you. And my action fed your anger. That's the last thing I wanted to do so please give back the money and I won't bother you again."

"What?"

"If you give the money back to me, you'll have one less target for your anger and more space for compassion."

"I'm warning you, lady, get out of my face!"

The man glanced toward me then back at Nina. His bravado was false. He knew it. Clutching the dirty cup, pressing it against his jutting rib cage, he protected his belongings.

"Let's go," I said and lightly took hold of Nina's arm. She didn't resist.

"Oh my goodness, I feel terrible for that man. He carries so much sadness with him. I wish I could help him but he doesn't know how to accept help." Nina's voice shook.

"You know how to do ear candling, don't you? Maybe purifying his ears would open him up."

"His energy is blocked in so many places."

"Of course, skeptics claim that candling is bogus and that insufficient pressure is created to vacuum out any impurities sullying the ear. Do you have another spell you could cast?"

"Don't make fun, Sam. I read people's energy. Energy transmissions are authentic; they're not conscious phenomena that can be disguised. I mean, that's what we are, right, a bundle of energy. At the most basic level, all living things are forms of energy. You know me, I'm tuned into the human spectrum of frequencies. This way, I'm not deceived by physical attraction or disingenuous words."

"I prefer to hang my hat on scent."

"I wish I had an off switch, like a radio knob, so I could tune out and be less empathetic. But I don't. It's not like I can take down my antennae and stop receiving other people's emotions. It's not just that I'm empathetic, I mean, I do empathize with people but more than that it's like I actually experience what the other person is experiencing. I'm on my side *and* their side at the same time so when someone is sad, not only do I feel badly for them but I also feel what they're feeling. And there's so much sadness in the world. It's all so heavy and I don't know how to stop it from bringing me down. It makes me wonder whether the human condition is wired primarily for suffering or *dukkha*, as my yogi says. Here and there, happiness displaces sorrow but why is the default condition sorrow? Is it because we're selfish, we pity ourselves when life doesn't go our way, when our dreams and wishes are not fulfilled? And because wishes rarely come true we nurse sorrow, so much that we burrow into behavioral ruts nearly impossible to climb out from, ruts chock-full of self-made troubles and worries that wouldn't even exist, or at least wouldn't be so deep if we focused on life's bounty instead of shortfalls, if we learned selflessness instead of greed, if we stopped craving and clinging and let our heart be our guide? Maybe then sorrow's hold would diminish. This is why I'm devoted to my yoga practice. The studio is my sanctuary; it's where toxic emotional overload runs off and I rejuvenate; it's where I'm working hard toward changing my lens and moving away from sadness so I'll be able to live my life from a place of contentment and if I'm content, I'll be filled with light, more than enough for myself and to help others along on their journey. That's a big part of who I am, you know, someone who is here to help less fortunate people. It's what I'm all about. Do you think that poor man was touched by my light?"

"If I know my liquor bouquet, I'm guessing he was more touched by vodka."

"Don't you feel fantastic after yoga class? It's such a wonderful feeling! I'm so peaceful and in love with life! And I'm in love with you! You don't mind if I lock you up in my dungeon and throw away the key, do you?"

"What's my energy reading now?"

"Oh, honey. It's such a beautiful day."

"Just for fun, Isis. Connect your sensors to me."

"I'm tired, honey. That man on the street depleted me. Oh my goodness! I forgot all about my meeting with Lily. Have I mentioned Lily? She's not well. She's a model you know, thin, attractive, absolutely gorgeous! But she let herself go on vacation in St. Barts, put on ten pounds and hasn't worked in the month since her return. She's in total panic mode. Her agent says no more shoots are coming her way until she loses weight. And her husband told her she's fat. Isn't that terrible? Lily's having a hard time and needs to talk with me. You go get something to eat, I'll see you later, okay? I really have to go, I'm sorry. I'll make it up to you. I love you, honey."

I watched Nina scamper toward the bus stop. She preferred traveling by bus, streetcar or subway but wouldn't be caught alive in a private vehicle, those bastions of seclusion, segregation and loneliness. Opposition wasn't based on environmental concern; rather, she felt uncomfortably isolated while locked inside four thousand pounds of heavy metal that, by its mere existence, thumbed its' nose at public transportation, a travel mode inherently supportive of public cohesion and the ties that bind the fabric of civilized society. I suggested she contact the Toronto Transit Commission with marketing campaign ideas aimed at increasing ridership.

To start her off in the right direction, I gave her a few taglines like, Forget Facebook: Hook Up on the Bus or Reach Out and Touch Someone ... on the Trolley. Surefire winners, I said. She declined, questioning my sincerity, of all things. I reminded her that the starting point of change is holding fast to one idea that is stridently, repeatedly ridiculed by conventional wisdom. This would easily be the second greatest marketing campaign ever, I said, setting in motion a revolution not seen since diamonds got messed up with love, commitment and being a best friend to girls. Sure, sure, it's all been said before but, come on, diamonds are a girl's best friend? What does this mean? Who are these *girls*? And how messed up are they that they need to buy a friend and fasten it tight to their finger? Or, could it be, heavens to betsy, the intent is to hold women in psychological bondage, reinforce infantilization, degradation, submission, inferiority, deficiency, inadequacy and subordination to the MALE, the beast ordained with decision-making power as to whom to make honest? As far as best friends go, while the pet rock splashed down during the disco decade, communing with the lonesome and mindless, the fad ran its course and not since the Bee Gees interminable stay at the top of the pop charts convinced Kim Jong-Il to curl his hair, squeeze into a purple velour jumpsuit and perturb macho men and kinsmen to the south by revealing his hairless chest while tripping over sequined platform shoes has man, woman, boy, girl or any stray combination of the four sidled up to an indifferent mineral.

Stringent analysis, meticulous debunking and pure objectivity aside, Debeers smacked a grand slam. Pure genius, marketing a carbon allotrope of extraordinarily hard composition that facilitates thermal conductivity within remarkable optical characteristics impervious to contamination; a stone birthed on the third rock from the sun available to all with inclination and means to search. But, if there be no such inclination coupled with means, then leave it to coifed men in the mining trade to wreck havoc, fundamentally disrupt animals, plants, marine life, communities and economies in search of glittering stones sold under the best friend banner. Are we to admire a masterly marketing campaign, pity untold numbers succumbing to the pitch or prudently purchase shares in the diamond king?

'Sir, may I remind you that barren fingers do not make for a happy wife. You do know that the English word *diamond* is a derivative of the Greek word *adamas*, meaning invincible. Sanctify your marriage with this lustrous stone, honor your woman and, by extension, adorn your relationship with invincibility. How could you not want what your wife wants; what *everyone* wants?'

Rather than contributing to the collection bowl of ruthless Edwardian dandies insatiably scouring gigantic underground holes for cubic crystals, my preference is to hark back to an age when diamonds were used as a talisman warding off evil. Be gone, diamond hunters!

'Collection bowl, eh?! Be careful what you mock. Diamonds are serious!'

No. Diamonds are diamonds. We the people accede to superimposing arbitrary value on a rock, a damn rock, for the illusory effect of creating material wealth, social division, disharmony and a singular form of human stupidity, as if our natural inclination toward lunacy isn't enough. Genuflecting to displays of a piece of earth on one's finger, in an ear, around a neck, tongue stapled, or *pipick* pierced, is optional. Do people not know any better?

'What does it matter? Fact is they don't.'

It does matter. It's one gauge of a person's symbolic affinity for recognition, status and inclusion in the moneyed or married world; it's intended as currency, announcing in which lane you place yourself in the human race.

'Sometimes, a diamond is a diamond is a diamond, is it not?'

A cigar is not only a cigar even when it's a cigar. Freud was hopped up on fine Austrian snow when he spit that one out. When we're talking diamonds, what are we really talking? That's right, money. Instead of plastering paper bills about our body in a desperate cry to be noticed and desire to belong, we get to exhibit wealth in the form of shiny stones. So much more convenient, so much prettier. Pretty counts not just for looks but at a glance we can measure our self against others, compare who is bigger which, of course, will determine who will feel better about themselves and whom will envy whom. Ahh, the stink of money! A perfume all too familiar to diamond hunters dressed in starched white, initial embroidered shirts tailor made on Savile Row who, as it happens, do not decorate themselves with carats but compensate for their own shortcomings by smoking truckloads of humidor stored Cubans.

The bus arrived. Surveying Nina's behind as she climbed aboard, I sensed trouble ahead. The unassuming vehicle belched exhaust soot and passed me by. I waved to Nina but she didn't notice. She was looking straight ahead, as if wearing blinders, as if she were alone in the crowd. Once the bus turned the corner I forgot about Nina and began retreating from the day, feeling smaller.

Chapter 5
Come As You Are

The bird a nest
the spider a web
the human friendship
– William Blake

I chose a roundabout route to cycle to Jack's home. Peddling through a maze of pot holed back alleys, I slowed once a tree-house jutting above an unpainted wood fence came into view.

The post and rail gate was unlocked. Entering the yard, I pushed out the bike's kickstand and walked toward the front door. Before arriving, pensiveness took hold and Psyche spoke.

'What color?'

What?

'What color do you want? I got red, I got white, I got green. I got red and white, green and white, and red and green. They all work the same. Don't make no difference which one you take. People like a choice. Makes 'em feel like they the man, like they in control.'

But they're all the same? Only difference is packaging?

'Uh huh. That's right.'

Doesn't make any sense.

'Don't got to make sense. Just got to satisfy the customer, make the customer feel good 'bout themself.'

I'll be fine. I don't need help.

'Suit yourself. You wanna wallow, that's cool. Lots o' folks they like to feed them shitty feelings, make 'em grow and feel all heavy 'cause they think they ain't got no better feelings that wanna hang out. When they like that, they always hiding somethin'. And when you hiding, you solitary. And the solitary man, he ain't a healthy man. Nope. The solitary man, he's denying the connection instinct, the need to commune with other folks for the sake of communion. That's it, nothing else but communion be the goal. We all got that instinct. That's how the Good Lord pieced us together. Doesn't matter what kind of fancy stuff you got or don't got, how many flags you planted, or the number of notches on your post, you gonna be one lonely fool if you don't step out of your cocoon and open yourself up. As long as you wallowing, you closed. You don't believe me? Take a chance, see what it's like when you flush that heavy shit away, when you trump that funk and step out from the shadows. Ain't nothing wrong with taking a little help from a friend; we all got to be a customer sometime. You change your mind; you call me. You got my number.'

Climbing long, narrow steps fitting for children's feet or ancient Mayan pyramids, I landed on the porch in front of a closed aluminum screen door. The door to the house was open. I could see Elise in the hallway on the phone.

Elise is the biological mother of her and Jacks only child. She's a mother who denies maternal instincts, believing them to be a fairy tale along the lines of Cinderella meant to bind women, plot against their freedom, negate their talents and dumb them down through mind numbing years spent in playpens and sandboxes.

Born with her middle finger extended, Elise is in complete possession of herself. She chain smokes Virginia Slims, chants after sundown, lectures on the evils of red meat, loses herself in Plath, head bangs to Black Sabbath, plays violin, drives a pink Vespa scooter, has a Karate black belt, swims naked in community pools to the alarm and delight of bystanders, competes in high level squash, chops wood, sips gunpowder tea at two o'clock every day, and ferociously brawls against daily ministrations of life.

'Why? What is the point?' she asks heatedly. 'If I clean up today then I will have to clean again tomorrow so why not leave the mess until it becomes unbearable? Why can it not sit for days, weeks, even months? I don't have time for this. Why should I waste my life cleaning? What is so important about being clean? Is cleanliness a virtue? It is not a virtue; it is not next to godliness; it's a sickness, an illness of the highest order, and I won't be infected with this germ phobic, compulsive hand washing obsession! Clutter helps the creative process. Dirt builds the immune system. I want clutter. I need clutter. Let the stupid people clean up after themselves, rejoice in tidiness and die wearing clean underwear.'

While Jack tolerated degrees of disorderliness, he wasn't a fan of filth. And when too many cockroaches bunked in corners, it was time to fetch the mop, pail and whatever poison was handy. Elise, however, refused to pay for cleaners. Strategically downplaying their comfortable financial position, she insisted they couldn't afford a bourgeois extravagance and, even if they could, under no circumstances would she lord over a servant. Fact is, she didn't want her territory disturbed. Jack, who loved Elise dearly, accepted her eccentricities and, out of respect, hired help when she wasn't home. Upon returning to a home free of insect colonies and plump mice, Elise said nothing. Theirs was an unspoken understanding that served them well.

Elise was talking louder now.

"It's in my blood! Why? Why? Idiot! I do not ask why. I know! Is that not enough, to know? Does a butterfly ask why it flutters? A porpoise why it swims? Do I get to choose who I am? Bah! What choose?! No one chooses. This is me. I am a creator, we are all creators, and I share my creations. I cannot deny my expression. You think I can deny? I can't deny. Why would I do that!? Stifle expression and you burst! Me, I speak out! What good am I if I hide away in a corner, refusing dialogue, withholding contributions? You know Vygotsky? Scaffolding he called it. Adding blocks to the foundation. The more we know, the broader the foundation, the more strength we have, the more we take life by the tail. And by 'we' I mean the individual and society as a whole. Like other artists, I cast my wares into the mix and from there who knows what will come next. That is not my concern. My concern is to participate. That is enough. And my work gives people pleasure, yes? Does the world know enough pleasure? Is there ever enough to lessen the emptiness of existence? Why would I deprive others of pleasure? If my work brings one moment of joy to one person, lights one candle for one instant, then I have contributed, I have made a difference."

I knocked loudly intending to interrupt. Elise looked up. Seeing me standing outside, she abruptly ended her conversation by dropping the corded phone on the floor then rushing to open the door.

"Sam! *Cherie*, it's Sam! Come in, come in! It has been so long, when did we last see you, look at you, you're tired, why are you tired, don't stand there like a stranger, follow me, I will get you a drink, please, come with me, what would you like, I know, I'll prepare a tequila, absinthe and rum. It is marvelous, my new favorite, this drink of mine, you will love it. Are you cold, I see you are cold, I'll get you a warm blanket, we have beautiful blankets, hand knitted from organic fed llamas on Salt Spring Island, oh, they are delightfully comfortable, you have no idea. You will like it so much you will want to steal it from me before you go, I bet! If this is what it takes to get you here, then it's yours! Whatever you want, I give to you. Jack will be so happy you are here! I didn't know you would be visiting, Jack didn't tell me. Did you tell Jack you would be visiting? Does he know? So what, you are here, that's what matters. You know we love to see you. You don't visit enough, always busy with work, work, work, ugh, I don't know how you stand it, spending so much time working, and for other people too, why do you do it? For the money? You waste your life! This is not good, I've told you before. You must listen to me. We will talk. For now, wrap yourself in the blanket. You look thin. You've lost weight. No wonder you're cold. Do you want another blanket? Jack misses you; I miss you. Come sit down and tell us everything, we want to know everything that is happening in your life. You will tell us, yes? Of course, you will, why wouldn't you? You have nothing to hide, right, or do you? Do you Sam, are you hiding something from us because if you are I want you to know right now that we will understand, whatever it is, we all have problems, of course, but you do know, yes, that we are safe. If you are burdened, talk to us, we are your friends, yes, we guard you with our life, because we love you.

"As for me, I am close, oh so close, to finishing my sculpture; I have been working on it for so long. But I cannot tell you how many days or months or years. Why should I keep track, catalogue time? When I have a project to complete, I do it and I finish when I finish! I get lost in my work. I forget the days of the week, sometimes I even forget to pee until the pain in my abdomen is too much and I think, uh oh, where is the toilet, I need a toilet. Fast. Then I relieve myself and I am so thankful for the toilet and I moan in relief and think to myself that I should remember to pee more often. I don't know why I forget. I am like a little boy, too busy having fun. I leave the door to the toilet open. Do you do that? Jack does not like this, he says peeing is a private matter and I should close the door. What does he know? I tell him he is uptight, a product of this Miss Manners society of ours. If he doesn't like to watch, then don't look. Why is he looking? If he looks, then that is his problem. I relieve myself, it's natural, is it not? Since when is it not natural? Between you and me, I think he likes watching. It excites him. There is no other explanation.

"Tell me, do you remember the sculpture? I'm sure I told you about it. Yes, you must remember, the sculpture of a little boy. No? Okay, I will remind you. Jack's spirit was my inspiration; from his spirit I created a physical representation. I didn't want to look at old photographs, no, that would have been terrible, absolutely ruin it for me, there would be no originality, none, so why bother if it is not original. Copies, imitation, they are no good. No, it must be original, it must come from within me, from my spirit. So when you look at it, you learn about my spirit. Others will say, so what, it is a sculpture of a boy, this is nothing new. But these idiots don't understand, they are simple, literal people who shouldn't speak. If it were up to me, they would not be allowed anywhere near my work.

"Oh, there are times when I think how much fun it would have been to know Jack when he was young, cunning, conniving, loveable Jackie. Him and his pack of rascals telling authority to fuck off. His mother tells me all the trouble he was but I don't believe her; a mother-in-law always has a self-serving agenda. Maybe Jack's mother saw problems but I see only beauty right down to the core. His mother is too limited to understand his spacious mind, his constant awe of life's wondrous happenings. If it were up to her, Jack would be like others, sacrificing selfhood for security of belonging to a caste, a culture, a nation, being absorbed by communal ideas rewarding obedience with inclusion. Inclusion in what?! In our society? Why would anyone want to be a part of our society? Society is in the business of murdering souls!

"The only way to live free is to steer clear of society. And stay away from prophets, sages and seers. You know the ones I'm talking about, fools wearing tall hats and white smiles, shrouding themselves in perspicacious scarves, promising to usher forlorn masses to the bright side of the moon. Liars, all of them!

"But demand is relentless from those dying to worship one form or another of organized or disorganized creeds, doctrines, dogmas, systems, codes, canons or tenets. Volunteers aplenty, waiting their turn to sit in eight pointed circles expecting, hoping, praying to rise from their padded tush having absorbed a wisdom that they wouldn't get if it kissed them on the ass. Round, round they go, seekers seeking, leaping from one sham savior to the next, complicating the simple, simplifying the complex, pleading to be made privy to magic powers and secret knowledge the possession of which is money back guaranteed to light up their life, never stopping long enough to attend a local showing of Happiness, An Inside Job, instead preferring to skim the surface, not questioning the efficacy of idolizing megalomaniacs.

"But not Jack. Even as a child, Jack bore through the mountains of bullshit thrown at him by adults. He opposed his mother not to cause trouble, as she thought, but because he knew no other way than to be true to himself, true to his character. And though his mother tried for a while to instill her ways in Jack, eventually she gave up, calling him a troubled boy and sending him away to boarding school in Montana because she couldn't shape Jack like other mothers shaped their gutless sons and daughters into hero worshipping, flag waving, brittle peons. Imbeciles!

"Do you think Jack has changed? You have known him since childhood. So fortunate the two of you are, to have this intricate history, to be able to observe each other's evolution and remain friends throughout. Oh, I can imagine the wild and crazy escapades you two went on, so innocent and real, as you were meant to be. My sculpture, I cannot show it to you now because it is not here but you will see it soon and you will tell me what you think. I want to know what you think; it is very important to me. Of course your opinion matters to me, you matter to me and I know you will like it because it is so, so, so *tres beau*! My show is next week at the Maison Bleu Gallery on Queen West Street, oooh la la, yes? Ha ha! You will be there of course and then you will see the sculpture and you will tell me whether it speaks to you, whether you feel Jack's vibes, whether Jack is brought to life by my work. Maybe you will not feel enough by looking so I will let you touch it, but we will do this when no one else is around. I cannot let other people touch my sculpture, no, I will not allow strangers to transfer their gloom to my work. Oh no, they would contaminate it, ruin everything. The area around the sculpture will be roped off and there will be big, stupid men carrying guns guarding it. I will tell them to shoot anyone who tries to touch my work. And they will because they must earn their keep.

"The show opens with a big gala, an evening black tie, hundreds of peacocks fanning their feathers, gathering to view my sculpture, only one, no more. And then dull people with too much money bursting from their crotch bid for the privilege of purchasing little Jackie and someone will pay an astronomical sum for my work because it is MY work and I have a NAME in this town. Do you want to know something? I like that I have my name and people know who I am because then people buy my work even if they know nothing about art and invariably they are ignorant but I will not think twice about taking their money because my work is done and I don't want it anymore. What use is it to me when it's finished? The process is complete. It's an end product, a trophy, an homage to the past. What, you take it home and sit and stare at the trophy? I want to be around the living, not the dead. Let them pay me lots of money to bring death into their home. They are the walking dead anyway. It's not my problem. Yes, the way I see it, I am helping these people. I bring a ray of sunshine into their miserable existence. They think that by spending money they capture enjoyment, so, let them spend! If they want to throw their money away, why not give it to me? Let them flaunt and boast to friends how much money they spend, believing this makes them worth something. Why not? This is what massages their pain, and they're too stupid to know how to live a life of meaning.

"It is almost always men, occasionally an obnoxious woman with too much testosterone coursing through her cunt shows up, but mostly men who can't help but put on a show. The big shots crave attention and, because they have a shriveled dick and no talent, only a ballpoint pen and checkbook, this is what they do, write checks. What do I care? I don't. Give me your money, I say, I will take it. It is good tender backed by full faith and credit of government printing presses. I am thankful for these people because without them I would not be able to pay for my home and fly to Paris in springtime and make love all day long with Jack on the grass in *Jardin du Luxembourg*, ha ha!

"At one time, I spurned these people who wanted my art. But then I realized, what does it matter if I like them or not? To be an artist, to be a great artist, does not mean I must starve! If this is how I get paid, so be it. Why should I be bothered? Human nature is human nature. We are all flawed in different ways and that's what makes us so appealing, our flaws. Perfection is dull. Never aspire to perfection; it can never be permanent, only fleeting. Once reached, there is nowhere else to go but down. If this is your goal, and if you live to be one hundred, most of your life you will be imperfect and you will see your imperfections and you will not like yourself. You will drive yourself crazy and become neurotic because you cannot enjoy, cannot live life until everything is exactly how you want it and that never happens for longer than a moment or two because nature is always changing so one moment you may be perfect but that moment melts, it always melts, and a new one appears, and you are no longer perfect but you are more neurotic and more pathetic than you were before, that I assure you.

"You will come to my show, yes? Tell me you will come. I need to know you will be there, that my handsome friend Samuel will share my evening with me. This will make me so happy! But I warn you, I will be busy much of the time because these money people they come not only to gawk at the sculpture but also to see the ARTIST, this is a big deal for them, to meet the artist, to talk with the artist, to shake hands with the artist, to buy the artist a drink, to feel sorry for the artist because she is not a millionaire and, after they drink too much, they offer me money, lots of money, to kiss me, to grope my tits, to fuck me, and if they touch me, if they invade my personal space, I move closer to them, pretending to accept their advance, and I knee them hard in the crotch, not stopping until they fall on their face. Then I take their money and move on to the next loser. But they like it. I know they do because they come back for more. I make the evening exciting and worthwhile for all these investment bankers and people with titles like vice-president, chief executive officer or maybe even prince! I have not yet had royalty attend one of my shows but you never know. To them, I am a curiosity, someone who has rejected their world and they have no inkling as to why, but they know that art is a good investment, especially if they are lucky enough to outlive the artist, and so they take a chance on buying art that may bring them even more money that they do not need. All of them, they like to be seen at these events, they like to appear well-rounded, as if they have knowledge beyond their own narrow existence or even care about anything but themselves. They rub shoulders with an artist so the next day they have something worthwhile to say when asked what is new and they can tell their friends what they did last night and where they have been and make it sound as if they KNOW me, an artist, deluding themselves into believing that, by association with me, their worth as a person has increased when in fact it merely tells the listener that they are in the presence of a neutered mutt.

"I do my job though, walking about the gallery, *beaujolais* guiding the way, speaking with these people, and they are always very excited to meet me and they ask me the same pedestrian questions and inside of me I am laughing. I have twin dialogue running in my head and I keep one dialogue secret and the other comes out of my mouth and I smile back at these people while they blather about themselves, telling me about their life and believing that I give a shit about what they say. But this does not bother me, oh no, this amuses me because I hear hardly anything of what they say because I am visualizing having sex with Jack and before I climax I am afraid that my secret dialogue will burst through so then I must end the conversation and say, nice to meet you, flashing a saccharine smile and leaving and taking a break to be by myself so I can redirect my thoughts and dry my thighs. Yes, it will be lots of fun. I am so glad you will be there. Go, go sit on the sofa and I will mix your drink. Where is Jack already? JACK! I know he is here. He knows you're here. He doesn't respond. Go sit, dear, he will be here in a moment."

"Elise, wait." I kissed her on the cheek.

"What was that for?"

"For being you."

"Such a sweetheart. Are you okay, Samuel? You don't seem yourself. You're antsy. Relax, you're among friends."

Wearing oversized stained shorts, sandals and a wrinkled, button down sport shirt, in clomped Jack.

"I'm wiped. You know that fifty-two story glass hi-rise going up on Adelaide Street? I've got three hundred and sixty people working for me on that one. We're four months in and every day we fall further behind. So long as they keep on shipping our fucking material on a second rate freighter from China, there's no way we'll complete on schedule. May as well send it by canoe paddled by a one armed panda bear! They're always late and when they get here, every goddamn shipment is missing supplies so we sit and wait another two weeks for the next one and that pushes us further back. I'm barely sleeping 'cause I can't stop thinking about the project and all the shit that's going wrong and the fact that I'll lose my bonus if we don't finish on schedule and I already promised Elise we'd go on vacation the month of August. She insists on taking August off. Likes to follow the European schedule. Only thing that calms my mind is fucking Elise but she refuses to come to the worksite for a quick one so I've got all this pent up energy that needs an outlet. That's why I'm working fourteen-hour days. By the time I get home I'm so burnt, there's no way I can get it up."

Forty-one years old, raccoon circled eyes, graying temple, high-strung, demanding, no-nonsense, ambitious, alpha Jack lived hard. So hard that his physician recently warned him to slow down and cut back on daily consumption of twelve cups of coffee if he wants to end blinding headaches and repair connective tissue covering weakening afferent nerves that were giving rise to digestive tract rebellion. If he didn't heed the yellow card warning him to terminate flow of gastric acids, a full blown ulcer might just turn the screws and bring Jack to a premature end. The physician's diagnosis was corroborated by thrice daily liquid stool blasts causing Jack's tormented bowels to scream mercy, mercy me.

'Jack' explained the physician, 'by antagonizing negative modulatory effects of adenosine receptors on dopamine receptors, excess caffeine intake leads to inhibition and blockade of adenosine A2 receptors, causing potentiation of dopaminergic neurotransmission. This means that neural pathways heartily chug along when pistons are pumping like they should but a faulty transmission line will bring the whole system crashing down. Your transmission line is a bag of whole beans away from melting down.'

Jack grudgingly followed the physician's counsel. Three weeks of debilitating withdrawal headaches, body tremors and volumes of bucketed vomit later, he was on the road to repair.

"Sam, it's been too long. What, three, four months?"

"You look like hell. You okay?"

"You have to start with that? What the fuck do I care? My focus is my work, my wife and my kid, that's it. I don't give a holy crap about what I look like. My body, your body, nothing but a display package. You don't love the body, you admire it, you fuck it, but you sure as hell don't love it. Like when a kid gets a gift. Sometimes the kid tosses the gift and only wants to play with the container. It's more fun than playing with what's inside. But, inevitably, the kid gets bored, loses interest and looks for another container furtively hoping that he'll discover a precious gift inside the next one. Elise and Adrien, they're my precious gifts. What I look like? That's bullshit. You think they care? What's on your mind, Sam? I know you well enough to know when you're off. What's going on?"

"I think I need some fresh air. I feel like I'm ..."

Unable to finish my thought, I barreled out of the room. Through the front door and down slippery steps, my feet touched ground in a moist Zen rock garden. Buckling over, sitting on my knees, I squirmed beside a six hundred year old majestic Oak tree ideally suited for hibernation. From its liberal trunk, so I believed, came the sound of a quaking baritone.

'I was once a nut like you.'

Mouth agape, short and shallow breaths, torrential downpour of conflicting emotions flooding seven major *chakras*, it didn't occur to me that a tree was talking, that a tree could talk, that I was certifiable and men in white coats would be approaching any minute. In the background, I heard Flamenco Sketches serenely trumpeting. First a tree talks and now music from ... from where?

'Patience is your ally,' murmured the Oak.

This is it, I thought. I'm crashing, I'm yearning, I'm breaking down.

"Sam? Please Sam, come back inside," came Elise's gentle plea.

The tree quieted, the music stopped and, hard and long as I looked, I didn't see any white coats. Bracing myself with trembling hands, I pushed up. Elise held open the door, escorting me back inside.

"Has the Oak ever spoken to you?"

"Sam, you're exhausted, come with me," said Elise, leading me to the living room.

"He's not exhausted, he just needs to learn a few things," said Jack. "You know what me and Elise were doing at six o'clock this morning? Banging like angry rabbits before falling back asleep. An hour later, I woke and poked another burning ember into her. You get what I'm saying? Yesterday was rough for me. So what? I start the day new, fresh. I don't carry yesterday forward. It's gone, leave it alone. Today started out as good as it could but after I leave the house, here comes the bullshit, hurdles, questions, doubt, the fucking negativity. What am I supposed to do? Fall apart? What, am I a loser?! Plow ahead! Sometimes it goes your way, other times not. You got plans? That's well and good but guess what, Napoleon? No one but you and your bloated head know about your plan and no one else cares about what you want to happen. The sooner you realize you're on your own, the sooner you'll step up to the plate and deal with whatever shit is on the table in the best way you know how. Your problems aren't that big and you're not the center, nobody is the center. You've got to keep it in perspective, man, perspective.

We're all inconsequential specks of dust doing the grandmaster's bidding before disintegrating. If you let crap infect your backbone, days will be long and nights longer. I know, I know, sometimes the teeter-totter flips and flops, flounders for balance. Happens to all of us. The trick is for you to recognize when that's happening. The trick is for you to work the seesaw back to the middle. You do this by constructing mental barriers that'll keep you afloat during tough times. You know why? Because the ultimate enemy is the mind. That's right, your mind is enemy number one. If you don't discipline the mind, then primal emotions like fear and doubt beat you with an ugly stick. This is important, Sam. Listen to what I'm saying and learn something. You're a mess. Running out of here, distraught like a high society woman whose husband has gone bankrupt, talking to a fucking tree! What the hell is going on with you?! Here, take this."

"What is it?"

"A *mandala*. My kid made it. He's a fucking brilliant artist just like his mother. Take it."

"Why?"

"Just take it. When you wake each morning, instead of wanking, hold this in your palms for fifteen minutes, focus on it and listen to yourself. I mean really hear your thoughts, the high-pitched drama rambling round your head. Then lock up those thoughts, put 'em away and make the *mandala* your sole focus and don't let anything else penetrate, not even a bullshit desire to talk to trees. Sound simple? It's not. You've got to practice until you've trained your mind to go where you want it to go, build strength to steady the teeter-totter. When that happens, you'll be sound enough to find yourself a woman instead of rubbing up against bark. Until then, I know an uptown girl with an enchanted snatch who'll back it up on a bearskin rug for fifty bucks and a double shot espresso."

"Jack," admonished Elise.

"What? You think there's violence in the world now? The planet would be barren and smoldering if it weren't for women willing to rent their snatch, doing their bit to take an edge off male aggression."

"Sam, I have an Aunt who talks to her flowers every morning. If it makes her happy, so what? If you want to talk to the tree then talk to the tree. You can visit anytime whether we're home or not. If you'd rather talk to us, we're here. Would you like to talk?"

"I've been having this weird dream."

"Do I need a drink for this?"

"Jack, listen to Sam," said Elise.

"It's pitch dark. I'm barefoot, descending a steep stairway, hands gripping railing for support. I see a dim light flickering underneath a door and move closer. I reach to turn the knob. But before touching it, the door opens automatically, as if expecting me, inviting me inside to a small, windowless, square-shaped room where fishhooks jut out of black walls and ceilings are so low I have to stoop. In one corner, there I am, as a fourteen-year old boy. The boy is crouching. Arms crossed. Defiant. Scared. Alone. He doesn't see me; doesn't know I'm in the room. Suddenly something, I don't know what, yanks the boy into the air and hangs him on one of the hooks. Terrified, the boy scrambles, tries to loosen himself, to lower his feet to the ground. The repetitive force of his own jerky movement causes his shirt collar to rip, freeing him from the hook and bringing him down. Desperately, the boy dashes about the room searching in vain for shelter. It doesn't take long before he tires from running and seeks refuge in an open corner. Then it happens again. The boy is slung onto another hook. But this time his reaction is different. This time, the boy doesn't flail. Methodically, he moves to and fro, managing to tear a hole in the fabric holding him in place. His feet now touching the ground, he reveals a menacing gaze, hones in on a target, and swipes at the air until closing his fist around something I can't see. Standing still for several seconds, as if savoring his catch, he unclenches his fist, furiously slamming his open hand against the wall. As this is happening, directly across from me, on the other side of the room, a second door suddenly appears. Swinging open, I'm shown a dirt trail bordered by waist high Bluegrass, a gentle breeze causing it to sway. The sun is shining. The boy turns to face me. He stares at me. I'm visible to him now. He seems to be waiting for my direction. Both of us stand motionless, taking each other in. I get the urge to embrace him but I suppress it. The door that suddenly opened now closes. Alone, I walk out of the room, exiting the same door through which I entered. The end."

"Why do you leave the boy behind?" asked Elise.

"Why should I take him with me?"

Jack interjected. "The kid's stuck in some craphole, you take him! You don't need to be a chin stroking shrink outfitted in a leather elbow patched tweed jacket to figure out that the only way you're twisted head is going to straighten out is for you to take hold of that boy and bring him with you. Don't you see, man?! The dream weaver is talking to you, telling you that unless you want to live your life alone in the trees munching snails, humpty dumpty has to put all the pieces back together again and that kid is one fucking crucial piece of the puzzle. Plain as day, that kid is you, man! Somewhere down the line your pilot light burned out when you fell into a black hole a hundred times the size of your wife's twat. And now that you left her, you're drowning in guilt, fucking guilt, the lowest, most hopeless, despicable emotion emanating from man's fucking reptilian brain. You think you're so important, that you're responsible for lives other than your own, that other people can't live without you? You think you owe her something more, that she won't survive without you? What do you owe her? What do you owe anyone? Huh, what? Where do you get this shit from?!

"This dream of yours is telling you to reignite, to take a spark from a dynamic, half-baked teenager. You know what happens if you ignore the kid, lock him up in the basement? You get old, stuck, stable, banal, lose your sense of wonder, your curiosity, your sense of adventure all in preparation for death. Death, man, not life, not living! And that's what happened to you. You died. But that's alright. It's good. You needed to die. Death is an opportunity to grow. Here's your opportunity. Grab it, otherwise why bother dying, why bother going through the pain of rebirth if you're gonna arrive stillborn? Man, you've got to move on. But you don't know how do you? You're about to turn onto the back nine of life and you've hit your balls into the woods. That's where you are, Hansel, lost in the forest but there's no breadcrumbs to help you find your way out. You're in there, panic stricken about the future, guilt ridden about the past, not realizing that living takes place today, only today. There is no future; there is no past!

How is it you don't know that? You're smart as hell and an idiot at the same time.

"Maybe I don't get to choose whether I grow."

"Sweet fucking Jesus! You don't have a choice? You, the cynic, the doubter, the mocker are telling me, what, you're raising the flag of fate, punting on personal responsibility? If you're not pulling the strings, who is, Geppetto? The man in the sky? That new one you're toying with, the tongue tied imitation Mother Teresa do gooder, is she bringing you down with her pacifist bullshit masquerading as divinity? Fucking women, they're like African Strangler plants, sizing up the meal ticket. Man, pull up your pants before Morticia swallows you whole. I need another drink."

"Why don't you have a choice, Sam?" inquired Elise.

"I'm just saying that maybe I've hit my end point, maybe for some of us growth ends before life ends."

"Sam!" interrupted Jack, "You're talking to fucking trees! Maybe Herr Doppelganger has his hand up your back. Maybe your prick disappeared and you've got a slit between your legs. Maybe if I punch you in the face with my fist you won't feel your jawbone cracking. Fuck the fucking maybes already! Goddamn, you're a train wreck!"

Jack stormed off to the kitchen, returning shortly with a tray carrying a worm infested bottle of tequila, shot glasses, lemon wedges, and salt. He placed the tray on a side table and sat on the sofa next to Elise. Pouring himself two shots, Jack threw them both back in quick succession before standing up to change the music then returning to the sofa to help himself to more.

Calmer, he began. "You think all the pieces are in your head and it's just a matter of putting them together. But they're not. And when you realize there's a slew of missing parts, you crumble 'cause you don't know where else to look; you don't know that your streaming commentary is fucking you up and running interference with your gut. Your gut's the kingmaker; you've got to listen to it. Forget about logic. Logic can't assuage the heart." Jack took hold of the gooseneck and tilted his head back.

"You want to break free? Listen to tunes and I'm not talking about looney tunes. Music comforts the soul, gives you strength, peace, courage, fires up endorphins. Take the Scots. They blast their screeching bagpipes and blood drips from the ear of every mammal within a three square mile radius. But for these skirt loving, red-faced bugle blowers, pipes are key to opening heaven's gate. *Salut*, eh!"

Elise spoke up as Jack went slip sliding away, mumbling along to the music.

"Do you see what's happening? When you think back to the fourteen-year old boy, you are dreaming of reuniting your self into one whole. This is good! Before you leave here today, you must promise that you will go back to the boy, embrace him like your life depended on it and never let him go. Do you understand, Samuel? Do you understand what I'm saying? You promise me, you will do this, yes? *Tres bon*! It is settled! Everyone is happy and we will celebrate my show next week. Now, drink up!"

I was sitting on one end of the sofa. Jack and Elise sat squished together on the other end. Half the tequila remained in my shot glass. I don't drink much, not because I don't like the taste nor because I'm bound to religious or philosophical edicts but because my hereditary stock is grounded in that fifty per cent of Jews who carry ALDH2, a gene ensuring sloth like metabolism of alcohol. Instead of experiencing the imbiber's predictable euphoric mirages and inanity, I slink straight away into melancholy. Given what happened next, I should have drank more.

Jack was snoring, holding the empty bottle in his left paw. With interest akin to that of Dian Fossey monitoring a female primate picking fleas off her mate, I watched Elise grope inside his pants. Once her object of desire sprung free, she fondled, patted and stroked the frenetic organ until achieving satisfactory length, girth and overall springiness. Dexterously cupping the delicate bag while systematically stroking and exerting shaft pressure in a style evidencing commitment to rehearsal begetting excellence and, importantly, results, Jack was bucking in less time than it takes an adolescent yellow tailed monkey to spray his reproductive balm. Proof of her impressive handiwork being in the pudding that coated her fingers that she rubbed onto her belly like sacred Dead Sea moisturizer, Elise then undressed and laid down on top of sleeping Jack before she too nodded off.

Attempting to erase the show from memory, I shuffled out of the house, straddled my bike and wondered whether I should go looking for some greens, reds, or whites.

Chapter 6
Double Trouble

*See, the problem is that God gives men a brain and a penis
and only enough blood to run one at a time*
– Robin Williams

Boy spoke.

'Come on Coach, you have to put me in! Henderson's got no offence, no defense, he's killing us. Come on, put me in!'

Coach replied.

'Shackleton, pipe down!'

Boy continued.

'Dontcha wanna win, Coach? I wanna win. My teammates wanna win. The cheerleaders want us to win, the whole damn school, I'll bet, want us to win! You for sure wanna win. You do wanna win, dontcha, Coach? Why dontcha wanna win? You've got to …'

Coach glared.

'Kid, I don't *got* to do nothing! Cut the crap. You're getting on my nerves.'

Boy persisted.

'Coach, Henderson's our weak link. You know it, I know it, the other team sure as hell knows it. They're running every play at him! Put me in, Coach. I'll get the job done. You'll see. Give me a chance, will ya?'

Coach yielded.

'Shackleton! Next whistle, you're in just so I don't have to listen to your bull anymore. I want you glued to Number Four. Pasted to him like a second skin. Think you can you handle it? He moves, you move. Glue! Got it? Now get your skinny ass out on the floor. What are you waiting for? Go!'

Boy beamed.

'I'll show you, Coach, I'll show you!'

Coach called time out. Boy bounded onto the court. Henderson slumped off. Boy sped toward Number Four who was taller, heavier and a better athlete than Boy. But Boy had resolve on his side. From the sidelines, Coach shouted encouragement. Three minutes passed. Number Four hadn't touched the ball. Boy was encouraged. Frustrated, out of the referee's view, Number Four hissed at Boy before lodging a pointed elbow into the side of Boy's head. Boy jerked, stumbled and fell. Coach grimaced. Dazed, Boy gathered himself, returning to face his opponent.

Game clock showed fifty-two seconds remaining. Score tied. Number Four had the ball, dribbling up court. Boy backpedaled. Number Four planted and shot. As the ball rose, Boy elevated, his fingertips brushing the rubber underbelly enough to send the shot wayward. Boy's barnyard wide teammate bullied to haul in the loose ball. Looking down court, the teammate passed to a streaking Boy who coasted in for an easy lay up. The ball went up but didn't drop in. Boy muscled inside to grab the rebound. Another shot from close range. The ball floated toward the basket, circled the rim, and circled and circled then fell out.

Just like that, all except Boy were freeze framed. Coach stopped shouting. Players stopped playing. Cheerleaders stopped cheering. Spectators stopped doing whatever it is that spectators do. Hearing nothing but the squeak of his own sneakers, Boy retrieved the rebound and shot again. The ball traveled an arcless path, straight up then down, returning to Boy's waiting hands. Try as he might, Boy couldn't get the ball into the basket.

Ω

Every night for the past month, I've dreamt the same dream.
'This concerns you?'
Should it concern me?
'If you think you should be concerned then it's a concern. Do you want to be concerned?'
What kind of question is that, do I want to be concerned?
'What kind? There are not kinds of questions. A question is a question.'
I'm here for answers, not questions.
'Aren't we all. But before we get to the answers, we must first ask the right questions. You want that I should interpret this dream? How can I solve a riddle without asking questions?'
Then you do think the dream has meaning?
'Everything has to have meaning? Who are you, Wittgenstein?'
We're side tracking here. Can we talk about my dream?
'You want to talk about the dream?'
Yes! Yes! The DREAM! That's why I'm here!
'What does it mean to you?'
Are you going to interpret the dream or not?
'You've got someplace else to be? Tell me, what's your hurry? Everyone's in a hurry. What's with all the running? Shuttling, dashing, bustling about with checklists, timetables and agendas,

caught up in modes of distraction, dodging and avoidance. Nothing but reacting and more reacting; the insistent propensity to react. What happened to patience, to movement in stillness, to cultivating reflection and reasoned action? Speed, convenience, this is what payment entitles you too? Ach! Fine. The dream. You want to talk about the dream, I'll tell you about your pokey dream.

'This game you play with the ball, a round sphere, speaks to the circle of life; birth to death and all that happens in between. You are alive yet you choose to sit on the sidelines, to withhold contribution. Who or what holds you back? The Coach? Number Four? Henderson? The bouncy cheerleaders? No. You are the coach just as you are both Number Four and Henderson. As for the cheerleaders, we'll get to that issue later. The dream is all about you, your life force grappling with death ... and losing. Standing stationary on the sidelines, you watch moments passing by, unwilling to call upon yourself to enter the court, to put yourself into the game, not a silly ball game but the game of life! Coach, put me in? No, what you are really asking is permission from yourself to join, to participate in living a life not in your head but in the company of others, in a community. You wait, you hesitate, you deliberately stall until the game is almost over. So, we must ask: why do you resist for so long? Why do you resist at all? What is it that you fear and what underlies this fear? When you do enter the game, your so-called opponent is effectively neutralized. But, in fact, there is no opponent; there does not exist a Number Four. Rather, the opponent is you, the part of you that resists, that inhibits and constructs defensive measures crafted to minimize failure, shun risk, relegate you to life's bench. And when opposition disappears? You step forward and freely shoot the ball yet you miss. Over and over, the ball passes up and down, no forward, no backward movement. No one blocking your way and still you don't score? Why? Because you're scared.

So you choose non-action thinking judgment will be avoided by making yourself a non-factor, taking yourself out of the game. This way, how can you fail to live up to your expectations or those of others? But what does this mean, to fail? Who is to say you have succeeded or failed? How is this measured? Who is doing the measuring and why? WHO IS YOUR JUDGE? Why do you think you're being judged? I see your restlessness, disquiet permeating your soul, thwarting your reach for fulfillment. And I see you have stopped the game clock. You must wind it back up, turn the inner wrestling match in favor of life instead of death.

'You don't know why the boy follows you in your dreams? He is there to remind you of who you once were, to encourage you to let yourself go, stop holding back, to help you be who you are today. Why? Because you've disconnected from the boy. Not good. Not helpful. The game clock will not resume and you will not feel fully alive until niggling insecurities are brought to light, healed, and all parts of you integrate, become one. So ask yourself, how do you wind the clock? How do you sidestep forty years in the desert, in exile from your self? A man begins by opening his arms. His heart will follow.'

What if the boy refuses my gesture?

'He won't.'

How can you be so sure?

'I am.'

But how do you KNOW?

'I have faith.'

I'm not religious.

'I said I have faith. What do I know? What do you know? What does anyone KNOW? To know suggests certainty. Don't for a minute think the idea of certainty is anything more than a contrived illusion of permanence designed to quell fear. Fear of what? Life? Death? Beans? You name it, humans are afraid.

Why be afraid? Is the unknown so scary? Hah! Preposterous! What we need is to NOT know. We want NOT to know. It is the unknown, the uncertain, that feeds our sense of anticipation, our excitement, our longing for adventure, for living! But you don't believe me, do you? You don't want to accept that existence is temporary so you cling to teachings predicated on believing in permanence of people, places and things. And because of this, you're wracked by anxieties and suffering.

'Tell me, everyone who lives will die, no? Or are we blessed with countless lives and reincarnations and every human who has ever lived has gone on to some other world or returned to this world in one form or another? There must be more; I MUST CONTINUE! I cannot accept my finite sojourn on this planet! Is that what you think? That you have been, and are forever, a permanent fixture on this or another planet? What you have right here, right now, this is it, this is life, whatever you make of it, this … is … your … life. And if you spend your limited time foolishly grasping for permanence, mourning what is past, impatient for the future, disregarding the present, then where are you? Think about it! Only in present moments do we truly live. To receive the *present* is to receive a gift, is it not? Neither future nor past are gifts, only present. But you reject it; you reject the present! And what happens? Anxieties fester, mutate and spread instigating fence building intended to stabilize delusions of continuity that must be achieved and maintained at all costs for fear your mortality be exposed!

'What must you do? You MUST dare to challenge this mindless gospel of permanence feeding inner turmoil from one hapless generation to the next. Is it not preferable to embrace rather than bar nature's proclivity for change? Will acceptance of who we are not slay our demons, offer a tonic for dismantling inner barriers serving no purpose other than to complicate our one life?

Welcoming life's uncertainties sets the stage for true liberation, true freedom, not despair. Samuel, the boy has been left behind far too long. Go to him, bring him with you, don't let him go for if …'

Ω

"No, not there Sam. Move it up a little, please. Let me do it. Ohhhhh! Oh, honey. That's it. Right there. You're so thick and hard in the morning. Oh, oh, baby, oh, you're so deep, oh Jesus I can feel you in my stomach. Oh, Sam! Sam? Baby, don't stop now. Why are you stopping? Are you awake? Sam? Sam! Wake up!"

"Mmmph," I grunted.

"Honey, I'm not doing this if you're half asleep."

"Mmmph."

"What were you dreaming?"

"I don't know."

"Well, I don't know where you were but you were tossing and groaning all night."

"Come here."

"Anything bothering you?"

"If I slip back inside you, life will be grand again."

Nina sat up. "What do you see when you look at me?"

"Depends on the angle?"

"I'm serious."

"Do you know that Egypt has a government department named the Serious Organized Crime Agency? The word *serious* was added to their title after too many people questioned their legitimacy. See if anyone doubts them now!"

"Honey, come on, what do you see?"

"Early Greek civilization worshipped righteous bovines as a mother goddess. I see you as a mother goddess, pure of heart, void of guile, mesmerizing in beauty. Sacred and delicious are you, oh lovely Nina. I am but a grateful worshipper, jinxed with insatiable thirst for your nectar and inexorable desire for mingling our spirits under watchful eyes of bewitching pyramids."

"Do you see me as sad, you know, depressed?"

"I don't know."

"What do you mean you don't know?"

"I haven't thought about it."

"Don't you pay attention to me?"

"At the moment, yes, I'd like to give you my full, unbending attention."

"That's not funny."

"Right. Twenty lashes for bad humor. Hit me hard. Make me feel it."

"Honey."

"Do you want me to see sadness? Okay, you're sad. Happy now?"

"I don't *want* you to see anything. I want you to be honest with me."

"Ah, you want truth. Then truth it shall be. The truth is I want to resume my post dream state. I want you on your back with your legs spread holding tight to your ankles with both hands. And moaning. Yes. The moaning bit helps."

"No, I don't feel like it anymore. I want to talk. I can't get my mother out of my head."

"I'm not so concerned with what's in your head."

"She brings me down so much. Ever since Dad left, she's been a wreck. I feel for her, really I do. But after four years shouldn't she be able to pick herself up and rebuild her life? It's hard for me. I see her wasting away and there's nothing I can do. I tell her that life is a gift to be treasured but she doesn't listen. She just goes on and on with her woe is me tales, wanting me to feel sorry for her. And I want to say to her, no wonder you feel so crappy, all day long you stare at the walls and watch television, why don't you do something with your life. But I don't say anything unkind because I don't want to hurt her. Instead, I listen and I pray for her and hope she doesn't give up."

"If you don't want to hold onto your ankles, that's okay, I'll hold them."

"Why won't you listen to me?"

"I will listen. We can do two things at once, can't we?"

"No, Sam, I can't. I can't make love to you at the same time that I'm telling you how I'm feeling about my mother or how I think I might be depressed. Is that all you want from me, to make love to me? Don't you care about me?"

"Don't do that. Don't turn it around on me and put me on the defensive. My wanting to fuck you has nothing to do with whether or not I care about you."

"I thought we had a deep connection. I thought we understood each other and that you care for me. If you did, you would respect what I want and what I want is to share myself with you in a way that is much more meaningful than sex."

"Alright then, I'm dropping your ankles. There. I'm listening."

"Honey, I'm sorry, I'm not feeling well. I love you and I'm so grateful for you. But I have this gloom that's been hanging over me for I don't know how long and I'm trying to figure out why and I'm afraid I may be more like my mother than I ever imagined. She used to be so passionate, so full of life! Her and Dad used to go out most every night or have friends in to visit. I know Dad went along to make her happy; he was content doing his own thing and didn't want people around so much. Not Mom. She fed off other people's energy; social activity plugged her in. And when no one but Dad was around, sure, she was more subdued but it's not like she was depressed. I don't think.

But since the divorce, she doesn't have anyone to sustain her and she just can't get it together. I mean, Mom has never been alone. Twenty years old and she jumps from her father to a husband eight years older than her. It happened more during her generation but I suppose it happens today, I mean women wanting to be carried off by an older mate, wanting a father figure. Psych 101, right? But the difference today is that women won't admit this is what they want, at least not to each other or to them self. Imagine how my friends would feel sorry for me if I told them I want a husband to support and take care of me? Not that I do, but imagine their reaction if I publicly gave up my independence. But I wouldn't care what they would say. Why should I? Is it so wrong to want a man in my life to share the daily burdens? I don't have to tell you we're made differently, inside and out, and we're made to complement, not oppose one another, not to say who's better or worse at this or that. We're different in some ways, that's all. On a fundamental level, women have to realize what they want and what we want is to fulfill our goals since fulfilling our goals realizes our spirit. Unlike men, women have no need to aspire to power without goals. Incarnation of the spirit, whoever or whatever the spirit may be, is what matters because we have to stay true to our destiny. You can't fight biological imperative and there's no reason why women should feel a need to emulate men. Why would we want to? We're not equal and those who say otherwise are caught up in political gamesmanship. I mean, equal? Equal to what? Are all women equal to each other? Are all men the same? So why should women be equal to men? That would be so dull if we were all the same.

"Mom's so lonely, thinking only of what she doesn't have instead of being thankful for what she has. When I tell her this, our conversation collapses, she slips into denial, attacks me, or says I'm being critical and sobs, telling me I must have inherited cruelty from my father. I feel terrible afterward! Is it right for her to make me feel guilty? Or to talk badly about Dad? I've tried being silent, being a sounding board. But when I'm too quiet she goads me into giving her advice, as if I'm a life coach, and I get sucked in and I feel obliged to tell her how she could brighten her life and I stupidly forget that the more I talk, the more likely she'll find offence in what I'm saying.

"When I stop talking long enough to realize I've been roped into her drama, I'm so angry with myself and then I lash out at her. I know I shouldn't but I do. After I hang up, I stew, regret sets in, and I call back. It's always me calling back, never her. One time I went three days without calling before giving in. I feign an apology, she accepts, and we exit the stage until next time. How do I get off this crazy stage? I have an obligation, don't I, to help her? I'm her only daughter after all. What should I do? Better yet, what can I do? I have to accept who she is and let go of who she was. Right? It's that habit of mine of fixing people in time, believing that the person she was yesterday, or two or ten years ago, is the same person today. And that just isn't so. Not with anyone.

"She's all alone in that huge house where she lived with Dad and refuses to move even though she claims money is tight and she can't afford the upkeep but I know that she can draw on her inheritance from Uncle Sal. She just wants to appear helpless. She likes telling people she lives alone in a cold, drafty mausoleum that, for added effect, has paper taped across the windows because she sold the curtains. Literally, she lives in the dark, refusing to turn on lights, instead burning candles and incense. I won't stay with her when I visit. It's too creepy. All except one of her friends has given up on her because she never returns phone calls or cancels plans at the last minute offering bizarre excuses like there are too many lunar ions in the air. Isn't that rude?

"Lately, she's been begging me to come live with her, sobbing to me about how lonely she is, that she's dying of loneliness and it's my duty as her daughter to be with her in old age. Oh my goodness! Am I supposed to accept this guilt trip? Does she think of anyone but herself? I guess I don't know why she'd start now when that's how she's lived her whole life. I would die within forty-eight hours if I went to live with her. Either that or I'd murder her. No, I don't mean that. I don't know where that came from. I love my mother. But how could I live with her? It's difficult enough when she visits for two weeks. One week is plenty, I've told her so, but she never listens, overstays her welcome and by day four I'm scheming how to avoid her, counting the days, the hours, the minutes until she goes home. Is that selfish of me? I have a life. I'm busy. Am I supposed to drop work, friends, yoga, stay up until two in the morning talking, cook her meals, clean up, entertain whenever she's in town to visit? I don't know how to manage an aging mother who's as dependent as a child and moody as a teenager. Doesn't she know she's not my responsibility? I leave for work and when I return she hasn't dressed, hasn't showered and is sitting with the cat on the sofa, staring out the window. This is what I come home to! It's not like my life is easy. I work hard and don't even make ends meet. I keep thinking that there must be a reason why I've been swimming under water for so long. Do you think she ever asks whether I need help? What about me?

"I don't know how to make it work with her. Is it my fault? I love her, I really do. Could that be the problem? I love her too much? I'm not blaming her. I mean, I have to own my emotions, right? I'm responsible for myself. I've known that since I was twelve. My therapist tells me I have abandonment issues because Dad left when I was a child; he says this explains why my first husband was eleven years older than me, because I wanted a father figure. But I don't agree because my first husband was a right wing zealot who treated me like a rival, not a partner. Dad always spoke to me like I was his friend, even when I was a kid. And now that we've reunited after fifteen years of not speaking, we're like best friends. We even talk about sex. Do you think it's weird that we have conversations about my sex life? The other day Dad asked me if you were good in bed. I mean, so what? It's not like he wanted to know details. What's the big deal to talk about sex with your parents? I can't stand people who are so secretive. Besides, I'm just happy to have Dad in my life again. Do you think I'm looking for a father figure, honey?

"For as long as I can remember, Mom's been so needy. Whenever I don't do as she says, she tells me it means I don't love her and if I don't love her then she wouldn't love me either. Then she shuts down, won't talk to me or anyone else for days on end and lies in bed in her ratty pajamas mutely watching television. And when I ask her to forgive me, to pay attention to me, she acts like she doesn't care. That's Mom. It's not like her character, her personality, has changed at all so why should I expect anything different from her? She's the same person she always was, selfish and competitive with me. When I was a teenager and one of my boyfriends came to the house, Mom would dress up like a skank and try to seduce him. Seriously, she would. I thought she was joking at first but then she did it again and again. Like, what was she doing competing with me for attention from boys? How do you think that made me feel? I try to understand, I try not to get mad at her, and for this I'm rewarded with being treated like her commiserating sounding board, every day the phone calls from her, hearing about how horrible life is. Do you think she's depressed, you know, not sad but actually depressed? If she is, and always has been, then I could be predisposed to depression.

Depression runs in families. What if my chronic sadness is a precursor to depression? Wait, I'm not always sad, am I?

"I want so badly to heal her because if I do, and Mom's sadness or depression or whatever it is goes away, then chances are I won't suffer. I've tried talking with her about this but she won't open up, says I'm blaming her for who I am, says my problems are my problems not hers and screeches that we're pawns in a universally ordained plan. We have to stand aside, she says, let our lives unfold as they will because we have no say in fate. Sometimes I agree. I mean, scratching and clawing usually doesn't get you anything except frustration. But, at the same time, I absolutely know that the universe is benevolent and whatever happens is part of the overall plan, a good plan."

"Nina, do you see it? The apparition? Two dark skinned, freckle faced Hawaiian girls shimmying in grass skirt and puka shells luring me into boundless space where the three of us hover together like slow motion whirlybirds. The girls place both their hands, one stacked flat on top of the other, upon my forehead and lean in close, each of them lip suctioning opposite cheeks; the sound of their slurrrrrp vibrating down to my baby toes."

"Honey, did you hear anything I said?"

"Don't you get it? Dancing spirits are leading indicators. The slurping signals how I should live life. With gusto baby, verve, gusto and a dash of panache. Verve I have; it's gusto and panache that are lagging and I'm trying to find them. Come to think of it, the delinquent duo may have sought refuge between your legs. Do you mind?"

"Sam, I'd really like you to listen when I have something to say. It's only fair."

"Did you hear a sound?"

"No."

"I thought I heard a knock on the door."

"No, I don't ..."

"Don't you hear that?"

"You go, honey. Bed's too cozy for me to leave."

Rubbing away sleep granules, I sauntered downstairs. The knocking grew louder, more urgent. Walking softly with hands held up in front like a kangaroo, I approached the door but gamely refused to open until the banging subsided. On the other side, I heard shuffling feet and profane mutterings.

"I know you're in there. Open the door!" shrieked a familiar voice.

Here we go, I thought.

"Amy, you shouldn't be here. You should ..."

"Don't tell me what to do! Where is she? I know she's here, you bastard, and I'm gong to put my hands around her scrawny neck and choke her till she's dead! After what you did to me, you don't deserve to be with anyone, even a stupid whore. You know why? Because you're sick. You're a sick, emotionally stunted, egotistical, primitive, psychopathic asshole! You never loved me, you never cared for me, you couldn't care less what happens to me, could you?

"Remember the time I was in the hospital, feet in stirrups, doctor sticking his cold, age spotted hand inside me scraping out diseased cells that you put there with your polluted sperm? And you left me there, alone, lying on a metal table, to be prodded like an experimental farm animal. Remember? You wouldn't stay with me, gave me no support whatsoever, too busy taking phone calls in the lobby, cutting deals, screwing other people out of their money and telling me that there wasn't anything you could do anyway and it's best to let the doctors handle this one. Handle this one? What does that mean?! Did it bother you to watch another man forearm deep in my uterus or were you afraid you would get off on the scene so you left the room? What in tarnation is wrong with you?! Nothing you could do? You could have been there with me, you could have given me hope, told me I would be fine and we would be home soon, you could have said you love me whether or not you meant it, you could have been my rock, my savior, my hero, my husband. My husband, damn it! Was it too much to ask for you to support me? Emotional support? I'm sure you've read about it in books. You like to read. Psychopaths have an exquisite knack for storing information. How do you live with yourself? How did you look at me everyday for all our years and lie to me?! Was everything a lie? Did we share anything real? Why did you do this to me?!"

"Your being here isn't helping anyone."

"Get out of my way, Sam."

Moving at the speed of a Venezuelan jet black guinea pig, Amy booted me in the shins, pushed past, and made for the stairs. Instinctively, I stooped down to rub my lower leg. Where were my soccer shin pads when I needed them? Hobbling, I lunged for the back of Amy's shirt as she was about to climb the first step up. Tugging a bit too hard, Amy fell backward into my arms where I held her comfortably until she regained composure and brusquely pushed herself away.

"Amy, enough already, you're a mess. Go home, run a hot bath, uncork a bottle of red wine, crank up Sinatra, whatever it takes to calm yourself before you do something crazy."

Red-faced, she howled, "Crazy? I'm crazy? You patronizing shit, let me go!"

"Come on, Amy, time to leave."

Seizing both her arms from the back, I pressed her toward the front door.

"Don't you ever call me again! Never! And when the day comes that you crawl back to me begging forgiveness and a second chance, and believe me you will, I'll crush you just like you crushed me!"

"Honey, who is it?" came Nina's deliberate chirping from the bedroom.

"Avon lady."

Amy called out in a small, sympathetic voice, "Nina, is that you? Please come down here right away. Ow! Sam's hurting me. Please hurry!"

Nervously, Nina waltzed into the foyer, her cotton robe pulled tight, just as I was about to close the door on Amy.

"Why is she here?" Nina asked while looking at me, her crossed arms belying outward calm.

"You bitch! You fucking bitch! Do you have any conscience whatsoever or are you truly as blank as your anorexic body suggests? Did you give any thought, any thought at all in that low wattage brain of yours, to the lives you ruined? I'll give you something to think about!"

Nostrils flaring like a bull staring down a Matador waving a red flag, Amy rushed at Nina. Strategically positioned, I intercepted her before the stampede gathered momentum. Her energy spent, she put up little resistance as I escorted her outside. Here, she glared at me one last time before turning away in a show of anger and disgust. If there was a crowd, which there wasn't, but if there was, it would have dispersed now that the excitement had petered out.

To soothe her rattled nerves, Nina retreated to the kitchen, tending to the urgent task of boiling hot water and brewing tea. I stood alone in the living room, peering out the window at Amy. She sat on the street curb, hunched over, arms hugging her knees.

The pain I imagined she felt, the humiliation. Given the circumstances, I suppose only retribution could do justice.

It was my fault. I did this to her. How could I? Never mind how, but why? Only now, separate and apart, was I coming to realize the depth of our bond. Still, as much as I was raised to be responsible, I refused to accept responsibility for puncturing her hopes and expectations. What are hopes and expectations anyway? Seeds planted in one's mind that may or may not flower. And who's to say it was my duty to cultivate her seeds? Just because we were married this duty, this burdensome expectation, falls upon me? What if her seeds were bad, or just didn't belong, and were better off not watered? Maybe my actions will, in the end, turn out to be best for her and neither she or I yet know it.

Or what if this isn't about me? What if she carries other wounds and scars that I know nothing about and it isn't my leaving that's made her feel unworthy? What if, as a child, she was taught to feel unworthy in a thousand different ways? That could be it. Maybe she was reared in an emotionally impoverished environment that did a bang up job of fostering a chronic sense of emptiness, a sense that something is profoundly wrong, that the world is not safe and she could fall apart at any moment. And, lacking an abiding center, through no fault of her own, she didn't form feelings of reassurance and safety, the result being an impermanent core self, one founded on fragmentation and Original Sin, one leaving her groping for sustenance. That could explain her insistence on converting to Judaism.

Become a Jew, she thought, magically effect a wholesale exchange of her soul. Like other converts, she may have convinced herself that changing religious affiliation would provide a fertile identity, filling up the proverbial glass that she believed was served half empty. As important, if not moreso, she bet that conversion would strengthen my attachment to her. But it didn't. First of all, her becoming a Jew dismantled our status: me the outsider, her the OTHER. Part of my attraction to her was in her being the OTHER, in adding spice to our mix. Second, she upset my perception of myself; by her act of conversion I was no longer a rebel, she had brought me into the tent, forcing me to do something my parents couldn't: conform to tribal custom. So now, on paper, I fit in. But in practice, I didn't know how to fit in nor did I want to. I was married to a Jew. Two married Jews. Plain vanilla. Where's the excitement in that?

    I couldn't understand, and still can't, why she wouldn't embrace her heritage. Sure, her religion came with the usual garbage but not any different than the rest of them. If it was pride she was looking for, her tribe offered much to be proud of, traits that anyone would want to teach their children, that I would want my children to learn, if I had any. I just didn't get it. Couldn't we call ourselves Human and call it a day?

    On a practical basis, it was beyond my comprehension as to why she would submit to the God squads' laborious regulatory process culminating with a written document certifying her renunciation of Jesus and simultaneous adoption of Larry, Curly and Moe. What she didn't get, and what I was certain of, was that the conversion game was just that, a game of make believe complete with mystical rituals and elaborate ceremony intended to pull one over on the anointed authorities as well as the newly dipped subject. You can't submerge yourself naked in water three times and, presto, the even-tempered WASP remodels to an intense Jew.

    No, it's not like that. You can't erase an individual's history, can't blot out their formative period, that first five to ten years of life, when the ways and means of family and surroundings are inhaled into your blood and bones with every breath. You can't go from an elder led culture endorsing obedience and protocol and demanding unwavering calm lest one be found guilty of the crime of exuberance, to one calling for passion, debate, opinions and ideas tossed together with moods, argument, conflict and vice.

Am I protesting too much? I'm getting carried away. I'm biased. Obviously. I'm rationalizing, trying to avoid responsibility for her hurt because avoiding responsibility lessens my conscious pain. I suppose that's why I'm with Nina, to ease my pain. And she does, or at least she initially did, help in that way. Warmth and affection are what I crave, and she gives that to me unconditionally. She makes it easy for me, accepting who I am, not making it difficult. Right, easy. What every man wants from a woman. But I don't do well with easy. I mean, it's fine for a short while, but without a challenge, without some sort of combat, restlessness soon returns. Then again, maybe its never gone away. I should have listened to the boomerang, the one that's been in my back pocket ever since I met Nina, the one that sent me into a metaphysical tailspin and forecast mutual passion dissolving, giving way to core differences.

Turning away from the window, stomach aching, tired of questioning, I sluggishly lowered myself into the black leather chair.

"Sweetie? Would you like chai with a cinnamon stick or chamomile?" spoke Nina's flat falsetto from behind the kitchen door. "Sweetie? Are you there? What kind of tea would you like?"

"Nothing for me."

"Are you okay?" Nina submissively inquired, setting her cup of tea on the chafed bamboo coffee table.

"Did I do the right thing? Maybe she needs help? Who does that? Who barges into someone else's home and threatens to hurt them? Is that chutzpah, psychosis or hysteria? It could be hysteria since, clearly, she is trying to cause trouble, one of the defined symptoms. On the other hand, I didn't notice any obvious fluid retention, did you?"

"Honey, you're not responsible for what she feels. You can't fix her. Why don't you stay away from her, at least until the anger subsides."

"Maybe pelvic massage would do the trick? You know, manual stimulation of genitals, a centuries old recommended treatment for hysteria. I'm not saying that I would administer the massage; that wouldn't go down well with anyone. A vibrator is better equipped than fingers anyway. Physicians will tell you so. They're the ones who invented the electric vibrator. They had to do something to prevent chapped finger tips. Seems that rubbing clitorises and vaginas for hours on end has its drawbacks beyond tedium (who would have thought?); revenue potential is minimized since duration of massage limits the number of patients treated each day. With self-medicating vibrator in hand, treatment of female hysteria became extraordinarily efficient and made for pleased patients and wealthier doctors. Needless to say, once the general female public caught wind of this revolutionary contraption, they wanted in. Pent up demand spurred manufacturers to expedite production. Hamilton Beach patented the first electric vibrator in 1902, about a decade before it introduced the electric iron and vacuum cleaner. The iconic department store, Sears, then peddled vibrators in their catalog under the title, Aids That Every Woman Appreciates. For less than six dollars, women could buy a portable vibrator, with attachments, that would prove to be *very useful and satisfactory for home service*."

"Honey, you're not getting it. The most help you can offer is to stay away and let her be. You'll only make it worse by showing signs of engagement. She wants engagement. She wants your relationship to continue. It doesn't matter whether it's positive or negative, engagement means connection. She wants to stay connected. She hasn't accepted that the roof you two shared has caved, the pillars crumbled. I'm saying this to you because I love you and I don't want to see you prolonging your hurt."

"I don't know. I like the vibrator idea. They say a climax a day keeps the blues away. I think it's worth a shot."

"Honey, you do whatever you think is right."

Nina leaned backward into the cushions. The belt on her robe loosened.

"What are you hiding in there?"

"Treats," she smiled mischievously.

"Yum."

"Want some?"

"Have I ever said no?"

"Maybe we could do it with you awake this time."

"Awake, asleep, either way works."

The phone rang.

"Hello," answered Nina.

The sound of her mother's canned voice squeaked out from the mouthpiece, clatter that could be patented as a new form of contraception. Kissing Nina on the forehead and waving nonsensical hand motions (I devised my own sign language), imminent departure was communicated. But before taking leave, I received a call of my own. Almighty bowels commanded honoring the Indian gooseberry; one powdered tablespoon of which was ingested yesterday. This noble fruit, righteous subject of prayers mumbled by countless minions bestowing gratitude for unfettered daily exit, is primarily responsible for setting the stage for the threefold rise of the Mahatma, glorious devotion to vegetables and worship of the holy cow. Nina, an *Ayurvedic* devotee, introduced me to the kindly berry after noticing the appearance of blue pulsating forehead veins following my daily constitution. It took but one meeting to persuade me. So enamored was I that proselytizing followed. Astonishingly, my gospel went unheeded.

It seems that mention of bowel maneuvers cause reflexive sphincter tightening in much of the population.

'Hush! Yes, yes, we shit everyday. We know we shit. Every second of every day, billions dump their waste. BUT, it is rather impolite to talk about, wouldn't you agree? The topic is, how shall I put it, *verboten*! Wipe, pretend it never happened and go about your business. The end.'

I couldn't help but wonder: did this venerated berry and I cross paths for a reason, namely, to send me on a mission to liberate assholes far and wide? Could the Indian gooseberry be the ever elusive elixir shepherding in world peace? John Lennon may have penned lyrics chanting about giving peace a chance but, really, a bed-in with Yoko at the King Edward Hotel wasn't about to steer the ship starboard. No, if Lenny truly wanted to influence others to follow Ghandi's smiling footprints and ease pervasive constipation stifling global political leaders holding the reins of peace in their soggy hands, he would have titled the tune, Give Gooseberry a Chance. I mean, face it, peace had, and still has, no chance unless the almighty berry is given its due. There are those who believe the squirrelly looking Beatle was holding out. What with the band's jaunts to Bharat, penchant for inhaling water piped smoke and consequent munching that plugged up internal pipes, you would think that Lenny, being the inquisitive type, as evidenced by eyeglasses betraying hints of intellect, would have learned a thing or two about natural irrigation. Then again, if the image reflected anything of the substance of the man, and the benefit of the doubt a lyrical man clearly deserves, attempts to publish the precept according to Gooseberry may quite likely have been snuffed out by an Axis of Pinheads comprised of Big Pharma, Big Food, Big Oil, and chameleon like politicians whose job it is to service all that is BIG. More than most, these folks are astutely aware that a gagged colon fundamentally stimulates persistent anger; fuel much needed to assist titans of industry slash, burn and conquer while stonewalling sissy empathetic leanings of the human rights and respect variety.

"Honey, I'll be off in a minute."

"Take your time. I have to go." With one foot out, I had the sensation that I was sinking, that I urgently needed to take to the sky.

Hastily, Nina ended her telephone conversation.

"Where are you going? I thought we were spending the morning together? Sweetie, come here."

She sat cross-legged, robe open, merchandise on full display.

Superego spoke.

'Be damned, temptations of Lilith! Quell thy primordial simmering! Possession of pleasure brings but ephemeral joy!'

If I didn't leave right then and there, I was afraid both feet would be right back in.

"I have to go meet Jack."

"Why? You were just with him. Stay with me, sweetie. I don't want you to go. I'll be lonely without you. You wouldn't want me to be lonely would you? We'll play. Whatever you want to do. I'll do anything you want." She purred like a hungry lioness stalking prey.

"I can't. I have to go to the orifice, I mean the office. When I get back, okay?"

"But sweetie," she said in a hoarse whisper, hands kneading succulent thighs, a hair's distance from alert labia minor.

"Your self control is better than mine; I'll be back in a few hours. Really, I have to go." I said half-heartedly, the dial on my brain setting to melt, balls stirring.

"Do you? Do you really, Sammy? Do you want to leave me? What will I do with myself? Oh, I have a few ideas but I'd rather they involve you. But if you have to work then go. I'm sure whatever you two need to do is more important. We wouldn't have much fun anyway, would we? On the way out, do me a favor honey and bring me a towel. There's a wet spot here."

She pinched her nipples as she spoke. As expected, I caved, my legs giving way, causing me to stumble. Her erect left nipple greeted me on the way down, poking me in the eye. Adjusting, moving three inches up and to the right, I latched. But the right nipple, inverted and feeling neglected, soon beckoned, demanding that the perversity of this bosomy imbalance be corrected.

"Mmmf."

"Shhh, I'm here for you, baby. You do know that, don't you? I'll always be here for you."

A lick or two later, the neglected nipple proudly popped out. Symmetry accomplished! In the face of two HB number two pencil eraser like protuberances, hardened nipples as insistent as nipples will be, my hesitation dissipated, opposition withered and I succumbed to the sucking sound of an estrogen vortex. Confronted by outstretched arms wielding French manicured fingernails digging into my back and a runway groomed apparatus waving me in for landing, there would be no abstaining.

Id piped up.

'Thou quivering shlong has spoken: *yin*'s aroma shall not be denied. Here ye!'

But before anything more could happen, superego once again intervened, leading me to ponder. Yes, I pondered. Pondering was safe. Not dithering but pondering. No one cares for a ditherer. A ponderer, however, invokes images of Rodin's Thinker. Ah yes, the Thinker, a serious man. The ditherer, having no such model, cannot be taken seriously. Surely, he cannot. And if anything, we want to be taken seriously.

Specifically, I pondered sexual energy. Dr. Bronner called it a cure all. Could pussy clear up confusion? I thought so. Prozac,

Zoloft, Paxil, were all amateurs compared to pussy's healing power. I'd go so far to advance, possibly contend, even assert, that sexual delight could treat and cure common and not so common ailments in addition to fog. Come to think of it, how could anyone doubt the validity of a theory based on personal observation, sample size of one and payment in forms other than money by non-arms length parties?

If this be the case, if sexual energy soothes the soul, then let's reach farther and boldly conclude that a preponderance of so-called mental afflictions, as anally delineated in the *Diagnostic and Statistical Manual of Mental Disorders* are, frankly, nothing more and nothing less than fables. Sure, fine, okay, I'll go with that but how do you propose to dislodge the incumbent, the Collection of American Psychiatrists Who Laugh At Talk Therapy (colloquially known as PILLS; the acronym's origin unclear), from its cranial perch? To suggest, merely to allude, to the remote possibility of resolving mental conflict through in and out friction and consequent release of sticky liquids would be met with swift ridicule, refutation and diabolical retaliation by a high strung man wearing black horn rimmed eyeglasses perched upon the crest of a middling nose and an immaculate three quarter length polyester coat dutifully broadcasting privilege and prestige, the type of man who shields his genitals from others when changing in the men's locker room at the YMCA.

'An industry and more is at risk, for God's sake! Who do you think you are? Expert diagnosis and related prescription is the only route to mental restoration. Spreading falsehoods, announcing that two or more people mixing genitalia, mingling odors, secreting secretions, reveling in hedonistic want and desire will somehow (here, the speaker grows angrier) conquer fears, phobias and neuroses is most damaging and highly irresponsible! We know. We know whereof we speak. For it is PILLS who defined and compiled the DSM, the bible of modern medical mental afflictions, the world's most comprehensive compendium of mind disorders. What do you know?! You, like the other charlatans are, quite simply, sick. But we don't hold this against you. No, no, no, not at all. Sickness is taking hold everywhere. If it weren't, if the masses were content or satisfied, then we would be out of a job. Be assured, whatever your flavor of suffering may be, it is catalogued in the DSM and once we slot you into the correct category, a cure will be had.

'First you need a category. Then you may progress toward a cure. If a category cannot be found, no need for worry since we add new listings in each new edition and each new edition brings millions more within our band of abnormality and millions more to our cash register. When we reach critical mass, and sufficient numbers of the population are diagnosed as abnormal, when derangement sheds its negative connotation, well then, being abnormal becomes the new normal.

'In 1952, when the DSM first edition was published, one hundred and six mental disorders, or conditions of normality, depending on your perspective, were listed. By 1994, the fourth edition reported a total of two hundred and ninety-seven separate classifications. In the intervening forty-two years, the world got a whole lot crazier! And now, in 2013, I'm pleased to report that the number of screwballs has ballooned higher and, according to DSM V (doesn't the Roman Numeral make it look more official and believable?) fully half the Western world's population should be medicated.

'So who are you to offer a catch-all cure, insinuating that all one need do is tap into a force discharged upon activation of sexual activity? You haven't even published a book to prove you're an expert. Hah! Besides, nature has nothing on synthetic remedies. That's right, nothing! Have you considered the danger, the bedlam, sure to happen upon dissemination of your quackery? Imagine the consequences to commerce's contribution to maintenance of civil society if individuals existed free of catalogued conditions; good heavens, in a state of persistently good health?! I'll tell you what would happen: empty hospitals, bankrupt pharmaceutical companies, media deprived of newsworthy horror stories, government tax receipts decimated, advertising agencies denied revenue sources and investors transferring capital to more reliable profit centers promising growth and higher returns! This is not how the almighty intends America to be. Our purpose is not to care for health but to create jobs to care for the sick. The sick is our priority and job creation is the number one goal! The more sickness, the more jobs, the healthier the economy.'

"Sam? Sam? Hellooo?"

"What? What?"

"You were spacing out, honey."

"I was pondering. Pondering is not the same as spacing out. Want to see me space out?"

"Another time, baby."

Nina wriggled off my pants. Pondering terminated when the drug, her name be desire, let loose vitality heretofore harnessed by cotton briefs. Naked, dropping into *malasana*, squat pose, she began fiddling, deftly ministering to an aqua veined instrument, hastening blood flow rushing from right atrium, surging onward to right ventricle, tricuspid valve, right and left pulmonary arteries, turning to the lungs, dipping into pulmonary vein, rounding left atrium and bicuspid valve, speeding through left ventricle, pumping into aortic valve and diving into aorta before heading back to pear shaped heart via superior and inferior vena cava. Vials of replenishing ounces marked for maximum engorgement detoured to a feverish scrotum. Endorphin flow gushed, grey matter exited and mental faculties ramped down.

Invigorated by her touch, I trembled and bounced like a maniacal puppet on a wispy string, one that was springing closer and closer to her mouth. Running on instinct, I urged her head forward, parted her plump, maroon painted lips and watched my sponge like head glide in and out. Being a simple man, as all men are when it comes to matters of the groin, the visual alone was almost enough to swiftly end this business. And though I didn't want the game of peek-a-boo to finish too soon, I couldn't help but watch.

Well versed in the oral arts, leisurely engulfing me, Nina confidently nodded her head back and forth to the beat of a sloth like metronome. Sucking the frenzied protuberance into fevered gyrations, she swallowed deeper to a place where the hallowed uvula was stroked and tickled (itself bearing remarkable likeness in size and shape to the clitoris thus providing further proof of the body's uncanny propensity toward symmetry not to mention that the clitoris is housed in the vulva; delete a 'u' and add a 'v' and uvula becomes vulva. Coincidence? I think not). Final expansion activated, she picked up speed, intermittently challenging herself to that rare feat of simultaneous suction and depth, and enthusiastically polished her palate so much so that emission's pulsating call came in a splendid hurry, a tablespoon's violent outpouring coating her throat. Even the most discerning Russian judge would have awarded high marks for her stirring performance.

No love, no intimacy, no emotional depth. A sex act. Cocksucking. Nothing more. And that was the problem.

Once blood flow routed back to my brain, and libidinous lunacy napped, I heard the thought train whistle. Flashing in the main corridor on the overhead screen were times of departure leaving station Nina. If I hurried, I could make the next train.

'Quick, now is the time to go; you must take your leave,' said Psyche.

I approached the ticket wicket but was rebuffed.

'Your money is no good here. Courage is the only acceptable currency,' growled the insulted conductor.

Evidently, I wasn't yet cured. Confusion persisted. Maybe my research is bunk. Maybe sex isn't a panacea. If I had an academic reputation, it would be in tatters. Maybe I should ask a real doc for a category and a prescription.

Chapter 7
A Handmaid's Bell

> There is a time for departure
> even when there is no certain place to go
> —*Tennessee Williams*

The whistle sounded at St. George subway station. It was a pea whistle and it was attached to a string necklace hung around the conductor's neck. He gave the all clear signal before closing the doors and shifting into gear.

I stood with one hand gripping a nickel metal bar securely bolted to floor and ceiling, the other loosely dangling. The subway car was jammed. Seats were occupied or generously caked with grunge lending a lovely pungent bouquet. Restricting breathing to shallow nose inhalations, I did what I could to minimize ingestion of free verse aromas and wonky passenger vibes. But it didn't matter much, the air I was breathing. At least I didn't feel like I was suffocating, like I had been lately with Nina.

Judiciously, I looked around, my gaze not resting too long on any one person. Near the back sat two boys, stone faced, circumaural headphones covering their ears out of which reverberated pounding lyrics to Hush. Involuntarily, my toes tapped. Looking down, I noticed another set of toes tapping. They belonged to an elfish, bespectacled, forty-something man outfitted in Sunday's best standing two feet across the tube like corridor holding a large briefcase crammed with too much reading material that may or may not have brought about a sloping right shoulder and creased forehead beyond his years. Next to him stood a mother and preschool aged child. The child craned his neck up, mutely inquiring about me. In return, I smiled a kindly, paternal smile. Witnessing this exchange, interpreting my expression as a danger sign, the mother protectively smothered child against her body and scuttled to the head of the car. Silently, I made a face protesting my innocence.

Watching the scene unfold was an elegant looking old world woman wearing long white gloves and carrying a classic umbrella. Staring at me, her expression severe, she whispered, *pedophile*, then feigned swinging the glossy u-shaped cane handle at my head like a baseball bat. Instinctively, I ducked, covering my head with my arms. Satisfied to have made her point, the woman receded into the crowd. And my smile waned until a mooing cow took up mental residence.

At Zurich airport, terminal connecting trains pacify weary passengers by piping in sounds of nature. Birds sing, wind rustles, waves lap and a Holstein-Friesian cow moos precisely (this being Switzerland) every sixty seconds accompanied by ringing of a handmaid's bell. These sounds elicit giggles, chuckles and a welcome shared experience among passengers green lighted to let go anxious anticipation of their destination and find pleasure in the journey.

Two women, oblivious to the alleged pedophile in their midst, squeezed into the area hitherto occupied by mother and child. The talker was of medium height, shoulder length dark hair and Mediterranean features. She was garnished in stylish low heel pump shoes, Gucci knockoff handbag, dark eyeliner, voluptuous curves and oddly thin legs that, in themselves, cast doubt on her character. The listener was taller, blond, British by design, who wore a long skirt, the bottom of which rested upon her calf, and a friendly expression. I listened to their conversation.

"My life is half over and what do I have?" cried the talker. "My friends, except you, live in Forest Hill mansions, travel to exotic places and have walk in closets full of clothes. Why do I have to struggle? Janet, why can't it be easy for me too?"

"Lisa, I would love to have your life! You're smart, pretty, you run your own business and you were just married. Who wouldn't envy you?"

"Oh, you don't understand the pressure I'm under! How could you? Except for four years with Bobby, I've been single my whole life. Remember him? The cuckoo who would have sex only in the missionary position, lights out, because he was convinced that the bible forbid any other position; who looked at me as if I was going to burn him at the stake when I asked that he go down on me and who, when I practically begged him to have sex during my period, telling him how horny I get, turned white as a holy ghost at the thought of his blood soaked penis. Oh, he was a barrel of laughs alright. I can't for the life of me recall why I was attracted to him. Then came fifteen years of singles life. Do you know what it's like to have family and friends pepper you with the same questions over and over: why aren't you married yet? Don't you want children? Your clock is ticking. Why haven't you met someone? Is there a problem with you we don't know about? I hate that! Why is it me? Why am I the one with the problem? I'm as normal as anyone else. I mean, as if I haven't been trying to find a nice guy! As if I don't want to be married and have children! As if it's anyone's business but my own! But what could I do except put on a plastic face and say how happy I am and that marriage isn't for everyone when the truth was that I've been mortified since turning thirty that I'd never meet someone who would love me and want to marry me but I couldn't tell that to anyone except you because you're my only single friend and you understand. For the others, I had to keep it together and act as if I were carefree and had everything I ever wanted when what I most wanted was a man I could come home to at the end of the day because that's the way it's supposed to be. But that's not what I had and the older I got, the less frequently men asked me out. It's like I turned sour and passed my mating expiry date! All men want a younger woman, even the old and ugly ones, they think it's their birthright to sleep with a young, pretty woman. But now look at me! I'm married and I'm pregnant! Did I tell you I'm pregnant? It all happened so fast and now I don't know if I'm ready. And after all this time, now that I'm where I wanted to be, I'm having second thoughts.

"Jason expects me to be a traditional wife but I don't know what tradition he's talking about so how can I meet his expectations?! I know he's disappointed in me. We've been married six months and already we're fighting. Last night, he tells me he doesn't like my cooking. What should I do? For six months he says nothing, he eats what I cook and now, all of a sudden, he doesn't like it? I like my cooking. I like the food I prepare. Am I supposed to change my diet and cook meals that I don't like so he'll be satisfied? Is it up to me to make him happy? Is this what a traditional wife does? If I have to change who I am then I was wrong, marriage isn't for me and if this marriage is falling apart then I'm leaving even if he is hypersexual. Oh my goodness, it's totally nuts how often he wants it! But he's strange too. Another one. Are there any normal guys out there? He tells me he can't get hard unless I'm lying on my side, head face down in the pillow and I'm not allowed to look at him. Why can't I look at him? Doesn't he want to look at my face when we're making love? I think lovers should look into each other's eyes when they're making love, don't you? I only want to close my eyes and feel my husband inside of me knowing he's the only one who will ever be inside of me for the rest of my life. Is that so wrong? Why can't I do what I want? Does it always have to be his way? And when I'm lying there face down he pulls my hair and yells at me if I don't talk to him, you know, telling him how much I like it. So I do it, you know, I do it, because if I don't, he shrivels up, blaming me for his impotence. But why should I talk dirty? I don't want to. It's not right and it's degrading, isn't it, what he makes me do? I feel so dirty after we're together. I don't think he loves me anymore. Or maybe he thinks I'm ugly. People tell me I'm as beautiful as I was ten years ago, that I haven't aged at all. And men still look me up and down on the street when I pass by so that means something, doesn't it?

"You're as beautiful as ever!"

"Does it matter if he doesn't love me? People stay married for reasons other than love, don't they? I read a book by a guy named, Jean de la Bruyere. He said that unhappiness comes from our inability to be alone. And he's right! Aloneness hurts. So we submerge our self in a relationship to forget we're alone, to forget that deep down we hurt. I mean, no one wants to be alone. Now that I think about it, does anyone really fall in love? Or are we acting out of self-interest, fulfilling a compelling need not to be alone? I don't know. I do know I don't want to be unhappy anymore. If Jason wants to pull my hair during sex that's okay. I suppose there are worse things he could do. Besides, it's not like he's really hurting me."

"Lisa, it's a matter of self-respect. He's abusing you and that's not right. You have to tell him you won't put up with it."

"At least it's not like he doesn't want me, right? If he didn't want me at all then I'd be concerned. His ex-wife was so frigid that he's like a schoolboy getting his first lay. How can I refuse his excitement, his cute puppy dog expression? And, oh my god, he's hung like a horse! The first time I saw it, I didn't think he'd able to get it in me. It hurts a little but he's worth it.

"I don't know if this has anything to do with his size but there have been a few times when he's been so excited that he makes a mess even before he pulls it out of his underwear. I feel bad for him when that happens because he gets embarrassed and then I have to console him, reassure him that it's no big deal. But, between you and me, I like it. It totally turns me on, knowing I can bring a man to orgasm just by him looking at me and thinking about being with me. Watching him ejaculate without touching himself or touching me, his body convulsing, his face all scrunched up, it's so erotic! And it makes me feel so sexual. I love that feeling! I wonder if other men think of me and spontaneously ejaculate? Or if they think of me when they're masturbating? That would be almost as much of a turn on. Anyway, I know I have to talk with Jason but our marriage is so new right now and I don't want to complicate things this early on since I was the one who pushed to get married. I think he had doubts; he even insisted I sign a prenuptial agreement. I couldn't believe it! I would never ask him to sign an agreement. Love isn't a business transaction!"

"Did you sign it?"

"What choice did I have? I love Jason. He said the agreement would protect both of us and that you never know what the future will bring and that if you fail to plan you plan to fail or some ridiculous idiom like that. After we went to the lawyer's office to sign the agreement, he changed, pretty much instantly, and started treating me like I was his possession, and no longer my own person. I don't know what happened. He became domineering and this distance opened up between us. But I'm sure it's only temporary. I'm sure he'll go back to being the man I knew before we married."

"Have you tried talking, telling him your concerns?"

"He thinks I need time to adjust. So what can I do? Nothing I suppose. It's not exactly fun, being married to Jason. Sometimes I think I may as well be single again because he doesn't come home as much as he used to and when he is home, we hardly talk. At least when I was single I could go out dancing and drinking and meet fun guys. Then again, the guys I would meet were assholes who didn't care about me and only wanted to sleep with me. Is that the trade off? The fun, wild guys are assholes and the sane, boring ones marriage material? Why do I have to compromise? Am I being too hard on Jason? It's still early in our relationship, isn't it? But what if our connection doesn't grow? What if Jason won't compromise for me? What if he leaves me after the baby is born? What would I do with the baby?! What if the baby is sick or deformed or has a terrible disease? I couldn't handle that! And then I'd be single again, a single parent! I could never be a single parent!"

"Lisa, everything will be fine. You'll see."

"Will it? Are you sure? What about my work? I've been working so hard to build my business and it's going so well now. What do I do when the baby arrives; give up everything I've worked for? I can't do that. What about my customers, who rely on me, who need me, where will they go if I close my doors? What will happen to me and my customers?!"

"Why not close for a few months or hire someone to help out while you're at home? Your customers will understand and I'm sure Jason will help you financially if you're worried about money."

"I'm not staying at home with the baby. Oh no. A few days after I'm out of the hospital I'll be back at work. And I've scheduled the delivery date for late in the day on a Friday to take advantage of the weekend and minimize my downtime. We'll hire a nanny to help out while I'm working. I haven't told Jason yet but I'm pretty sure he'll agree. Besides, I don't ask him for money. We keep separate bank accounts. That way, we're each responsible for our own expenses. We think it's better that way."

"But if you have a nanny so soon, how will you nurse the baby? Will you at least take the baby to work with you?"

"My baby will be born on February 14. Isn't that romantic? A Valentine's Day baby! And did I tell you it's a girl? It was so amazing; I saw an ultrasound photo of her and she looks just like me!"

"You're delivering in three months? I can barely see your belly."

Lisa beamed. "I know. Don't I look great!"

"Is the baby healthy? Are you healthy? You know the average weight gain for a pregnant woman is twenty-five to thirty-five pounds?"

"Ugghh! Not if I can help it. I will not let this baby make me fat. Isn't it enough that I'm hungry and tired and grumpy most of the time? I can't imagine being fat; that's so gross. Did you know that you look two years older for every five pounds you're overweight? I don't plan on looking any older than I do right now. Ever. Do you know how many people ask me my secret to looking young?"

I was waiting for Lisa to parrot the doltish refrain, forty is the new thirty, and I began thinking about our fear of death; a fear responsible for concocting legends of eternal youth, making believe others die but we won't. All because we're so ready, willing and able to fool our self that, on a wink and a grin, Earth's spin will pass us by, seasons changing for others but not for us.

To prove it, we buy - hook, line and wads of fiat currency - into pop culture images of a photo shopped reality. And we store these images, believing this is who we should be, who we want to be, who we need to be, and we subject ourself to scalpels, implants and chemical injectables wreaking havoc inside, creating clownish imagery outside all to feed growth of fictional armor built to bottle awareness of the inescapable march of decay. We seek empowerment, whether it be real or illusory doesn't matter; whether it be four leaf clovers or horse shoes doesn't matter; what matters is that we employ buffers, be they fairy tale, superstition, myth, fable, or fantasy, to relieve inner scuffle, sandbag the psychological fort against mortality's pounding waves of awareness.

'But...what if there's an alternative ... what if truth shall indeed set you free?'

What, pray tell, is Truth?

'Truth is acknowledging that our mind is prone to jilt, spin, sputter and stick strong to destructive historical archetypes etched into our seven levels of being, and we would do well to recognize our deficiencies. Truth is believing all that is, all that was, and all that will be is perfectly adequate, even sublimely stupendous so much so that delusions may be cast aside!'

Why?

'Because ... well because, we exist as we exist and we are who we are and we live and we die, not on account of error. For if our finite existence is accepted and embraced, if our imperfections are nothing of the kind, rather, we and our world are just as we are meant to be, then foundations of fear and suffering dissolve and we may sojourn, however briefly, through annals of time welcoming the absurd experiment that is humanity.

"Get away from me!" shrieked Lisa.

A stocky, unwashed, bereft of neck male leaking jungle stench through pierced nipples stood in front of Lisa. Jethro (as

I christened him) had Lisa pinned in the crowded subway car. Lisa had Jethro excited. Must have been that sexual aura she proudly emitted.

"Yu age wouldn't none matter to me lady. You daaaamn fine. Oh ya."

Deftly transitioning her nose upward, possibly on account of beef jerky breath, Lisa intoned, "I'm warning you, I've got a gun and if you come any closer I'll shoot you between the eyes!"

Jethro laughed. "Lady, I hear yous talkin' and my ole' lady talks the same way and I learned that ladies like you, you know, fine lookin' ones, they don't want to change but sure as the yellow sun rises in the west, ya do change no tellin' what yous want. All that prettiness yous got can't do nothin' to put a stop to winter comin' and summer goin'. Yous only sabotaging yourself. I seen my ole' lady do the same thing, in a bad way, by payin' some slick surgeon to slice her up and tell her she gonna look younger and more beautiful but it didn happen and you knows what happened is that she don't look like herself no mores and she don't feel like herself no mores. She gots no lines on her face and she gots these crazy comic book size rock hard jugs and now no one sees who she is no more, all they sees is that plastic face and those big jugs. She ain't a person no more; she be better off if she were in a comic book. So don't do that, lady, don't turn yourself into plastic and don't you be so much worried about what yous looks are cause if yous do, it'll be the death o' yous. And your old man he gonna leave and probably take your baby with him if yous keep this shit up. Now, as for yous, I betcha I can put smile on yous face. How about yous come home with me and we go lookin' at the mirror on my ceilin' and I shows you how darn pretty yous are."

"Shut up! Shut up!" screamed Lisa piercing passenger malaise.

Jethro, sensing weakness, plowed forward.

"If yous don't believe me, look here this magazine I been readin' and listen what it says: 'self-absorption convolutes the mystery that is life, destabilizes balance and feeds feelings of fundamental sadness, the pervasiveness of which is only fleetingly punctured by glimpses of joy. Persistently painting pretty pictures of other people's lives while denigrating your own serves to perpetuate and reinforce belief in one's own inadequacy'. How 'bout that? I think they talking 'bout yous when they wrote it. Yous come home with me and I make yous all better. Oh ya, I be sure to make you better alright."

Jethro shimmied still closer. Attempting a broken tooth smile, he stroked her sleeve as if petting scales on a lizard. Lisa looked like she was going to *plotz*.

Summoning bravery or stupidity, little difference between the two, I inserted myself between Jethro and Lisa.

"Jethro, leave the lady alone."

"Who you fruitcake and why'd ya call me Jethro? My name ain't Jethro so don't yous call me that. I don't like it. Hear me? If I have to say it agin, there gonna be trouble. Now get out of here if yous wanna keep your face."

Fruitcake? Where was I, junior high school? Built to move heavy furniture out of large trucks, Jethro came across like a stereotypical short man turned gym rat to broaden physique to enlarge footprint to expand appeal to himself. What was I thinking, squaring off against this pock marked Hun? Lisa, suddenly reveling in the role of damsel in distress contested by two men, subtly retreated, her eyelashes involuntarily fluttering.

Lucky for me, a showdown was averted when my attention diverted to a female form exhibited in silver lycra skin. Jethro couldn't help but follow my gaze. The prehistoric relic and I stood on the same side, mutually enthralled. Silently, a peace treaty was executed after which, for no clear reason, as if rehearsed, both of us pressed the palms of our hands together, thumbs touching chest, in symbolic gratitude for thy creature named woman. Disturbingly, Jethro and I being of one mind, even if that mind be fleeting, or not, served to reinforce genome project findings of pervasive Neanderthal-Human interbreeding.

But our treaty came undone after the vision vaporized into a fast forming blob jockeying for exit position once the conductor announced the next stop. Through the sound system crackled a monotone voice. "Arriving Museum. Next station, Museum."

Separated from Jethro by the herd, the inner wheels spun once again, questioning why I was here and why now? Was my squiggly path preordained to cross this juncture? Did the entire planetary history need to unfold exactly how it unfolded in order for me to be exactly where I am at this precise moment or is it mere happenstance that I am where I am? The discussion with myself was interrupted by the crowd's motion carrying me up and out from underground. On emerging, my cell phone rang. It was Nina.

"Hi honey, where are you?"

"At the farm."

"You're on a farm? I thought you were meeting Jack? What are you doing?"

"Sprinkling fertilizer. Apparently, farmers know that manure gets life moving; manure is good for growth."

"Sweetheart, please remember to be here by six o'clock. We're having dinner with Rita and Mikael."

"The lesbians."

"No, our friends."

"Just saying they're lesbians. That's all. Your friends."

"Don't judge like that, Sam. They're nice people. Please be on time. Is everything okay? You were acting funny this morning."

"I'm parched. The Lehua blossom unfolds only when rain treads on it."

"I don't know what you're talking about half the time, honey. If you come home early we can play again."

"Uh huh."

"Sam? Did you hear what I said?"

"Bad connection. You're cutting out."

Oh, man. That's exactly what I needed to do, cut out. But that would happen later. For now, I was keeping a peripheral look out for lumbering Jethro in case he forgot the route back to the Pleistocene epoch and decided to follow me. Nearing the Queens Park Crescent exit, I looked up and saw Lisa and Janet climbing the stairs ahead of me. I remembered the quote Lisa threw out about not being happy when you're alone. This was reason enough for me to hustle after the women, catching up as they strolled along lost in conversation.

"Pardon me. That was quite a scene wasn't it?" Pardon me? Who was I, Cary Grant?

"What do you want?" said Lisa coldly.

"I'm the guy who saved you from Jethro," I said, a bit winded. "Wanted to make sure you're alright. Maybe I could buy you both a black licorice ice cream cone."

I lingered on Janet as I spoke. Perturbed by a lack of attention, Lisa threw back her hair and unzipped her coat, flaunting cleavage in a vain attempt to reclaim the spotlight.

"Ice cream? Are you for real? Uh, no, I don't think so," Lisa shot back.

"Janet, right? Okay, how about you?"

Janet took Lisa aside and whispered to her. Moving out in front of Lisa, she said, "Black licorice ice cream, huh? I haven't had that forever. I used to like how it would make my tongue all black."

Searching for SHACKLETON   **135**

"Forever's a long time. Maybe you're due?"

"What do you do when you're not saving women from subway monsters?"

"Aside from ridding the world of wall to wall carpeting?"

"Why did you chase after us?"

"Isn't it obvious?"

"Not yet."

"Your elbows make me salivate."

"That's the best you have?"

"You don't like elbows?"

"What's your sign?" asked Janet.

"Do I know sign language?"

"Your astrological sign."

"Virgo."

The corners of her mouth upturned slightly.

"What's your name?"

"Sam."

"You're odd Sam the Virgo. I like that. You're welcome to walk with us on two conditions: you take us for ice cream and you're not boring."

"Cash for beverage and ben-wah balls for juggling. Count me in." I had no idea where I was going with this but momentum pushed me onward.

Lisa, her charms wasted, manner boorish, zipped up her coat and brooded. Janet, manifestly self-contained in skirt covered legs, enticed me with bare knobby ankles.

As a conversation starter, I announced, "Did you know that the word 'astrology' comes from the Latin term *astrologia* which means 'astronomy' and astronomy derives from the Greek noun *astron* meaning 'constellation' or 'star' and, of course, *logia* refers to 'study'. The movements and alignment of stars, planets, moons …"

"You're telling us this because I asked you your sign?"

"No, I'm telling you this because your ankles are driving me crazy."

"Ankles and elbows, huh? This is what does if for you?"

Before I could carry on with my end of this ludicrous conversation, cords of anxiety surged out of the blue and into me. Instead of talking to a tree, I was rapidly spewing thoughts and words the full meaning of which were incomprehensible to me but, in reading Janet's expression, maintained a semblance of coherence for her. A voice, my voice so it seemed, spoke deliberately:

"Every infinitesimal event, every action and non-action happening on planet Earth shall be destined, by relative positioning of celestial bodies holding keys to understanding past and predicting future; though never revelatory to its inhabitants, for knowledge within celestial bodies is forever to remain shrouded in mystery for the sake of human experience;

"... denying the human intellect's desire to know compels the challenge to learn the art of surrender to a benevolent universe and to appreciate each moment of life since, to do otherwise, to get caught up in what has been or should be, to grasp, to heedlessly disregard organic unfolding of events beyond our control, is a sure recipe for emptiness;

"... ultimately, our focus on the body, on the material, on our personal wants, is counterproductive to soul fulfillment; it is a life led under cover of darkness; if stardust sparkle is the objective then pursuit of the external is a misdirected detour;

"... it is known that stillness is, and always will be, drawn from within; tapping into contentment, quieting the mind, nurturing perspective conducive to muting noise and making possible silent permeation of birdsong within our soul opens gates of introspection leading to fine tuning of our heart's vibration and, in time, we are welcomed to freely root among an awareness that brings pebbles into focus where others see distorted mountains."

"Sam? How did you go from black licorice ice cream to THAT?"

"I wish I knew. Um, listen, I just remembered that I have to be somewhere but, um, Janet, how about we go out sometime? Here's my telephone number. Call me if you'd like to share a cone one day soon." I pulled a torn piece of paper out of my wallet, scribbled my number on the back and said goodbye.

"I just might," replied Janet, not entirely sure where eccentric humor crossed the line into mental illness.

Once outside, Psyche continued.

'For a seed to grow to perfection, it must develop beyond its initial form, it must decompose, shatter, fall apart. Only then may shoots expand, reconfigure and flower.'

Have I fallen apart?

'Let's say you have.'

That could be a problem.

'No, it's quite good in fact.'

Why?

'Because to grow, you must fall apart.'

Leaving my wife, hitching my wagon to a woman who howls at the moon, almost being beaten to a pulp by a stone age relic, this is growing?

'Every experience you have is exactly as it should be, exactly as it must be.'

You think so?

"Hey asshole, wake up!" shouted a man driving a BMW that screeched to a halt as I crossed the street oblivious to oncoming traffic.

I approached.

"Hey, what time is it?" I asked.

Exasperated, he shook his head and sped away.

Maharishi, what do I do now?

'Ask for nothing and much will be provided. Kismetic tussles, not chicken soup, are good for the soul.'

Chapter 8
Animal Plane

Illusion is the first of all pleasures
— Oscar Wilde

Standing curbside off Harbord and Bathurst, I sent a telepathic message and a long armed wave to the approaching yellow cab. Picking up my signal, the driver stopped. I opened the front door. Settling into the front seat, color photo identification taped to the dashboard immediately grabbed me. Under the photo was written the name, YHWH. Given the absence of vowels, I surmised Eastern European origin. Then I recalled her telepathic receptivity and, taken together with an other worldly name, concluded she could be an angel. Few of us meet angels, I thought. Fewer still would recognize one.

The driver asked where I was going. I gave her the address. She punched it into the car's global positioning system and what sounded like Lucille Ball's disembodied voice began pointing the way. But I couldn't say for certain whether it was Lucille; the voice was muffled by a blaring radio. We were listening to a news report, spoken, I imagined, by an insipid man with a noticeable gap between his two front teeth.

"Coming to you LIVE from the kitchen of Schmendricks Bagels, we're here speaking with Arnold Schmendrick about unconfirmed reports of excessive black fly infestation. Arnold, do you care to comment?"

Boldly swatting away insinuations of wrongdoing, Arnold told his story.

"They nosh here, they nosh there, then they're gone. Pfttt! Fly fly away. No harm done. So what's the problem? Are there this many flies at other bagel joints? No, and I'll tell you why: because Schmendricks makes bagels like no other, that's why. Flies are hungry; they eat at Schmendricks. People are hungry; they eat at Schmendricks. We don't discriminate. Here, try a bagel! Go on, eat! Tell me it's not the best bagel you've ever eaten! Here, have another one. Eat at Schmendricks Bagels and you support small business, our employees, the local economy and the patriotic men and woman who put their lives on the line for our great country all so we have the freedom to make and eat bagels. Is this a great country or what?!"

The program cut to commercial. I asked the driver to lower the volume.

"On, off, do what you want. You're paying the fare."

Lucille (I was now sure it was her) patiently instructed the driver to continue straight on Bathurst for several kilometers, turn left onto Eglinton and continue straight for one kilometer before taking another left onto Old Park Road. I wondered, if the driver really was an angel, would she need Lucille for directions? Then again, maybe even angels have someone looking over their shoulder.

"Why'd you choose that voice for the GPS?"

"It's a voice. What do I care? It tells me where to go and that's where I go."

"Do you have choice of voice?"

"I don't know."

"You might get tired of listening to Lucille. A change might be nice."

"This is important to you? The GPS voice?"

"I'm just saying that ..."

"What happens if there is no choice for another voice? Should I be disappointed? Are you going to tell me that I *should* have a choice, and if this GPS doesn't provide options then I ought to find one that does? Why? Why can't I accept this GPS? Why must I look for another? And if I do change and find myself another voice, what then? Will there come a time when I tire of that one too? I make do with what I have."

"But if you want another voice, and you can have it, why not take it?"

"Me, I have everything I need. I am integrated. When you're integrated, you want for nothing. When you're not, fires of transformation burn out of control."

"What do you mean by integrated?"

"Buddy, we're here. Twenty-two dollars."

"I'm interested. Tell me what you mean?"

"Twenty-four dollars."

"First twenty-two, now twenty-four? You didn't turn on the meter. Now that I mention it, where is the meter?"

"Thirty. You want to keep talking? See how high we can go?"

I paid. YHWH sped off. I may have caught a glimpse of wings fluttering but I wasn't sure.

I stepped out of the cab and peered into the front window. The lights were on. Nina was lying on the couch. Her feathered black hair draped over the top of a green *sari* covering all but her feet. Complementing the rest of her, she had beautiful feet. Delicate, strong, smooth, unblemished, magnificently coordinated, their exquisiteness indicative of a clear foot *chakra*.

Nina complained her beauty was a curse, causing women to despise her as competition, men to want her as nothing more than a trophy. Sure, that's what she said but she didn't convince anyone, least of all herself. Appearance was everything to her. And vanity was her guidepost.

There was a short time, however, after her last love lost, when she was able to see through her own cloak of conceit and question whether undue focus on appearance was largely responsible for sorrow. Convinced it was, she determined to reinvent herself. Only through across the board rejection of her current self could anguish be alleviated thus creating room for a new self to grow, so she thought.

She started by reducing her bodyprint, by becoming smaller, eating less, training for marathons instead of half marathons, all in a lamentable effort to narrow her hips and flatten her chest thereby removing all titillating evidence from the immutable offense of womanhood.

Once pardoned, so she hoped, the right kind of man would be attracted, women would befriend her and happiness would result. But, far from a receding body and sunken face fulfilling her desire to consort with more desirable types, she simply attracted a different, equally disagreeable, kind. Reinforcing the thesis that like attracts like, similarly self-loathing men and women pushed into her circle. Dejected, unsure of her next step, she joined a Tuesday evening Buddhist loving kindness meditation group in hopes of breaking loose from despair.

Sessions were held in the basement of a Catholic church. The leader was a short, wiry bald monk named Geshe Kelsang Gyoto (tagged G-Kel by devout followers who felt more of a personal connection when using an insider's nickname). This is where she asked that I meet her on our second date, in the basement.

There were twenty metal chairs in the room set out in orderly fashion in two rows of ten. When I entered, only the chair beside Nina was unoccupied. After taking my place, I visually roamed the low ceiling room, searching out unfamiliar faces before landing back on Nina. Her hands rested on her lap. Her attention, and that of the group, was locked onto GKG. He spoke in a melodious tone, going on at length about the meaning of happiness until, without warning, a gong struck three times signaling commencement of a thirty-minute mediation period. Participants bowed their head and lowered eyelids. The room turned silent and still. Except for me. I couldn't stay at rest more than a few seconds never mind freeze for half an hour like a mime. Then I remembered I was carrying a packet of fairy dust. Taking it out of my jacket pocket, I read the front side. Lavender ink colored capital letters cautioned the age old Be Careful What You Wish For. Smaller print instructions said to 'sprinkle a speck between object's toes and object will be yours.' Clear enough but to get between Nina's toes her socks would have to come off.

So I thought and I considered and I mused and I contemplated how to remove her socks. Before I came up with a solution, the gong sounded again. Thirty minutes had passed and caramel colored G-Kel began clearing his throat in preparation for more speech.

"Reality exists only in our senses. When we die, when our senses stop functioning, our reality dies too. Does this mean life is mere illusion propagated by sensory interpretation? If so, and if we have some level of authority over our senses, may we not shape interpretation to err on the side of happiness, ergo happiness is within our power?"

Low vibrations emanated from the Church's ventilation system.

"We must work for happiness. And this work takes the form of meditation. When we meditate, manifestations of suffering are subdued. How so? We train in the art of meditation to build a platform on which to develop essential skills of right understanding, right speech, right action, right livelihood, right effort and right concentration. With effort, these skills are permeated with awareness of all that you do, all that you say, all that you think. It is then that we arrive at a peace speaking of happiness."

Leaning over, brushing up against Nina's backside, I whispered in her ear, "If you please, sir, do you mind removing your socks? Just one will do."

Apparently, the room's acoustics caused my words to echo and transmit on a frequency known only to little brown bats and G-Kel. He smiled and went on with his lecture. Nina, meanwhile, acted as if I hadn't said a word. Maybe she hadn't heard me. Maybe she had. Maybe I hadn't paid enough attention to the cautionary warning written in lavender ink. Either way, I put the fairy dust back in my jacket.

Since that session in the basement, Nina hasn't seen G-Kel. And she's back to her old self, a slightly meatier, curvier, narcissistic prize. This I suppose may have been what attracted me to her. I liked winning.

And now, here I stood in front of her home. The houses on her block, arranged on the east side, were modest. Each property horizontally separated by four feet of empty space and vertically by a twenty-foot long stone walkway that looked like it had been there for a long time. The west side boasted an open, undeveloped field full of weeds and grass, sporadically interrupted by sugar maple trees.

I watched as a flight of swallows swooped low to the ground, got lost among the brush, then abruptly jetted upward, gracefully resuming their acrobatics. I'd noticed swallows before. No matter what the weather, they were playing, having fun with each other, letting wind carry them or diving straight into hurricane like gusts; daredevils who gained strength from challenging the elements.

Where was I going? Back to Nina? Why? I should turn around right now. It would be so easy. I wouldn't have to speak a word or go through the break up mess. Cowardly? So what. It's clean from my end. I think. Okay, that's what I should do. Yes. Shouldn't I? Why play charades any longer? Adolescent passion has fizzled; time to go. Right. If I leave now and never see her again then there's no way I'll fall back into her trap. Hmm, what if I miss her trap? It's some kind of trap. No, no I have to walk away. Why is it so hard to walk away!? Pleasure. Is this my driving force?

'Profit from pleasure. Pleasure from profit. This should be enough' declared Psyche.

Far from it. In carrying on like this, I'm ruining myself.

'Ruining yourself? You finally found someone who makes you feel like a real man!'

But we don't talk about anything. Shouldn't we able to talk about subjects other than Betty and Veronica? I mean, there's all that dead space to fill after playtime.

'Archie thinks he can transcend man? Come on! What postpubescent male doesn't want to mingle with that flesh, stomp around in that orchard even if the fruit is starting to hang a bit low? She knows well enough the power of those gams; any mortal man would be squashed by the mere thought of tilling those grounds. Believe me, she knows how dangerous she can be. Ever since she was a baby powder scented sweet sixteen seducing old men for kicks she's known the havoc she wrecks with that feminine power. Is it a surprise she didn't bother cultivating anything but her appearance; trim and polish anything but her front lawn? If brains were what you wanted, you wouldn't be here now would you? You want full blown tête-à-tête? You want raucous conversation? You want to recite poetry under moonlight, debate Spinoza and Leibniz's positions on rationalism? Then turn left at the University and scour graduate classes for decidedly unsightly intellectuals. What you have here is an unabridged bombshell unburdened by intellectual trappings. Believe me, SHE is what men want. You're a man, aren't you?'

No, I can't do it anymore. She may not be burdened by brains but I am. I'm burdened and she's only complicating my misery. I have to end this, for my sake and hers.

'Oh my, look at you! Sprouting a conscience are we?'

Do I enjoy weighing my actions against high falutin notions of morality formed not by me? No, no, no! I'd much prefer the shapely dimwit who leaves me weak and spent and wanting more and more and more but what choice do I have? None! I have no choice! This conscience of mine is holding me hostage! Tormented by this damn cerebral cortex and vigilant occipital lobe, I have no choice but to access audio and visual playback of an over stocked inter-generational library, organized and catalogued in obsessive fatherland order, a library whose purpose is to teach me right from wrong.

I know what you're going to say; there are no mistakes in life so stop fighting the inevitable and stop faulting inherited grey matter when I should be thankful for a memory that serves conscience; a conscience abetting moral compass; and a moral compass bumping up the human animal that is me in the evolutionary scheme of things. Up is where we want to go, where we must go, where we have no choice but to go, like it or not. Well then, if that's so, let me ask you this: how did I get tangled in this mess in the first place? Where was conscience when I needed it?

The swallows mischievously tease a blossoming school girl; she with chestnut colored hair tied back in a lazy ponytail, outfitted in standard dress grey and blue private school uniform, ivory white socks, mid-length plaid skirt and roomy white button down blouse. Nubile, spring time breasts bounce ever so slightly, athletic, cream hued legs forcefully stride, newly widened hips hint at the woman she is to become. I'm frozen by her budding form but, unlike Polanski, the reins to my bobble headed penis are pulled tight, my animal drive hobbled once I consider that this girl is someone's daughter, sister, granddaughter. Once I humanize her.

The girl passes by. I wipe my sullied brow and redirect my gaze to long dandelions having gone to seed in Nina's overgrown garden. What do I do now? I have to end it or commit. No more in between. Maybe I should do it, commit to her? Maybe this would bring order to my life, maybe this is what I need. Or would it spawn even more chaos?

'Neither'

Why?

'You flee, you commit, so what? You're in the same or different physical space, you're with Nina or with another woman, so what? What's changed? You go on creating pain for yourself and others, chained to the wheel of suffering by the affliction of desire, the obsession with *I*; futilely searching for liberation through an intellect ensnared in ego, thinking that you are your thoughts, relations, work, physical body and possessions; living a life in ignorance disconnected from the core of Self, you've forgotten who you are. Or it could be you've never known. Yet, there is hope. For you have embarked on the road of trials, destroying that which no longer serves your needs, disorganizing, journeying into the unknown from which you will not emerge UNTIL you run the risk of complete and total self-reflection thus allowing for the possibility of your world collapsing. And if you are privileged enough to collapse, then you will awake, connecting to the divine Self and reorganizing with new energy, new life and order.'

Sensing my presence, Nina turned her head to face the street. Upon seeing me, she gave a look that said, why are you standing there? Once I was inside, she patted the sofa beside her, wanting me to sit. I sat. Ever affectionate, she wrapped her arms around my neck, leaning forward for a kiss.

"Mmmm, wet lips."

"You like? There's more where that came from."

"When are the lady and gentleman arriving?"

"They'll be here soon. Rita called to say traffic is heavy but they're on the way. As it turned out, I had time to get everything done by myself. I missed you! I'm so glad you're here."

"Do we have time to play?"

"I'd love to baby but they could be here any minute. Let's kiss. I like how you kiss."

"Where's the phone?"

"Why?"

"Rita? Hi, how are you? This is Sam. That's right, Nina's friend. I'm calling to see when we might expect you because we forgot something for dinner and if you won't be here for five or ten minutes, then we were going to run out to the store."

"I'm not sure. I'm guessing forty-five minutes or so. Would you like us to stop at the store for you, Sam? We don't mind."

"No, no, don't bother yourselves. We'll leave now and be back by the time you arrive. Take your time. Look forward to seeing you. Bye."

"We have forty-five minutes," I declared.

Nina was light. I picked her up, carried her upstairs and laid her down on the bed. Slowly unwinding the sari until she was naked from the waist up, the sight of her supple breasts laid waste to my conscience.

"I was thinking about you all day, baby. Why didn't you come home earlier when I asked?" she cooed. "That's okay. I forgive you. Come here. I want to show you how much I forgive you."

Helping lift off my shirt, unbuckle my pants and slide them off, it was made plain to both of us that I missed her too.

"Oh baby, what's yours is mine, right?!"

There she stood, all five feet two of her on ornamental display, feet anchoring muscular runner's thighs, hands resting on taut hourglass hips decorated with white lace panties riding halfway up her dimpled cheeks. Blessed with the long slender fingers of a seductress, I watched her dip two fingers into a wide jar of shea butter conveniently set upon the bedside table. Scooping out a sizeable mound, she melted it between her palms, rubbing it on her arms, midsection and bottom. Stricken by her sexual vibes, I waited. She was in charge. All women are in charge. Men can fool themselves into believing they're dominant in the sexual arena but, really, sooner or later they must submit.

"Lie down. I want to sit on you," she said. Grinning like a Cheshire cat, she eased her slippery bottom onto my chest and stomach and slid back and forth. She liked being on top, felt more powerful with me looking up at her, admiring her face, her small tits, her sparse pubic hair; believing that I looked at her as approvingly as she looked at herself.

"Asana number eighteen. Deep breathing before tender movement."

"I must have missed that class."

"It's special. Only for you, baby. Remember to breathe and soon we'll be joined as one."

Steady went the succulent drip from between her legs. Kerplunk, went my mind, short circuited by gyrating hips and a blood supply detouring to a rapidly swelling bi-polar organ. Wobbling, salivating, no more able to contain myself than a kid who hears the ice cream truck ringing its bell on a sweltering summer day, and she says I'm supposed to breathe?!

She scooped another mound of shea butter and placed it in my hand.

"Baby, rub it all over me, make me all slippery."

Oh, blessed Nefertiti, keys to the Queendom were as good as mine! Her torso stretched forward, Nina rested her head on my chest and shimmied her backside upward, making accessible smooth crevices, moist puckers and trickling petals. Arching her back, knees set in line with hips, she motioned me in from behind. But the uniform laws of kinesiology prevented my squirming out from underneath to accept her offering of union. Desperate to take hold of delicious nipples swinging a smidgen or two removed from tongue's tip, I lifted myself onto forearms until thy mushroom head could do no more than tickle her belly. Alas, the keys were rendered inoperable!

"Patience, dear," she counseled.

Disembarking, Nina sat cross-legged on the bed. Reaching down, reaching inside, she gathered natural lubricant to be applied to one agonizing shaft. Literally and figuratively in the palm of her hands, tantalizing me with what was to come, catapulting me into a state of religious frenzy as I inched closer and closer to the folds of nirvana, I feverishly swore I would love her to the end of time. Then the lesbians rang.

"Nooooo!"

"To be continued," said Nina. "Come on honey, time to get dressed. Be a sweetheart and greet our guests, okay? I need a few minutes to clean up."

"What am I supposed to do with this?"

Nina laughed. "Ice?"

"One more minute, that's all I'm asking."

"Honey, we can't. Our guests are here."

"Thirty seconds then," I pleaded to no avail.

Left to my own devices, I grudgingly chose a long shirttail over a friendly hand and stomped off to usher in the girlfriends.

April, the dom, spoke first.

"Sam, you're flushed. Are you feeling okay? Not coming down with the flu are you because if you're not well then this isn't a good time for a visit. I don't want to catch your germs. I can't afford to be sick. Do you have any Purell I could use? No? You should. Everyone has it. It's called consideration. Ever think of anyone but yourself? Look at your shirt. Don't you own an iron? Why don't you tuck it in? This is the respect we get? I'm starving. Did you get what you needed at the store? When are we eating? I could use a drink. Where's Nina?"

Not needing ice after April spoke, I tucked in my shirt.

"She'll be down in a minute. Putting on finishing touches. Come on in. Let me take your coats."

I hung the coats in the front hall closet, which was otherwise empty except for six bare hangars.

"We've got fruit and veg juices or I could whip up a smoothie, add in a shot of wheatgrass, protein, enzymes, whatever you want."

"You two are wild aren't you," retorted April. "Give me a gin straight up."

"We're running a dry joint here, Humphrey."

"Well, I'm going to need something!"

"April, don't you think you'll be fine without alcohol for one evening," suggested Rita, timidly.

"You think I'll be fine? YOU think I'll be fine do you?! Rita, I'm not having this conversation…"

Nina, dry, dressed and made up, bounded into the room.

"Oh, there she is! Nina, it's good to see you. You look lovely," enthused Rita as she hugged Nina, kissing her on both cheeks.

"I'm so glad you two are here!"

"Nina, Sam says you don't have any booze. Is that right?" interrogated April.

"It's possible I'm hiding the last bottle in my pants."

"Right, about the size of the ones they give you on an airplane. Back off will you, Sam. It's Nina's house so I'm asking her, alright? You got a problem with that?"

"I don't drink alcohol, April. I'm sorry," offered Nina.

"You might want to think about having some around for guests. It's only considerate for those of us who drink. People do drink you know."

"Yes, of course. Sam, sweetheart, would you do me a favor and go pick up a bottle of gin for our guests."

"No, Sam, that won't be necessary," interrupted Rita. "I apologize for April's behavior, we've been having …"

"YOU apologize for MY behavior? Since when does asking for a drink constitute behavior?! Who the hell are you to apologize for me because I committed the heinous sin of asking for a drink? You know what? I don't need this; I'm outta here! I knew I never should have agreed to tolerate an evening with your exhilarating friends. Nina, Sam, let's do it again sometime. Real soon."

Bullying her way into the closet, April grabbed her coat and slammed the front door on her way out.

"Doesn't even have the manners to say goodbye."

"Don't be glib, Sam!" Nina scolded.

"I'm so sorry. I really am. She's not usually like this. I was looking forward to this evening. Now look what's happened. This is terrible. I should go too," offered Rita.

"No, no, please stay. It'll be best to let April go. She needs time alone. This has nothing to do with you or us. This is April's issue. You chasing after her will only make it worse," proclaimed Nina.

"Thanks Nina but I think I should be with her."

"Of course you should be with her, just not now. It'll be helpful for both of you to wait until she calms down."

"Please don't counsel me Nina. I love you, you're my friend but I didn't ask for your advice. You don't know what's been going on between April and I."

"I'm sorry if you interpreted my words that way. I didn't mean to offend you. I'm not trying to be your counselor. I'm only trying to give you the benefit of my experience. Believe me, I know what it's like when someone you love lashes out at you. I've been there too often. And I know the impulse that says, go, run to her, heal her and fix what's wrong. But you can't. Despite your best intentions, you'll make it worse if you run after April. Because she doesn't want to heal yet. She's not ready. She's full of anger, she wants to be angry and she needs to let it out. Unfortunately, she'll let it out on you because it's easier to blame someone else than to take responsibility. Please, Rita, stay here a while. April will be fine. What she needs is to be alone. What you need is a friend."

Nina extended both hands to Rita who permitted herself to be guided to the sofa while fighting back tears.

"It's been so difficult," Rita whimpered. "I don't know who we are anymore. We used to be so good for each other, so light and carefree, supportive and loving. Then one day I woke up and realized that, after five years, we changed. April doesn't know we're not who we used to be so how can I get through to her? She acts as if nothing has changed, as if our relationship is just as good as its always been. Does she really think nothing has changed? Does she believe that her binge drinking, pot smoking and bar hopping hasn't affected her or us? That we're not totally out of sync with each other? When I confront her, she yells at me and tells me that I'm the one with the problem, not her. Why won't she talk with me? I've tried so many times and every time

I get the same depressing response. I'm so tired Nina. Tired of the arguing, the fighting, the stale air. Her love used to give me so much strength; now, we deplete each other. Is this what love does? Tear you apart? Before love you're whole and once you're in love, the whole breaks, never to be fixed unless you leave the person you love and strike out on your own again? I love April but I hate what we've become, the wretched state of our relationship. All the little things are gone. Hand holding, good night kisses, kind words. We lead separate, parallel lives. I don't know if we share anything anymore. We're like distant sisters. Dysfunctional sisters. What's the point of continuing? How do I get through to her that we're far from hunky dory?"

I crossed my legs and my balls inadvertently wedged between my thighs and I grimaced and yelped and hobbled to the kitchen to nurse the ache in isolation like a wounded animal seeking relief in a hospitable forest. At least I didn't have to listen to the chatter any longer. That's what I thought until my own inner dialogue took over.

'Drama, a drug more poisonous than love, craved by a mind gleefully anticipating action, demanding perpetual movement. Don't just stand there, says the mind. DO something, anything! Just do!'

Why do we need to do? What if we don't want drama?

'You witnessed April's tantrum, yes? Did she know of the tantrum? Is a three year old aware of their behavior? Do we ever outgrow believing we are at the universe's center? DEMANDING we be the center? Why should we THINK to change? Why should we consider there may an alternative way? April will get what she wants, won't she? Her behavior thus validated, she'll repeat it, again and again. Dr. Skinner (a most excellent name) says that pacification is tantamount to dousing flames with oil. If that's the case then April's got an inferno raging inside.

Every time Rita resorts to appeasement, she's turning up the heat. Only when fire extinguishes organically will fertile soil present, allowing consciousness to take root, wisdom to sprout, suffering to cease, and tranquility to grow.'

What's this? Engaged in a spirited discussion with myself and, will you look at that, out of nowhere pops an erection that should have been spent on Nina. But it wasn't and now I have no use for it. Back, back, I say, vile beast! You see, this is my fear. Not death, old age or disease but the unsolicited, surprise erection. I didn't ask for it. I don't want it. Not now. It's not like I'm sixteen anymore, sitting at my school desk, snickering with Stevie and Morty about pounding nails or drooling over ninety-five pound pigtailed Cindy, an early onset child woman classmate acutely aware of the hex cast by her cupped charms snuggled in two sizes too small blouses; a hex hypnotizing all the straight boys to participate in daily jack rabbit tribute to little Cindy who willingly inserted her soft body front and center, rear and back, this way and that, into our mentally insatiable masturbation skits. Unlike the rest of our gang, however, Morty wasn't satisfied with private fantasies; he wanted to put on a show of his own.

Informal Jewish education is resolute in its belief that experience is central to the individual's development. Subsequent to a boy's Bar Mitzvah, when he is culturally obligated as if an adult to observe The Commandments, emphasis on experience begins in earnest, derived from the notion that participating in an event (first we shall do, then we shall understand) or a moment is integral to learning, understanding and reinforcing beliefs in a direct and unmediated way.

P.B.M.E. (Post Bar Mitzvah Era), Morty's parents showed increasing concern about time spent behind locked doors, questioning the speed and determination with which this aspect of his education was delivered.

'The boy,' said his father, 'we should take the lock off his bedroom door. What does he do in there all day, anyway? If it's what I think it is, how many times can he do it? Doesn't he get tired? What, he has a bionic *putz*? Why isn't he outside playing with his friends instead of himself? With your powers, you can't redirect his education to something more productive?'

Moses replied, 'Mine is not to command thee; mine is but to provide guidance through delivery of words.'

'Words? That's all you've got? Words?! Fine, do me a favor will you, talk to him. He won't listen to me. Tell him to let up on the pull and jerk and get some sun.'

'Soon, the boy will learn to nurture his soul.'

'Soul shmole! This kid is a slave to his penis! Exodus or no exodus, that's not freedom. That girlfriend of his was here yesterday. The whole neighborhood heard her screaming. From the sounds of it, they did it six times in two hours. Six times! What, is he a farm animal!? Do, do, do! The tribe and their doing. Why always must we do? Can we not be? You broke the tablets once, why not twice? Engrave a new set, write something about the price you pay for sexual obsession and I'm not talking shekels. Strike 'thou shall not covet thy neighbor' and scribble in 'thou shall not know thyself more than twice per week and never on the Sabbath. Why not? Who says you can't make amendments? God will understand. Anyway, it's not like it's written in stone. Alright, I take that back.'

'In time, he will get there.'

'In time, we'll all be dead! Is the altitude too high up there? Not enough oxygen?'

As Morty grew, he left the solitude of his bedroom and held daily lunch hour whack sessions in the high school library stacks for a gaggle of wide-eyed girls. At precisely ten minutes past twelve, Monday through Friday, the show started. The kid with the circus size dick dropped his pants behind shelves housing titles beginning with letters C through E, ferociously jerking until haphazardly splotching a row of spines. Morty's proclivity for self-flagellation invited a mix of amusement, fascination, derision and disgust from innocent, curious girls who departed each show wet, horny and confused as to how, and why, females willingly allow, even desire, the SHLONG inside their body, or anywhere near them for that matter. Socially inept, Morty was certain that his comic endowment would lead to greater attraction of the fairer sex. Thus, his public demonstrations. How else would the girls know his strength of character? Morty's male classmates, knowing they couldn't compete with him in the library, were keen to play out their envy on the soccer field, on which Morty endured friendly beatings though, out of fraternal respect, no one hit him in the *kishkes*.

One fateful day, along came Mrs. Beatty, school librarian, sent by the gods of humility and proponents of semen free bookshelves. It was Mrs. Beatty's habit to lunch in the staff room. On this day, however, the librarian's workload kept her cloistered to her desk through the noon hour.

The entertainment began on time. Working with typical haste and resolve, Morty spewed in less than sixty seconds. The crowd oohed and ahhed, reflexively jumping back when the salty load wrenchingly ejected. Hearing the moaning kerfuffle, Mrs. Beatty rose from her desk to investigate. The girls, alert to sounds of sensible shoes striding on the wood floor, hastily dispersed. Poor Morty, however, was left alone holding his bag. Pants bundled about ankles, nursing his spent dink, waiting for the smattering of applause that usually accompanied the shows' climax, Morty stood strong, exuding pleasure with his performance. He was not wise to the approaching librarian (who, from that day forward refused to check out the school's stained copy of Catcher in the

Rye). Mortified, the good librarian seized the star performer by the ear, dragging him through hallways to the principal's office, pants and underwear still drooped around his ankles. Students and teachers alike gawked and pointed. The principal, controller of Autocratic Scales of Justice, balanced the clamor of the lunch time crowd, who pleaded for the show to go on, against the outraged librarian whose territory had been soiled. In the end, the principal, more a fan of home movies than live theatre, drew the curtain on Morty's Masturbation Sideshow. When word of lunch time hijinks spread through the community, Morty's parents were shamed into relocating to the other side of town and shuffling Morty off to a boys only boarding school in Manitoba. Though he never did acquire friends through public display of his prodigious member, time spent alone in the Keystone Province was a blessing in disguise. Because of the cold, frigid winters, Morty kept his pants on most of the time and redirected energy flow to a brain that was adept enough to gain entrance to medical school where, to the delight of his parents and rabbi, he eventually completed residency in psychiatry. Nevertheless, so I've heard through the cranberry vine, today he continues paying late night visits to local libraries.

"Sam? Who are you talking to? Honey, would you do us a favor and bring out the vegetable plate in the fridge?"

I entered the living room with a plate full of red and yellow peppers, zucchini, cucumber, celery, broccoli, green onions, carrots, black olives, green olives, goat cheese and raw crackers along with a large bottle of mineral water and wide mouthed glasses. The food and drink was placed on the coffee table within reach of Nina and Rita. After which, needing something to help me redirect my thoughts away from Morty and masturbation, I excused myself and went upstairs to shower. The water would do me good.

Ancient Greeks, Romans and Aboriginal cultures were tuned into water's power to mysteriously heal injury, disease, emotional upset, sexual longing and plain ole' malaise. Hippocrates, master sorcerer, affirmed water's Expulsive Virtue, one that washes away waste from the body for it is a Universal Solvent, ph balanced nourishment for body-mind-spirit, salvation to self-discipline, secret to loving oneself and others, uniter of fractured divisions, lifter of souls, preventer of excessive self-polluting. Listen children to eternal father; heed the pre-eminence of this indispensable life blood, a one of a kind liquid prone to dissolving and softening plethoras, thickenings, hardenings and accretions; its' fluid surface tension enabling infiltration, gripping and drawing out toxins and impurities. Make it hot and watch untold caloric energy be transferred to the body. Conversely, cold acts as a potent coolant, refrigerant and absorber of excess heat, inflammation and fever. At whatever temperature, water stimulates skin's touch receptors, boosts blood circulation, releases tight muscles, enhances immune functioning, influences stress hormone production, invigorates circulation and digestion, encourages blood flow, lessens pain sensitivity and calms lungs, heart, stomach, and endocrine system by stimulating spinal cord nerve reflexes. Submerged in a bath, witness feelings of weightlessness, the body relieved from gravitational pull ...

Stop! Stop! The streaming verbiage has got to stop! The relentless swirling among grooves worn down by neurotic forebearers must stop! Coming from a long line of thinkers, my whole life I've been thinking, thinking, thinking, priding myself on my thinking. May I not chew Black Jack gum, lounge in Alabama cotton pajamas, star gaze beyond the Milky Way without being interrupted by agitating forces compelling reading of lengthy essays detailing inner workings, machinations and metaphorical meanings of elevators manufactured by Otis, ThyssenKrupp and

Schindler and the advantages/disadvantages presented by each maker and their product?

'BUILD A WALL, SAM. ASSEMBLE UNBUSTABLE AMERICAN CONCRETE AND CHINESE REBAR. THIRTY-SIX FEET HIGH. TO REPEL NON-BELONGING THOUGHTS. TO TURN AWAY THE SELF DRAMATIZING MIND.'

But then nothing would penetrate, even light. Isn't there another way?

'You choose to invent your world. You choose to process life through your mind's eye, however that may be.'

I choose? It's that easy? I don't know.

'Sure, sure, why take a chance? Do as you've always done; stay the course, wear down behavioral patterns, dig cavernous ruts, don't even try to climb out. Go on, rationalize all you want, reinforce psychological defenses, renew ego's term of office for another four years. How's that working for you so far?'

Will the questions never end?! Must I always be reflecting, considering, mulling, ruminating, cogitating or contemplating? Do as I've always done because that's the only way I know? Are there no other options?

'None. Why should there be? This is it. This is life: as good and as bad as it gets. There's nothing else. Nothing! Avoid, repress, strangle and life shall be splendid. If not splendid, then tolerable. If not tolerable, then that's the way it goes. It has been written thus it shall be done.'

"Sam. Sam? You've been in the shower for twenty minutes. I wanted to check on you. Are you okay?" Nina's melodious voice snapped me back.

"What? Sure, I'm coming out."

"You sure you're okay, honey?"

"Yes Nina. I'm fine."

"No need to be rude. Join us after you dress, please."

"While you're here, um, how about you hop in?"

"Honey, I love you. I'll see you downstairs."

Too calm from the shower to argue, I dressed and joined the women, choosing a chair across from Nina and Rita.

"I didn't know if you were coming back, Sam," said Rita.

"And miss chatting with you two?"

Nina shot me a look.

"So, what's the subject?" I asked.

"April."

"Right."

"Sam," Rita started, "You're a man, right?"

"Ever since the operation, yes."

"Well, men harbor more anger than women, right? Then again, there are exceptions to every rule and April seems to be that exception. I thought that you, being a man, could share your insights on anger. It might help me better understand Roxy's behavior of late."

"Ahhh, you want my esteemed opinion, to cross the vaunted threshold into my store of knowledge, inhale the essence of wisdom borne of experience and intuition, expose yourself to piercing insight, acumen and ..."

"Sam," Nina chided, devoid of humor.

"Dearest Nina, never may there be too much amusement. Yet, you favor being earnest. So be it. For what it's worth, I'll tell you what I think. But first, I will say this: in defense of the emotionally screwed gender, I wouldn't pin the anger tail on men alone; I've seen torrents of molten lava gush from women and I'm not referring to vaginal discharge because, I mean, who's ever had an angry orgasm, I mean, not an angry orgasm but been with someone who is angry and who ..."

"Sam!" Nina reprimanded.

"Did I cross the bounds of common decency? My, what was I thinking? Shame on me. May I continue? Alright then. Flip the coin of anger and fear abounds. Anger gushes from many wells be it fear of the future, grasping for desired outcomes (the more we grasp, the more we suffer), or being terrified of letting go of an imagined past, imagined because yesterday's gone. Anger's cancerous invaders burrow deep within our trillions of cells, camouflage true sources of conflict, obscure resolution and, like any effective parasite, thrive on contaminating innumerable hosts for pervasive destruction is anger's end goal! And the longer it goes undetected, the deeper it anchors, building intensity and constructing an inner atmosphere secreting scorn, mockery and ridicule poorly disguised as irritability, frustration, disharmony and discord. Anger is inner bedlam, anarchy and mayhem that injures and rips into those who have the misfortune of crossing its track."

Rita replied, "Let me ask you, when I'm with April and she …"

A northern chill entered the room. Nina, sensing territory encroachment, cut her off.

"Rita," said Nina, gathering herself, "Sam may not be the best person to help you with this. What I know for sure is that Sam and I built our relationship on a foundation of acceptance. We show love, respect and kindness to each other, we try to give more than we take. Sure, we have our moments but it's in these moments when it's most necessary to show compassion, to remember that we love each other and that our words and actions should be considerate. Isn't that right, Sam? I'm not saying we're perfect, not at all. I mean, Sam thinks it's fun to lick my armpits. It's revolting to me but I let him because I love him despite how weird he can be."

"Since when don't you like armpit hickeys?"

"Rita," Nina continued, "When April gets angry, do you call her karma?"

"Call her karma?"

"Yes. This is her issue, not yours. You are not the cause of April's suffering, you're not to blame. You didn't do anything to her; no one is capable of DOING anything to her. She can only do or not do for herself. It's her suffering, not yours. As long as she holds onto anger, she's stuck in her own prison. You have to be careful not to let her draw you in. You have to set boundaries, not let her step on you. If this means protecting yourself by walking away, then walk away and go back to her when she's calm. Only when she's calm will you have a chance to restore harmony."

"I know you mean well, Nina, but I've tried everything. Nothing works. Whatever I do, April hates me."

"No, she doesn't hate you, she's in pain. The screaming and slamming doors, that's all venting, releasing frustration. Obviously she's angry but anger is a passing state; it's not who she is.

Still, loving her doesn't mean you allow yourself to receive that anger. I tell you this as a friend, Rita. I'm concerned about you. I see how you carry yourself: slumped shoulders, curved spine, quiet voice. Emotional turmoil manifests not only in our mind but also our body. You have to take care of yourself too, Rita."

"I'm glad that you and Sam are able to manage your relationship to make it work but I'm not you and I don't know how to deal with April anymore. I don't want to be afraid to come home fearing not if but when she'll explode; walking on eggshells never knowing what will set her off. I don't want to feel the need to placate her or feel frightened that I've done something to upset her but I don't even know why she's upset! It's madness and I can't take it anymore! All I'm asking is to be able to love her and for her to show me love in return. Is that too much to ask? Lately, I've been thinking it is."

"Keep the dream alive, Rita."

"Sam! Don't listen to his sarcasm. Listen to your heart, Rita, your heart speaks truth."

"I'm so torn. I can't think about my life without April but I also can't imagine continuing as we are. If she gets help, I know she'll return to being the sweet person she was, the person whom I pledged to spend the rest of my life. But she refuses to even acknowledge she has a problem! What do I do? Do I end our relationship, give up hope, accept that she's changed and isn't coming back?"

"Why not focus more on yourself, figure out what you want in your life, what will be best for you. And if April is best for you, then you two will figure it out. "

"It's so difficult to know," said Rita, gazing right through Nina.

Chapter 9
Blame Granola

Desire is the creator
Desire is the destroyer
– Hari Das Baba

Next morning I woke on the living room chair, contorted. Pasted to the coffee table beside me was a square, yellow sticky note. Nina's elementary handwriting reminded me to follow proper etiquette and call Rita. It would only be polite, she wrote, since I fell asleep before saying goodbye. Not caring one way or another, I dialed. Fortunately, voicemail answered.

"Hi Rita, it's Sam. Sorry about not seeing you out last night. I was wiped. Guess I fell asleep. Hope you're feeling better today. Bye."

Before I could hang up, April got on the line. "Sam? This is April. Rita's not here."

"Oh, April, ok, um, well, we missed you last night. How are you feeling?"

"Asshole! What the hell did you and Nina say to Rita last night? She left me, you know, she goddamn left me! And it's your fault. The two of you. What did I ever do to you that would make you destroy my relationship with the woman I love?!"

"It could have been the jalapenos. Wow, they were hot! Rita was throwing them back like candy and when you eat too many, look out. I know because I indulged too. Woke up at three in the morning, scared out of bed by a techno color dream of bighead carp jumping fifteen feet out of the water and slapping me silly. Funny thing is, I don't fish. Never have. Wouldn't know one end from the other of a fishing pole. So why am I dreaming of fish? Better yet, why bighead carp? And why are they called bighead? Is this how they differentiate types of carp? By head size? I had all these questions coming at me and I couldn't get back to sleep so I spent time trying to figure out what the dream meant by learning a whole lot about carp. For instance, did you know ..."

"I don't care about you and your dreams, Sam! I woke up in bed alone this morning. Rita wasn't here. Laying on her pillow was a letter. Should I read it to you?"

Dearest April, by the time you read this, I'll be on an airplane to Vancouver. As much as I love you, and I do still love you, I now realize that we're at the end of our road. I've tried, god only knows I've tried, but all the trying in the world hasn't stopped our fighting and I can't take anymore. To salvage what remains of my sanity, I had to leave. I hope you forgive me one day. I will always love you. Be well. Rita.

"This is bullshit, bullshit, bullshit! You have ruined my life!"

"The thing is, after the jalapeno heat settled down, I fell asleep and ..."

"I don't want to hear your lies, Sam! Do you know how much Rita means to me? How much I love her? She's my life, you moron! You and your prissy girlfriend did this to me!"

"Well, prissy I won't argue with but I don't know how comfortable I am with you referring to Nina as my girlfriend, kind of a juvenile term don't you ..."

"Why the hell did she go to Vancouver? Is there another woman? Some granola eating bitch? She doesn't know anyone on the West Coast. You screwed with her head so bad that she had to leave town without even talking to me? Without saying goodbye she moves to the end of the earth? That's it? We're done, over, five years down the drain? She walks out because of one stupid fight? Who's going to take care of the house, pay the bills, feed the dog? Am I supposed to do all that by myself? Is that fair? She owes me, that wench, she owes me. I'm not paying for her irresponsibility. Everything always falls on me. No way. This is her doing. I don't deserve this. Am I being punished? For what, for god's sake, what did I do that would cause Rita to disappear from my life? She's going to pay for doing this to me, so help me. You're going to pay too. I know where you and your girlfriend live. Tell me where she went. Tell me right now or so help me I'll drive over there and rip you apart. Where did she go, Sam? Where did she go?!"

Click. I called Nina to bring her up to speed.

"Hey, listen, I was speaking with jolly April and ..."

"I know. Rita called and left me a message. I feel terrible. Did I have something to do with this? Do you think I caused Rita to leave?"

"Of course it was you. Absolutely."

"Don't even joke like that, Sam! For Rita to up and leave like that there must have been awful problems between those two. Oh my goodness, I can't imagine getting to the point in a relationship where I wouldn't be willing to try to work things out. Do you think that could happen to us? I mean, if you were upset with me, wouldn't you talk to me and try to patch things up, not just run off? Of course you would. I know you would. Because our relationship is so wonderful and we completely, totally, absolutely trust each other. You mean the world to me, Sam. I love you, and we're going to spend the rest of our long lives together. I've been thinking, remember when you were talking about marriage and I said I didn't think it was a good idea? Well, I thought it over and I've changed my mind. I think we should get married, make it official. I mean, why not? We love each other right so why shouldn't we announce our love to the world and get married?"

"You want to talk about this now? Your friend just ran away. Shouldn't you be thinking about her or trying to find out where she went?"

"Now is as good a time as any. So what do you say, should we tie the knot?"

"Do you not recall your recent reading to me of the riot act on why we should never get married, why marriage is a prison, why we don't need the state's stamp of approval, why if other people can't accept our relationship then that's their problem, why our lives are about us and not them, why we don't have to fit the mold as long as we have each other. You've been married before; it fell apart and you spent two years post separation in therapy trying to understand why you hitched your wagon to an emotionally stunted leech who only wanted to lock you up, tie you down, barricade you in a stone turret and cut off all your hair. Your Cinderella fantasy turned into a Grimm Brothers nightmare. You said so yourself."

"You're being a little harsh in your assessment, sweetheart. Besides, you're not my ex-husband and you don't know what happened between us. Am I not allowed to change my mind about marriage?"

"Where did this come from? Out of the blue, you don't just declare we're getting married. We have to talk about this. It takes two. Remember what you said when I brought it up several weeks back, when we spent that Sunday morning in bed? Do you remember your response? You got all intense on me and said we're fine as we are and there's no need to fix what isn't broken, and then you refused to talk about it anymore."

"Why are you getting angry with me? We weren't ready then. Today is different. Today I'm ready and I'm saying yes, I do want to get married, I do want to commit to living my life with you because now is the right time. Don't you think it's the right time? Why aren't you happy? If it were me, I'd be ecstatic, not angry. What's gotten into you? I'm saying I love you and I want to be with you. You know, it's not every day I tell a man that I'll marry him."

"I'm not angry. I'm confused. You've hammered home the 'say no to marriage' message to me ever since we met and now you're telling me you're primed to light up the airwaves broadcasting born again devotion to the staid institution? Because you're pulling a u-turn doesn't mean I am. I bought your story, Nina. You convinced me that marriage stifles freedom. Voluntary bondage, you called it. Said you wouldn't be anyone's chattel. What's changed? As much as I enjoy the blindfolding, handcuffing and baton slapping, I can do all that without being an owner. Maybe that's why we haven't lost our passion for each other, because the illicit thrill remains, because we're unchained.

"It wasn't too long ago that I ended a marriage. And I thought, that's it, once is enough, never again. And then, THEN, you happened! I fell for you. Chin deep from the start. Way in, as far as the unnatural order of things allowed. I wanted you or at least I thought I wanted you in my life.

But, in retrospect, maybe I was driven to you not from a place of affection but from profound loneliness and you and I are meant to be temporary, to last only as long as my suffering persists and once it dissipates, once I stop groping, it'll be time for me to move on. What I'm saying is, I'm thinking maybe you're right, let's take our time, what's the hurry?"

"I only said it would be *okay* with me if we got married. I didn't say I wanted to get married."

"So now you don't want to get married? Why are you playing games?"

"Whether or not we get married is something I'm happy to discuss when you're not so agitated. I don't like talking with you when you're upset."

"Don't do that. Don't tell me I'm upset when I'm not and then put me in the position of defending myself and then, yes, I become upset! Why are we having this conversation? You do or you do not want to marry me! Deciphering Protestant subtleties of speech is not a talent of mine. Directness is what I understand. Blame it on the commandments. Notably, number eleven. Remember number eleven? No coveting sheep, white, black or any combination of the two. You could try to finagle wiggle room by nailing down a restrictive definition of what constitutes a sheep, whether it would be the whole sheep or part of a sheep and if so what part but if a reasonable person were to look at the context or the whole chiseled text, which included not coveting someone else's wife, manservant or maidservant, there's little room for argument about meaning."

"Please don't insult me and don't try to bait me into an argument, Sam."

"This is insulting you? How am I insulting you?! You, who wholeheartedly falls for gibberish from shmos off the street think what I'm saying now is insulting? Perfect. Just perfect. I suppose the buffoon you met last week, who was vibrating the same energy as you, who touted the merits of his brilliant, Feed the Children of Africa project, the premise of which was to blanket the continent with enough apple trees to sauce a billion people, who responded to your inquiry about the minor predisposition toward drought with his belief that Africa was in the Amazon rainforest so the suggestion of drought was laughable, who stuck photos of abdomen bloated children in your face while raging about the project's guaranteed success if only he could raise enough money, and you believed him and you wrote a check for him, after which you spoke with your friend Sheila who told you the project was a scam and that she'd been burned by the same guy, and even then, after you'd been swindled and it was too late to place a stop payment on your check, you expressed sympathy for this guy.

"Then there was the moron who claimed to be a Julliard trained pianist, a photographer on par with Annie Leibowitz, expert archeologist and Nobel peace prize nominee owing to his role in eliminating athlete's foot in Australian pygmy tribes, who relentlessly pushed you to donate five thousand dollars to a charity funding his research and, owing to research of my own, I showed you that the charity was bogus and its only activity was making wallets out of foreskin that were sold to Baltic nouveau riche willing to pay top dollar for unique luxury items exuding special charms. By the way, that's why you'll never hear Baltic people voice any opposition to circumcision but, and this is important, the international community has released a statement saying that they do not approve of commercial trade in foreskin wallets and may, at some unspecified time in the future, take action against offending parties.

"Where was I? Right. In deluding yourself into believing in a divine subtext, one nimwit after another senses your vulnerability and barges into your space because you let them. You then rationalize that boundaries are not being violated because these supposed hominids cross your path for a divine reason so you must welcome them, and the drama is played out until they hit you up for money or sex or both whereupon the production ends in disappointment, disillusionment, a lighter bank account and potentially messy underpants. Not everyone is meant to be in your life Nina! No one, including you, is being addressed by the universe. You are not the sun around which others revolve! If today's Pope can understand this why can't you? I know what you're going to say; that you don't judge people, everyone's equal and everyone has a good soul. Hell, you have to judge, you have to discern if you want to avoid soul infection, not to mention bladder infection, especially if you believe you're meant to help people. Well, how are you going to help anyone if you're not taking care of yourself, if you're busy minding greedy rugrats who invade you and poison you without permission? If you could only differentiate healthy from rotten, stop obsessively ministering to the lost and forlorn, then before you know it you'd be fiddling on rooftops lifting more spirits than you could ever dream. Do you know … "

"Enough! When did this become a personal attack? Why are you doing this?! You know I don't fight. I won't. Am I supposed to attack you now? Is it my turn? It's not enough that I blow you on demand; you have to shit all over me too? Do you have any idea how you're making me feel? You say you love me. This is how you show love? This is how you show your care, your devotion, by verbally abusing me, running me down, treating me horribly? Is this what marriage to you will look like? I won't fight on your terms, Sam. I won't fight at all. I don't need to defend myself against your attack, I don't need to persuade you that I'm not the person you say I am. I know who I am. Everything you said to me just now, was that about me or you? I'm sorry. I've said all I should say. I will not be mean like you. You should leave; we need a break. I need time to digest your outburst, to consider who you are and where you're going with your life and whether I should be there with you. I can't be with another paternalistic, paranoid man. I know the beginning and the ending of that story all too well and there's no way I'm bringing that back into my life. Since we met, every fiber of my being told me that you were the one I've been waiting for, that I had to wade through the assholes, the break ups, the pain, the lies, the abuse, the heartbreak, the therapy to bring me to this point, to the point where I met you, and that you would be the last man who I'd ever lay my head on and, until today, I've had no doubt. In fact, every day I'm with you I'm grateful for you being here with me, believing that whatever happens, happiness or grief, we're in it together, supporting each other, looking out for each other. I love you. I do. If I used plasticine to craft my perfect mate, he would look, feel, think and be who you are, warts and all. And you do have warts but I have no interest in trying to change a purple flower to red. I accept you, I embrace all of you but it doesn't mean I'm going to take to heart your ramblings about what's wrong with me and how I should improve myself. Who do you think you are lecturing me about the spiritual domain, interpreting the meaning of cosmic forces? You're a smart guy, but wisdom is not the sole domain of the intellect. You haven't yet learned what it means to feel your way through life and that we don't have all the answers and it's okay to say you don't know; it's okay to accept circumstances beyond our control and to accept people, all people, to let them be who they are because who are we to insist that someone change? With tremendous effort, we can change our self, but not others. And why would we want to even if we could? Ask yourself why are you trying to shape me into something that I'm not. Is that what you want, someone other than me? Because that's what it sounds like. Or are you just afraid of a woman who is her own person, who prances about naked in her backyard, singing and dancing, and who doesn't care about hurtful rumors spread by sexually repressed neighbors? If you can't love me for who I am, if you can't accept me part and parcel, then I was mistaken, and I was never intended to roam the earth by your side. Maybe I'm destined to be alone, not to walk with anyone for any length of time. I haven't made it past two years with any man. Maybe that's the way it's meant to be. Maybe perpetual transition is my fate and you're doing me a favor by opening my eyes to what is and what will be.

"You know, when my marriage ended, I was all set to join a nunnery, to live outside mainstream society, avoid men and give up sex. I wasn't willing to again endure the pain of a relationship. I couldn't. But before committing, I was struck by the thought that I would be running away from myself, hurting only myself by locking myself away, letting others dictate my terms of existence. Then I went to visit Jacob who helped me see that this was true. He said that wherever I run to, there I am. Have I told you about Jacob? He's an eighty-year old blind man whose purpose in life is to give of himself to others. Jacob convinced me not to live my life in hiding but to help others and for this I would be rewarded; maybe not in this lifetime but rewards would surely come. I believed Jacob and I still believe him. And rewards did come; if not for Jacob, you and I never would have met."

"You've told me about Jacob. A saint."

"You should go."

"You want me to go? Where?"

"We need a break, Sam. You hurt me and I'm scared for our relationship. I need to rest and think about what just happened. Please go."

This is it. This is my out. What am I waiting for?

Psyche, not one to stay quiet, answered, 'Flip a coin. If it lands on heads, you make amends, apologize and propose marriage. If its tails, well if its tails, we'll know that this verbal aggression of yours is camouflage for adolescent like inability to say what you mean, to say goodbye. Instead, you bundle stealth attacks with covert meaning propelling you to slur, slight and offend the woman, not letting up until she breaks. You want her to break so she can do the dirty work of telling you to get out of her life; this saves you the trouble of severing ties.

So, what do you think? Marriage? Nope. Not going to happen, man. That's a two-headed coin there. Both sides will turn up tails and I'll tell you why. Because when it's time to go it's time to go. You knew this wasn't going anywhere beyond the bedroom. You had your fun now get out. You don't hang on when there's nothing to hang on to. You go. The crying, name-calling, threats, recriminations, none of this is your concern. Block it out. What matters is that you live according to your needs. If you don't, if you live by someone else's terms, you suffer. That's the way it works. Either you call the shots or someone else does. No way around it. I've known guys like you. Guys who think they're too nice to pull the trigger. Guys who beat themselves up whether they stay or go. If they go, there's trouble. If they stay, it's double trouble. That's what happens to dopes. You want to be a dope the rest of your life? That's what nice guys are, dopes. I'm taking the time to talk to you so listen. Heed what I say. You pull that trigger as many times as you need to and you don't stop pulling till the deed is done and you've made your get away. You've got to be tough. That's what a man is, tough. You'll see, once you kill the relationship, you know what you're in for? Peace of mind, that's what. You got it? Tell her your out. Tell her now. Make it cut and dried. People need that; they need to know their place.'

Nina was silent on her end of the line, waiting for my response. I was stalling. I wanted to say goodbye but the words wouldn't come out. And I was distracted by my mind replaying a commercial I heard last week.

Don't miss tonight's two-hour special presentation on your local PBS channel featuring Dr. Blaine Myer sharing his secrets for unlocking doors to happiness. Dr. Myer explains how human biology is not programmed to tolerate stasis for extended periods.

Drawing on ground breaking research, Dr. Myer explains that stability is sustained by intermittent instability. Meaning: our inner state basks in the experience of regular change. If left unchanged for too long, distress preempts equilibrium.

It is this distress that lures individuals into downward spirals of internal conflict, otherwise known as the danger zone. And conflict, in itself, is a form of self-medication perpetuating prolongation of imbalance. Riveting, unnerving and exciting, conflict unleashes instant adrenaline rushes serving to reinforce craving for even more conflict thereby strengthening a vicious circle.

Dr. Myer will show you how to remove yourself from the circle and regain your balance free of harmful addiction. To unlock your doors to happiness, be sure to watch Dr. Myer tonight at seven o'clock on your local station.

"You're right," I said to Nina. "I should go. Goodbye Nina."

"Sam?! All I said was I need time to think! I didn't mean ..."

I hung up the telephone. Afterward, not sure what to do, I got myself dressed and walked out. Once outside, I closed my eyes and counted steps toward the intersection between the front yard pathway and the boulevard. I'd counted before and knew that there were twenty-two steps. Except today, for some reason, I miscounted, went too far, stumbled on a rock and fell to the ground. Looking up, I was met by a small child. Six years old or so, squinting from the sun, she stared at me and snickered.

"Funny, huh," I said, her sparkle and laughter contagious.

Giggle, giggle. "Mister, why were you walking with your eyes closed? My Mom says if I do that, I could bump into something and get hurt just like you did. Didn't your mother ever tell you not to do that?" said the child with inquisitive eyes and a shock of curly blond hair.

"I was trying to run away from my shadow. Aren't you supposed to be in school?"

"That's dumb. Everyone knows you can't run from your own shadow. Your face looks funny. You're old. Did you hurt yourself when you fell?"

"I'll be fine. You live in the green bungalow down the street, right? What's your name?"

The little girl darted off. Skipping and laughing all the way back to her home without looking back. Honoring the child's wisdom, I picked myself up and, enlisting the aid of sight, cautiously maneuvered past rocks and stones.

Chapter 10
Tumbling Up

*There is no terror in a bang,
only in the anticipation of it
— Alfred Hitchcock*

Running with a comatose pack of rabid bipeds chasing dreams dreamt not by me, youth internalized cultural messages implore me to reach for a time honored podium offering golden pigs as reward. Spongelike, an immature core sops up middle of the road storylines, unable to differentiate purposeful from red herrings.

'The game, son. Don't be a fool. Play our game.'

The game. I wanted to be a player. I wanted to be like them. To do like them. It looked so exciting, all those people grinning and patting their stomachs. So I played their game. Under wing of those who HAD IT ALL, charging forward, head down, tapered focus, for the better part of two decades, on intimate terms with pleasure, possession and position, cunning and chutzpah propelling me around barriers and up summits. Yet, I never failed to land at the top with a hard THUMP! Surveying the landscape below, clutching seized spoils, I would force out a terse smile lasting little more than the time it took strategic planning knobs to shove self-satisfaction aside and get on with the business of mapping out ways to get me back in the action, to do what needed to be done to ensure return to the winner's circle where I would bow, await placement of red ribbons and consequent spiritual depletion.

There I was, beholden to a supersized self, fueled by bottomless drive toward achievement and acquisition, unable to resist the pull of material gratification and personal recognition. And I thought to myself that something wasn't right. But thoughts weren't enough to stop me. There was no resisting ego, my sustaining life force. That's the way it was, the way I was. I hadn't yet come to the turning point, that place where we seek liberation from impulse, peek out from under cover of routine and conformity to explore the unchartered, the hidden, the cryptic, the veiled, and jump the queue to (horrors!) query what else is out there.

Yes, the turning point. Not a cliff to jump off, rather more like a slow twist. And twist I did. Vacillate too. But why? I had a good thing going. Why chuck it away? For what? To interfere in areas I know nothing about? I would have to make a list, I thought. It would help to write down the pros and cons. So I did. And on reading it over, I realized my decision had already been made. As the *uber* trendy people told me, IT IS what it is. Well if in fact IT IS then I took that to mean whatever I know is all there is to know and all I need to know. That being the case, there's no need to ask what or why, to go looking in places where I don't belong if there's nothing to look for. I should stay put.

Enter guide number one.

'*Macher*! You think you know it all? If you do not know that there is vastly more to know than what you know then there is little you know. What are you afraid of? WHAT?! A little chaos? Life is chaos! It's a constant fight exactly because we're in eternal flux, shuffling this way and that. There is no straight-line linear progression. Change, contradiction, inconsistency IS the architect of nature herself. You cut your heart and now it's happening to you; searching for answers, for understanding. Questioning is only the starting point. For what, you ask? For facilitating progress, for bringing the soul alive. So stop being afraid. Open up and do your best to navigate through life's turns, coils and bends; be excited to discover what lies ahead. Now, follow that man.'

Enter guide number two.

'Walk this way, sir. Please, please come with us won't you? Yes, yes, that's it. Here we are.'

What's behind the door?

'We prefer the term *entryway*. Hearty congratulations for making it this far but let's not dwell then shall we? Please. Go ahead, open your door.'

But I don't have the code.

'What do you mean you don't have the code? Alright then, I suppose you'll have to wait until it arrives.'

When will it arrive?

'Did I say arrive? I should have said, recognize. I expect you will recognize the code any moment.'

How?

'Look inside.'

Where do I look?

'Inside.'

Inside is a big place. Maybe it's obvious to you but for me, stark revelations are a rarity. More likely I'll encounter revolving medleys of cryptic symbols that I can't decipher. That's how it usually works. And if I do stumble upon this code, how will I know that it's the code I'm searching for? Maybe it's a code for something else? If it isn't, if it's the code of which you speak, will I understand its meaning? You imply I'm capable but I don't know. If I am, that's good. The search comes to an end and in flows perspicuity of self thus initiating dissolution of confusion. Yes, well, be that as it may, I'll still need your guidance. I've never done this before. You will stay with me, won't you?

Ω

I hesitated before stepping through the familiar marble arched entryway. It fronted a one hundred and two story tower where Hayes and Winter occupy floors fifty-two through fifty-five. It's where I used to work. It's where my office was, my home field. This was where I made my mark, where I played the part of trickster ace quarterback calling Merger and Acquisition plays for the venerable law firm. I was the go to guy because I was good at what I did. But I'm being humble. I was better than good. I was the best this law firm ever had, by far bringing in more money than any other lawyer.

Maybe I didn't walk on water but, as far as clients were concerned, I inhabited rarefied air. That's why they trusted me. That's why they paid one thousand dollars an hour for my services. I could extort fees like that because I won often and I won big. Winning made me worth the cost. When orchestrating deals to client's advantage, I did whatever needed to be done. Charm, needling, cajoling, arm twisting, threatening, blackmail or intimidation, none of it was below me. Only winning mattered. Not fair play. Not old school, out dated notions of right and wrong. Not anyone or anything but me and my clients. And under my leadership deals closed, old malt scotch flowed, and Hayes and Winter went swimming in it.

That was then, in another lifetime. More accurately, it lasted until three weeks ago. I was on my way to the office, following a familiar route, one I've been taking for more than ten years.

About to enter the building, to my left I noticed a chuba wearing albino Tibetan sitting cross-legged and stirring a singing bowl with a Himalayan hardwood mallet. Stopping to listen, I was drawn closer by his sing-song high-pitched voice. Lyrics didn't accompany his song but chanting did. He chanted to the mesmerizing tone rising from the musical bowl.

As if being pulled forward by invisible hands, I moved closer to the Tibetan until I was practically on top of him. Though he didn't move, didn't flinch at all, the sound grew quieter, simpler yet more beautiful, as if only one note were playing, speaking to me, only me. I don't know how long I stood there but it was long enough for the music to send me a message, to let me see that this part of my life, this work, was over. It was time to change. I didn't go into the office building that day. Instead, I walked off the field.

That evening, Dean Hayes called me at home.

"Samuel! Where were you today? Were you here? Why weren't you here? I didn't see you in the office. Why? Are you dying? Unless you're on your deathbed, I want you here tomorrow. We've got three major deals on the go, you know that, there's a mountain of work to get through and it can't wait."

I hadn't prepared a speech for Dean. Sure, I knew the call was coming but how many ways could I say I quit?

"No, Dean, I wasn't in today and I won't be there for a while. In fact, never. I'm not coming back." My tone was flat. But my message was clear because my thinking was clear. Above all else, I wanted to be clear, as much for Dean as for myself.

Apparently, I wasn't. "I'm not talking about today. It's late. I know that. I'm still working but, hey, that's me. Be here tomorrow, will you? Before sunrise. Some of us are working round the clock until these transactions close. They don't get much bigger, Samuel."

"Dean, I'm not coming back today, tomorrow or the next day. I'm done."

"These deals will take us global. We'll become a fucking worldwide powerhouse drawing business from every corner! And with you running the show, guess who'll be getting the glory? After this, they'll be naming libraries after you. Have you thought about that? Every numbskull lawyer out there will know who you are if they don't already. You'll be slapping a sticker tag on future deals. Taking a piece of the transaction instead of an hourly wage. That's where serious money is made. Not to mention we'll set a new record for partnership revenue and year end bonuses."

"Dean, listen to what I'm saying."

"Samuel, it's late, I'm tired, don't joke with me. I'm not in the mood. Just be here early tomorrow."

"This isn't a joke. I'm not joking."

"Did I call at a bad time? What, you've been fighting with the girlfriend? What's she saying? Headache, stomach ache, moon cycle? She won't give you what you want? Who cares? Leave her. Find another one. With the amount of money you make, that won't be a problem."

"Look, I want to thank you for taking a chance on me way back when and ..."

"You've been drinking. I can hear it in your voice. Even smell it on your breath from this far away. Early celebration of our impending good fortune or drowning out some kind of misery? Either way, I don't care. Get over whatever it is and get your head on straight. There's work to be done."

"Dean, I haven't been drinking. You know I rarely touch the stuff. You'll have my resignation letter in the morning."

"Don't piss me off, Samuel! What the hell are you saying? What do you mean you're not coming back?! What's wrong, your slice isn't big enough? Is this your way of negotiating? You want to negotiate before the deals are done? Fine, you son of a bitch, hold my feet to the fire, let's do it your way, let's negotiate. Give me a number. I've been meaning to up your share anyway. You're underpaid. I know that. I know what you bring in. I know your worth to this firm and I know we want you to be happy. I've been so damn busy it slipped my mind, that's all. How much do you want? Give me a number that'll put a smile on your face and I'll take it to the other partners in the morning and have it stamped."

"It's not about money."

"Not about money he says. Funny. You're very funny this evening. Bullshit! It's always about the money!"

"Not this time."

"Fifteen per cent of net billings on every deal you lead plus a fifty per cent bump in salary."

"No."

"I said, fifteen per cent! Do the math. You'll make triple this year compared to last. You'll be able to live in a damn mansion, have a maid sponge wash your dick every morning for christ sake! You think all the partners get a piece that big? Only the names, Winter and me, that's it! No one else comes close. You'll be at the top, Samuel, you can't go any higher! You review our financials, you know what we're taking in, who gets paid what. I'm not playing games here. I'm giving you my best offer right off the top. You've built your career on the back of Hayes and Winter and now I'm offering to set you up for life as a rich man; to cement your reputation as the toughest, smartest M & A lawyer in town. I'm giving you the opportunity to really make something of yourself, to go down in the history books. What more do your want?!"

"That's just it. I don't want more. I don't even want what I have."

"You irresponsible, selfish, ungrateful fuck! You don't decide when to leave, I decide. Do you hear me? I expect to see you in the office tomorrow. Screw me on this and I'll destroy you. That's a promise, Samuel!"

That evening, Dean called back every ten minutes until two in the morning, lacing into voicemail whenever I didn't pick up. His telephone harangues continued for the next few days, messages alternating between threats and bribes in an attempt to woo me back. But I didn't return his calls. As for his warnings of retribution, I wasn't concerned. He would prosper without me, as would Hayes and Winter. Ultimately, like everyone else, I was dispensable and my departure would be nothing but a temporary glitch in the machine.

Now, three weeks later, I was around the corner from the familiar black skyscraper, intending to clean out what was my office. Meandering down the sidewalk, I passed through a rickety safety tunnel erected next to a construction site where Jack happened to be working. A few old men were peering through intentional gaps punched into plywood barriers obstructing views of the gargantuan hole in the ground. Wherever there's a construction site, you'll find old men looking in. What's the curb appeal? Sand, soil, rock, steel girders, heavy equipment machines, cranes, what is there to look at? Curious, I called dibs on a gap to the right of which was a stapled leaflet.

'*Ubiquitous media blurs boundaries between public and private behavior. Sex has become a Commodity. Immaturity is Idealized. Pervasive Sexual Exhibitionistic display undermines physiological Value of long-term personal Attachments and Punctures sense of Self. Emotional/psychological Fulfillment is Not attainable except through Intimate relations.*'

The old men and I, each with a gap of our own, were looking at a piece of earth big enough to house a small town. Densely scattered about were an abundance of yellow hats; workers in blue jeans and wide tool belts. One blue hat, the alpha, the headmaster, patrolled the site bellowing commands. It was Jack. Strutting, megaphone in hand, his hawk's eye zeroed in on every workman, analyzing form and function, pouncing on sloppiness. Ten feet away from an unsuspecting hatless employee, Jack let loose.

"Hey! Your hardhat? Where's your hardhat, Diane?" Jack hollered.

"Name's not Diane, dude, it's Jimmy."

"Don't you EVER take that hat off again while you're working for me Diane or you'll be out of here faster than you can pluck your eyebrows."

"Dude, I told you, name's Jimmy."

Jack beared down on the bigger man.

"You like your job, Diane? Get the fuckin' hat on!" Jack screamed, spittle bunching at the corners of his mouth.

Jimmy blinked. He put on the hardhat, his slow moving acquiescence intended as a futile statement that he was acting of his own volition. Other workers paid no attention to the dust up. They saw that Jimmy was offside. Besides, they respected Jack. Whether or not they liked him didn't matter: making friends wasn't a priority. The priority was earning a paycheck, taking care of themselves and family. And Jack paid his men well, more than they would make at unionized sites ('unions are the same as herpes' he would say, 'unpleasant, inconvenient, and you do what's necessary to avoid contact') and he didn't ask them to work overtime knowing that, when fatigue sets in, accidents happen and accidents diminish morale and that, in turn, lessens work efficiency and product quality.

On top of higher wages and no overtime, Jack bought each of his men a customized tool belt embossed with the worker's name. The belt was essential not only for the utilitarian purpose of carrying equipment but, as important, strapping the belt around their waist first thing every day reinforced masculine identity and weighted their psyche on the side of *yang*. The belt, he was sure, also served as a constant symbolic reminder that Jack looked out for his team. If the men wore the same belt everyday, if it became indispensable to them, then so did Jack, and stronger loyalty meant less employee turnover, less administrative headache and greater likelihood of project completion on time and on budget.

Some men would ask to take the belts home. Wearing it around the home, they said, helped their relationships; the women would see the belt on their man's waist and revert to traditional roles and responsibilities. There was less fighting, more lovemaking (and once man and woman had exhausted themselves, man would strut around the immediate vicinity with belt held high in air, celebrating himself). It reinforced, they said, normal roles and identity of the two genders. But Jack said no and told them to buy a second belt if they wanted to swagger in front of the missus. Jack believed that the belts' power lay in it remaining on site, untainted by the scent of *yin*, by feminine contamination that could upset the men's loyalty to their work and to Jack.

"Strong boys, aren't they?" said an elderly, weathered man standing ten feet away. He was guarding his lookout, smoking a cigarette, ashes precariously hanging on.

"Excuse me?"

"I'm here most everyday watching those boys work. My wife doesn't like it, thinks I'm wasting my life, so I tell her I mostly go to McDonalds and drink coffee with my friends. But that doesn't satisfy her either and she gets on me, says she doesn't believe me, says I don't have any friends. Know what? She's right. She says I should get a hobby and I say I got a hobby, coming here everyday and watching the men build. Then she looks at me with that disapproving look of hers, as if I'm a kid and she's my mother, and that's the end of that. Ach, what do I care? She doesn't understand. She spends her days with her lady friends anyway, playing bridge or baking or gardening or sewing or going to the movies and whatever else it is those ladies get up to. And when they're together, you never heard so much talking; you'd think they hadn't seen each other for years when its been only a day or two. They talk and talk and talk and somehow they never run out of words. Who's got so much to say?

"I don't know how she stands it, all that socializing. But when it comes to me and her, you think we talk? Hardly ever. Been married fifty years this March and we hardly got more than one word for each other anymore. Only time we're in the same room is when we're staring at the dumb television or reading the newspaper. You'd think we could at least talk about something in the news. We could talk about the weather. Who can't talk about weather? But we never say much to each other, don't discuss current events or if there's gonna be a hurricane or a heat wave tomorrow. After fifty years, what is there to say?

"I read that leaflet, you know the one about abstinence, and it made me think that I don't get no inner or outer fulfillment from the wife and I'm not only talking sexually. Let's face it, at my age, the pecker isn't popping up too often. And if it does, the wife's dry as a whale bone and ain't got no interest in lubricating. She says the days of puttin' out, having to lie on her back and wait for me to finish my business are long gone. That's what she says. Then she turns her back on me and goes about doing the dishes or laundry. I tell her she's not making me feel so good by telling me that. She's taking away my dignity is what she's doing, my manly dignity, and that's not right. But she don't care none. Why should she?

"I don't love her no more, haven't loved her for the longest time but what can I do? I tell her she's gonna drive me away one day and it'll be her fault. How so, she says. Because you're not giving me what I need, I tell her. Like the poster says, I got the right to be fulfilled. The Americans know that. They've been sounding off about their rights ever since some smart cookies wrote the Bill of Rights. Do you know where the founding fathers got the idea for that line about life, liberty and happiness? Lifted it from a marriage contract. Being married themselves, they knew it was best to put it in writing cause sometimes you forget why got married in the first place. If you've got it down on paper, it's more likely you'll remember, more likely you'll stick around and try to get things right. That's what I heard anyway. Do you think that's true? But if you have to put it in writing, then there's a problem right from the get go wouldn't you say? Where's the trust? Is it in a piece of paper or each other? Ah well, married or not, at my age it's too late for me to do much of anything but look around."

The old man stuck his head back in the hole. Walking away, I melded into the hurried crowd, my pace instinctively falling in lockstep. Once inside the building lobby, I swiped my identification card through security, waiting for the buzz of approval before moving forward. Ahead of me were three corridors. Four elevators lined each corridor, two on each side. Corridor three, elevator two carried passengers to floors thirty through sixty-six. Shepherding myself inside the rectangular lift, I prepared for Eustachian tube blockage from the NASA shuttle like velocity sustained on elevation by swallowing frequently until the doors opened at floor fifty-four. Stepping out, I was greeted by two familiar wide glass doors emblazoned with the law firm's name and logo. I pushed through.

"Mr. Shackleton! Oh my goodness! Where have you been? We haven't seen you for so long! Were you on vacation? Have you been ill? We missed you. May I give you a hug? Oh, it's so good to see you!"

"Hi Vivian. Good to see you too. I won't be staying long."

"Why not? Do you have to go out of town on business? How long will you be gone?"

"I resigned. I'm only here to pack up my office."

"Oh my gosh! You're leaving us? What happened?!" Vivian lowered her voice to a whisper. "Did Mr. Hayes fire you? He's been angrier than usual these past few weeks."

"It's time for me to leave, that's all. I'll see you on the way out, Vivian."

"Mr. Shackleton, wait! Your office is locked. Mr. Hayes asked me to lock it. I didn't know why and I didn't ask. I was only following his instructions."

"Of course you were. Not a problem. Do you have a key?"

"Uh huh, right here."

"Good. I'll return it once I'm done."

"Oh, this is really, really awkward for me to say but, um, Mr. Hayes told me not to give the key to anyone and, in particular, not to give it to you. I'm sorry Mr. Shackleton. I would if I could but he's my boss and I have to listen to him."

"How about you walk with me to the office and open the door. This way, the key never leaves your hands."

"Sounds sneaky but that should be fine! So what are you doing now? Do you have another job? Are you working for another law firm? What about your wife, what does she say about you not working here anymore?"

"No job yet, I'm taking some time sorting things out. As for my wife, we're no longer together."

"I'm so sorry to hear that, about you and your wife I mean. Um, I don't mean to pry but does that mean you're divorced?" Vivian asked as she turned the key to open the door.

"Thanks for your help. And not just for today but for all the times you helped me out over the years. I'll come and get you when I'm done so you can lock up."

Vivian stood in the middle of the oblong shaped office, pools gathering in her eyes. "I'm sorry, I'm really sorry. It's just that, I'll miss you, Mr. Shackleton. I like it when you're here."

Then came the tears. I wasn't sure whether to toss files into a box or console her. I wanted to get my stuff and get out. I liked Vivian, exchanged pleasantries with her for more than ten years but gave her no more thought than the Cyperus Alternifolius standing in the corner. She was thirty-six years old, plain but pleasant in appearance, preferring retro clothing that shrouded generous feminine attributes. Her infectious enthusiasm and benevolent quirkiness endeared her to co-workers and management alike. Single, conscientious, respectful, willing to work weekends and late on weekdays, she was the ideal employee who showered me with an effusive, heartfelt welcome each morning on my arrival that never registered as anything more than affability. In response, I kept my distance, greeting her properly, civil, formal, rarely engaging in small talk. I wasn't one for small talk. I was busy. There were more important things to do than talk with support staff.

"Vivian, why don't you sit down until you feel better?" I offered, thinking that would be enough to avoid discussion and allow me to get what I needed.

Uncovering her face, cheeks moist, eyes dreamy, she edged forward. Uh oh, here comes the hug, I thought. Should I slip away or accept her embrace, pretend that I care? How was I going to get out by noon? Not that I had to be out by noon but I didn't want to stay any longer than necessary. And this? An emotional outpouring? This I wasn't prepared for. Vivian didn't wait for my response. Instead, she reached out to take hold my forearms, letting her head lean into my shoulders, dampening my blue shirt with tears. Stiff, awkward, wondering why this woman was leaning on me and why she was crying at all, I kept looking at my watch, waiting for her to be done.

"Mr. Shackleton, you've been so nice to me. You always took the time to say hello. I know that my work isn't as important as yours but you always treated me kindly and most of the lawyers don't so much as acknowledge my existence or if they do, they aren't in the least bit respectful to me. Why are they like that? Is there a course you take at law school teaching you to look down on hired help? Don't they know it hurts to be treated shabbily or outright ignored? I mean, everyone wants to be acknowledged, to know that they matter, that they're needed, if only in a small way. I do matter. All of us who aren't lawyers are very important to this office. How could you get your work done without us? I'm sorry. I don't mean to bother you with dramatics. I know you're leaving and probably going through a difficult period yourself and I don't want to dump my problems on you. I do like working here but it's not the friendliest place sometimes. That's why it was nice to know you would be here everyday; you have a big heart, I saw it in your face the first time we met. Remember? March 23, 2003."

Oh boy. She's reciting dates. This isn't good. It's never good when a woman recites dates. She knows what the date refers to but you, well, you draw a blank. Other than a birthday or two, you don't attach dates to events. Why would you? But she does. She's built that way. March 23, 2003? I'm supposed to know this? I sensed danger. I couldn't wait any longer. I'd have to push her aside. My waterproof watch read 11:38. I could still make it out by noon if I started packing now.

"Vivian," I started to extricate myself, "I don't have much time, I need to take care of my files."

Sniffling now, the top of her head brushing the bottom of my neck, she unbuttoned her blouse revealing a uniformly white shaded smooth navel of a pigment common to redheads though she was brunette. Tilting her head up, one hand snuck behind my neck, nudging my face toward her pursed lips.

'Run, run as fast as you can,' cautioned a small voice. But in an instant, the voice was steamrolled by male frailty.

Fully unbuttoned, Vivian removed her blouse, letting it fall to the floor, exposing full breasts detained in a canary yellow lace bra. First she's reciting dates, now she's exposing these breasts. Look at those things! Oy. May as well tie me down to railroad tracks. I was beaten, back in that familiar place, caught up in inner battle.

'Ha, ha, ha,' howled Libido, 'thou shalt not be overcome!'

Turn it off. Off I say. Go away.

'Never! Mine is not to restrain hunger, mine is to satisfy desire.'

My desire is to be like the good people, those who recognize satisfaction of their wants as secondary to the well being of others who don't know any better.

'Sure, sure, but last time I checked you weren't among them.'

But I want to be.

'You can't.'

Why not? Why can't I be like them and have the strength to resist such an offering?

Cue HOWLING from main gallery.

'Resist? Is that what you want to do? Why resist? You're a man. You're supposed to buckle upon dissemination of female essence. You're expected to subjugate discipline to pleasure. Did Zeus, Apollo and Hermes, the GODS, not dine on strength replenishing nectar? Should you, a loyal subject, not consume as they did?'

What are you saying? That a feast is placed before me for a reason, that I must partake because I'm a man and that's what a man does because that's what the GODS do? Isn't there more to being a man or a GOD for that matter? Hmm. Okay, what about this; what if this is an opening of another kind altogether; what if I have a responsibility to fulfill? Yes, that's it! A responsibility to this woman, this fellow human being, to support her and not take advantage.

Upper Balconies join resumption of Boisterous Hooting.

'You're saying you can look at those breasts and not want to touch them, to fondle and suckle? You can ignore your growing erection? Tame your self? Yes? Impressive, this willingness to put someone else before you.'

Sure. That's what I'm doing. That's what I could do, if I wanted. But … what was that you said about Zeus and the others? I should do as they did? They didn't get to be Gods without knowing a thing or two. Maybe they knew it was just sex. That's it. Nothing more than physical contact. An amorous act. I'm not here to hurt anyone. I take my penis, stick it in somewhere, repeat until liberated and that's that. What's the problem? If I walk out of here with a smile, let me tell you who benefits; me, her, everyone we come into contact with BECAUSE we're happy. It's a win win. Where is it written that recreational breast play or orifice penetration leads one to conclude that love is in the air? Love. You know where that leads; manacles of possession, domination and control, restraints giving rise to dreadful emotions of jealousy, insecurity, hurt and rage. Who needs it? I don't. No, let's stick with sex; sidestep the rest.

SLAP! 'Wake up Dorothy, it CANNOT be done! Sure, Toto can hump all the four-pound furry ass he wants without repercussion but you, unlike the barking mongrel, do not run on instinct alone.'

"Vivian, maybe we shouldn't …"

But I was too late. Her top was completely off, her soft breasts were pushing against me and jam packed arousal negated meddlesome thoughts of doing the righteous thing. Reaching inside my pants, she artlessly clutched a vigorously expanding cock before leaning forward to smother me in between cleavage's sweet spot. After getting my fill of slithering up and down her chest, I motioned for a change up, intimating she drop her skirt but leave the matching yellow g-string in place. Compliant, Vivian turned away from me to face the desk, her hands laid flat on top for support. Visually inhaling her from behind, I prepared to burrow in. Then I looked. And I saw it. Damn. She was utterly native! This not being the 1970s, I had no choice but to step back, way back.

"Vivian, as much as it pains me to say this, I can't. I don't have a condom, we can't ..."

"I'm not worried, Mr. Shackleton. My period ended three days ago. I won't get pregnant."

"Flow or no flow, pregnancy may happen anytime."

"Mr. Shackleton, please, I want you. I really, really want you."

For what man would spoken words imploring him to enter not be stimulation enough to restore blood rush to a softening *shlong*? When a woman like Vivian says they want you, ego responds and the woman becomes irresistible, for a short time anyway.

Steeling my nerves for a second go, trying to maintain level focus on the task at hand, I did my best to block out sight of the untamed mane. And I was almost there, almost in, when field of vision expanded and ... there it was. Retreat! I had to retreat. I knew, surely I knew I shouldn't have looked, that I would ruin it for myself, but I did look, I did sabotage desire. It was too much hair. I would get lost; never find my way out. I couldn't do it.

Oddly enough, I thought, maybe conscience did win this battle. Limp, I accepted defeat. Vivian, however, oblivious to my distressed musings, but sensing lost momentum, turned round and ground her freshly matted pelvis against mine, territorially varnishing me and giving all she had to coax me into a romp in and out of the wild. But, alas, this bang was not to be.

"Sam? Sam! Is that you in there? Who's in there?"

It was Dean Hayes. Alarmed, Vivian rushed to dress and I buckled up.

"Why is this door locked? Open it!" growled Dean.

I waited before opening, giving Vivian time to regain composure.

"Dean, good to see you. Vivian here was kind enough to help me empty my drawers and pack. I shouldn't be more than twenty minutes."

Dean was too riled up to take notice of the room's pungent fragrance or Vivian's crimson cheeks. Impatiently, he sternly instructed Vivian to return to her desk.

"You really fucked us, Samuel. No notice, no time to adjust or create a credible story to feed to clients and media. Do you know we lost Simmons today and the Henderson account yesterday? Because of you; you selfish son of a bitch. They wanted you directing those deals, no one else. With those accounts gone, our revenue is sliced by more than sixty-seven million this fiscal year. And that's only the beginning. People gossip. Word is spreading that those assholes fired us. You know what'll happen now? We'll take more hits from the trickle down of the minion lemmings who can't think for themselves and take their business wherever the big boys go. You happy. I hope you're happy. Your happiness is my only concern. It's all about Samuel, isn't it? I made you, damn it! I made your career, I made your fortune, I made your life! Do you give two fucks about me, the firm, people who work here, who make a living from the work we do? Have you given any thought to the carnage you've wrought, the lives you've ruined?"

Dean was right. I didn't care what he had done for me. I was groomed as much for his benefit as mine. As far as I was concerned, I had already paid him back fifty times over. Fading out while he spewed his particular brand of vitriol, I zeroed in on Vivian's bra laying on the floor. In the commotion, she forgot to put it on. Dean saw it too. He interrupted himself to bend over, pick up the bra and hold it aloft with two fingers, as if being careful not to tamper with crime scene evidence.

"What the hell is this?"

Dean paused, glanced at the open door then back at me.

"Christ! What happened to you? You were one of the brightest guys I knew, analytical skills and judgment second to none. With you on board, our M & A marketing budget was non-existent. We didn't have to pitch clients; they knocked on our door because of you. Now look what you've become! Why are you doing this to me, Samuel? You're here to clean house and, what, spur of the moment decide to donate a few more droppings for me to clean up? Farewell *shtupping* of the help? It's not enough that you're screwing yourself and the firm? Class act, real class act. I tell you what, go to my office, take the samurai sword hanging on the wall, you know the gift from Takamatsi and Partners for running the mining deal that put this firm on the map and vaulted your career into superstar status, and do what's honorable. Be sure you don't miss the organs that matter and I'm not talking about your dick, shithead. You've obliterated your career, ruined your marriage and now you're begging me to call up your little girlfriend and share today's events. One fucking deserves another wouldn't you say? Certainly I owe you that much after what you've done to me. Think I'll have Vivian by my side on speakerphone when calling the girlfriend just in case she wants size and shape corroboration. The future's never looked brighter for you, has it, Samuel?

"When reception told me you were here I decided to take one last shot at talking sense into you. Offer him more money, I thought, he's the best in the business and I can't afford having a competitor scooping him up down the road. The other partners will have to suck it up and reduce their take. This is Shackleton we're talking about, my right hand man. He's the guy I can always count on to get the job done, the guy who's been devoted to me all these years. And that's worth something. It's worth a hell of a lot. So I'm told you're in the office and I come to see you, to talk to you, to get you to see what's right, and I open the door and this is what I find? I swear if this firm is hit with a sexual harassment suit, you're coming along for the ride! You're done, Samuel, and not only at Hayes and Winter, I'll make sure of that. Fuck you. We'll be fine without you. We'll be better than ever. Get your shit and get out of here! I don't want to see your face or hear your voice again. I'm giving you five minutes then I'm calling security."

Dean stormed out of the office.

"Hey Dean," I called out to him as he rumbled down the hallway. "You can look at this as a beginning or an ending. Adjust your lens and you'll be anticipating the next race instead of bemoaning a finish line. Our paths diverge here; nothing more, nothing less."

My homily was as much a surprise to me as it was to Dean. Nobody spoke to him like this. In his own eyes and others, Dean was revered as a rainmaking star, corporate saint, feared dictator, politically connected aspiring aristocrat who dreams of one day being knighted by the Queen of England. Behold, Dean Hayes, barrister and solicitor, working exclusively for material gain thus building his own prison, never knowing the true meaning of wealth.

Dean stopped marching. Turning to face me, his face was on fire. Raging closer, lacerating me with his look, we stood toe to toe like two boxers hamming for a promotional photo op. We were so close that I could have puckered and kissed him. That's what I was thinking because the seriousness that he brought to the situation made it all the more comical. His upper lip was twitching as he opened his mouth to speak. Before saying a word, he reconsidered and left.

Returning to my task, I filled a bankers box with documents, knickknacks and Vivian's bra. It was 12:15 and I was on my way out. Vivian had her head buried in the computer monitor as I passed by the reception area.

"Vivian, I'm sorry for what happened."

"Is Mr. Hayes going to fire me?"

"Nah. Stay away from him for a few days. He'll cool down."

"Will I see you again, Mr. Shackleton?"

"I don't imagine I'll be returning to this office."

"Then where will I see you?"

Where will you see me? Why should she see me? What more is there to see? I didn't have to answer. I shouldn't have answered. I could have kept on walking. That's what I should have done. But I didn't. Her breasts were still on my mind and her bra in my box.

"Well, um, how about the Avenue Grill, say 5:30, we'll get a drink and a bite."

"That would be wonderful!" she beamed.

I joined a crowd of six Brooks Brothers look a likes impatiently waiting near the elevator doors. On hearing the bell of arrival, we quickly entered, arranging ourselves in an orderly manner. A light touch to the control panel ordered up our descent. Sightlines of fourteen eyeballs (maybe thirteen, a prematurely bald man may have had a glass eye) aligned straight ahead, as if wearing horse blinders. During the twenty-second drop to the ground floor, I re-considered why I suggested meeting up with Vivian. What could possibly come of it? Then again, how could I say no? How could I reject her youthful exuberance, her unblemished skin, her desire? But what about the bush? Oy, the bush!

Ding Ding. Exiting the elevator, holding my box in both arms, I passed the security guard sitting on a black swivel chair behind a square black aluminum desk leaning against a massive off white shaded wall seventy-five feet in length and thirty feet high. Plastered to the wall's expanse was a painting that could have been a Pollock or unschooled renderings of eighteen kindergarten children. Who could tell the difference?

Atop the guard's desk were eight computer monitors relaying real time visuals of the lobby, capturing pixeled images of every intruder to be used for future, as yet unknown, purposes. This man, the security guard, I passed by countless times during the years I called this building home.

"Do you mind if I leave this box here for ten minutes?" The box was getting heavy, I was hungry and there was a café in the building.

"I'm working, sir. I'm not your doorman. You can go ahead and leave it but I can't guarantee it'll be here when you get back. Your box is your responsibility, not mine."

"By the way, name's Sam. I've worked in this building for a long time. I see you every morning and I've never introduced myself."

The guard ignored my extended hand. "I'm busy, sir. May I help you with something other than your box?"

Picking up the box, I made my way to the revolving doors leading outside. Halfway through, my forehead smacked against the glass when the doors abruptly stopped. Glancing back, I saw

Vivian on the opposite side, frantic and in tears once again. I motioned for her to go the other way so we could both get out.

"Vivian, what's going on?"

Throwing her arms around me, she said nothing. The box nearly fell but I steadied myself. She planted salty lips on mine, swiftly wedging her tongue down my throat, the tip snaking its way down my trachea. Gagging, I promptly pushed her away but not before marveling at my cleanly swept mouth.

"Mr. Hayes fired me," Vivian said, nibbling her lower lip.

You share your genitals with someone and now you're their confidant?

"Dean wouldn't do that. The office would fall apart without you. You're a fixture at Hayes and Winter."

"A fixture? Is that what I am to you? A fixture!? Do you think I ask other men in the office to go for a spin on this fixture? For your information, I can count on one hand, with fingers to spare, the number of men I've slept with in my entire life and I've never, ever been with anyone from the office! You tell me how much you love me and now you say I'm a fixture, an inanimate object with no feelings?"

"Whoa! Back up. We rubbed, we tickled, you played with the pickle, but love, I'm sure, wasn't in the brine."

"Do you know that I haven't slept with a man for more than two years? Do you know why? Because I'm tired of being with one-inch deep men terrified of their own vulnerability. Men who don't understand that to be vulnerable is a sign of strength, not weakness. I thought you were different Mr. Shackleton. I truly believed you weren't like the other men who couldn't care less about the real me, who didn't know my favorite color or which song I sing when I'm sad or why I don't eat potatoes, who didn't even pretend to want to know who I am, who saw me only as a plaything to be mounted and ejaculated upon. That's not true with you is it, Mr. Shackleton? I mean more to you don't I?

"Do you know why I chose to work in a law office? Because I was hoping to meet a sweet, charming, intelligent man because that's the type of man I'm attracted to and I was sure that one day someone like you would come along. And you did and I was so excited but you didn't take much notice of me until today when I had my chance with you so I took that chance because if I don't take chances, nothing happens in life, and I thought that if this is my one and only chance then I better show you everything I have, everything that you could have, if you stay with me and maybe I'll even embarrass myself by having sex with you in your office, by exposing myself more than I should because I thought that's what you wanted and, in the scheme of things, what does it matter if we have sex now or later? And I thought what we shared was beautiful and that you are in love with me just like I'm in love with you so I did what you wanted because I believed you were a gentleman, a decent, considerate person who wants to care for me like I want to take care of you and you'll show your love for me by marrying me at sunrise, barefoot on the beach in Maui and we'll sip champagne and throw our empty glasses into the ocean and make love on the warm sand and never again will I work as a receptionist and, even better, never again have to scout for a man and I'd thank heaven above that you would be by my side.

"But like I've foolishly done in the past, it's clear to me now that I got ahead of myself and made a mistake in thinking that you're in love with me, that you wanted more than a wham bam thank you ma'am, that you wanted everything about me, but the fact is you don't, the fact is you only want a trollop and you don't give a hoot about me and I'm just another play thing for you and I'm so angry with you I want to hurt you but I know if I did that then I'd only be hurting myself and I'm even angrier at myself for letting this happen, for letting you do this to me, and for playing out this love story fantasy in my head and allowing my heart to be broken and having to spend the next year, or who knows how long, mending myself and I'm crestfallen because you don't care, because you never cared, and because I never learn that men are all the same, programmed to relentlessly wax their pole because they're so pathetically insecure about their masculinity and they think that demonstrating sexual prowess buttresses their sense of self and they believe it every time when you tell them they're huge because that's what they want to believe and they're so stupid and I swear this will never happen again and the next time I'll find someone who will take care of me, who understands what I want, who understands me, who gets me, and if I don't find anyone then I'll be fine being alone because I've had it with this merry-go-round and I can't do it anymore and I'd rather be a barren receptionist holding onto my dream that one day I'll find the right one because I can't let go, I won't let go, of my dream! I'm heartbroken! All these years you've been so nice to me. I could see it in your eyes, the way they sparkled when you spoke to me. Our feelings for each other grew stronger as the months and years went by. Then today, you told me that you left your wife and I wanted to kiss you so bad but there were other people around. That was your signal, I knew, that you were finally ready to consummate our love. And when you were making love to me today, I felt like we had known each other our whole lives. Mr. Shackleton, I've loved you since the day we met. Did our lovemaking mean nothing to you? Do I mean nothing? Nothing at all? Why did you make love to me if you don't love me! How could you? I don't understand!"

Out of my depth, possibly on the wrong planet, I played it safe, played the straight man. "Vivian, it was a misunderstanding, okay? It's best that I leave."

Raising her voice, she cried, "You're leaving?!"

This is the price I pay for not being able to resist her tits. But before I could run like the wind, Vivian, the brewing tempest, suddenly transformed.

"I'll see you later this afternoon, Mr. Shackleton. 5:30. Don't be late," Vivian smiled as she took leave, as if the words she just spoke carried no weight, as if all was forgiven and we were best friends and lovers, as if she were perfectly deranged.

What a mistake. Big, BIG mistake. But what could I do? How was I to know about her fantasy life, her distorted inner world? By invitation only do we become privy to others' musings. Unfortunately, I opened the envelope. I had to. I have no control over this. Oh, sure, 1 Thessalonians 5:6-8 babbles on about putting on faith and love as a breastplate. But that was Paul babbling! Babblings aren't genuine. No way was Paul so naïve as to believe the human male could control his drive for sexual gratification. And triumph over it to boot? Not a chance! Puberty hits and BOOM, we scheme to get laid every day of our life.

Somber historians (there are no other kind) write that this Paul character was on to something, that he recognized inherent limits etched into our psychological make-up, limits preventing males from transcending procreative forces. Because we are bound by these forces, for society to function peacefully, males need help defending against nature's call. And this help was delivered in the form of SINS; prohibitive exhortations, restrictive covenants and penal offences furnished to serve as ungodly restrictions on horny man.

But Paul was no dupe. He knew full well that nature doesn't heel to man made demotion. Still, as long as the masses could be swayed by published restraints, small numbers of miscreants slipping through the net could be tolerated. The broader purpose, you see, was to draw a black line, spelling out consequences for those who crossed into thoust sweaty dalliance, thereby inhibiting the herd by means of communal morals.

Detractors claim that Paul's rantings had no such higher purpose and were merely those of a cynical fear mongerer interested only in usurping leadership from James the Just and advancing up the canonical pole. In Paul's defense, can you blame him? I mean, anyone tying The Just to the back end of their name is asking to be taken down a notch; there is no blessed humility in self-promotion.

Passing by Jack's worksite again, I saw the same old man standing in the same spot, his head plastered through the same hole.

"Mr. Shackleton!"

Oh no! I thought she left; why is she back?

"I'm so glad I found you! You were right about Mr. Hayes; he didn't fire me even when I told him about us. In fact, he said he would give me a month end bonus if I told you the good news as soon as I could. Can you believe it?! He's paying me for taking the time to tell you I love you! Underneath that gruff exterior, Mr. Hayes is a romantic, don't you think? I know he's upset that you're not working at the office any longer but really he's a kind man. The two of you are kind of alike. I mean, you were cold and indifferent to me today but I know that you care. I know you want me as much as I want you. I have to go back up to the office now but I'll see you later. I love you!"

Never saw it coming. *Touché*, Dean.

The old man had turned his attention to Vivian. When she finished, he glanced over at me then back at Vivian, inspecting her top to bottom. Resting his gaze on her braless chest, he spoke to her nipples as if they were magnetic microphones.

"Creation. One bolt, one screw, one nail, one plank, one brick, one steel beam, one girder and another and another and slowly, steadily, the building grows. See the man wearing the blue hat; he's the foreman. The man with the red hat is the engineer. Once a week, they walk the site together and review progress. If there's a mistake, and mistakes do happen, they figure out plans to rectify the problem. Then construction continues until all pieces fall into place as intended. What's your name dear?"

"Vivian."

"Vivian, it's not likely that pieces of your life will go where you want them to go. Nope. From the moment you're born to the time of departure, life marches toward death and we struggle and suffer and try to muddle our way through."

Jumping toward her and pressing his brittle body against hers, the nimble old man surprised Vivian, forcibly pushing his cracked lips upon hers. Vivian screamed. The old man fell back, covering his ears.

"Nice to feel a woman. Haven't felt a woman in the longest time. Been married forever but it's been almost as long since I felt my wife."

Vivian stood by my side, arms crossed, pale.

"You're alive, aren't you Viv? You got spirit; you got fight. I like that. But are you, beyond doubt, alive? Have you been shown the passageway? Do you step in line behind admonishing words of men who lived before you? Do you sheepishly follow literal translations, rotely mumble ancient teachings telling us to rail against evils of modernity and cling to the ways of our father? Or are you one of those who reject dogma and fasten your lifeline to the table of hard science and cold facts? Black hats, red hats, non-believers, all laying claim to opposite ends of the same spectrum, fanatical beliefs, blocking all hints of grey, repelling any creep of compromise. To veer off course, to question, is unthinkable, would shake the core of existence to its bare bones, leaving you wholly exposed to elements of unsacred diffidence, adrift from the knowers and no one except a lunatic wears nothing but bare bones. Few dare to be apart, to sport the hat of absurdity. Instead, we prefer multiple means of disassociation, lifelines in and of themself, adaptive disorders reinforcing comfortable delusions making tolerable ticks and tocks between birth and death. Who's right? Who's wrong? What I ask myself is why? Why did God make life so difficult? And why did he make me incompatible with HIM?"

The old man returned to his peephole. Vivian stood by my side waiting for direction. Concerned that, along with opening her box I had opened Pandora's too, I head faked a sense of urgency while pointing behind us toward nothing specific. She turned her head and off I darted.

Chapter 11
Bird's Eye View

*One who is of sound mind keeps
the inner madman under lock and key*
— Paul Valery

Gobs of writhing seed sputter into compliant fallopian tube prompting mechanical release of enzymes bent on busting through the lonesome egg's fetching jelly like membrane.

Traveling at the speed of sperm, one triumphant lottery winner jingles molecular chimes, activating energetic depolarization and subsequent dumping of cortical granules into vast gelatinous sea turned graveyard for swarms of unsuccessful suitors.

Fertilization launched, zany spirits enter on cue, colliding, colluding, conspiratorially hashing out the developing zygotes unearthly configuration. It is here, in utero, under shelter of a one hundred and twenty year universal patent, where human programs are written and irrevocably published, where benedictions are mumbled, and where elemental material fuses, to be awakened or not, some time post vaginal exit.

Swaddled in psychological bondage by those who have come before, self-knowledge is stymied, assuring one of nothing more than fleeting fulfillment and lasting frustration should the taboo against knowing who you are not be broken.

'You and your nattering about a soul mate; this was the starting point of your bondage, thinking you arrive in this world incomplete, remaining so unless and until sacrosanct vows are pledged, roles delegated and bed sides chosen, setting in motion fostering of union, one that predictably transforms into states of dysfunction engendering not winged hearts but bound feet. Too green to appreciate your wholeness never mind the terrific cost of buying into the moronic notion of til' death do us part, THIS was what you sought, THIS was what you wanted, to celebrate a golden anniversary, a life sentence bereft of easily accessible escape clauses. LOVE cannot be controlled, orchestrated according to your wishes. It doesn't work that way. No. Smart money wagers on the rose wilting, the journey ending before you turn to ash for love is forever subject to permutations, transformations, incarnations, snafus, bobbles, flubs and FINALES. Hear me? Finales! Sure, go ahead and pledge but know there's an end point, that forever doesn't translate into a lifetime. Who said it did? And why do you listen?

'God Willing (isn't that the trite phrase?), may your coalition flourish, may you coast through life with the top down, wind in your hair, sun at your back; may you dodge a bitter end, your union enduring until one of you goes gentle into the good night, for if premature rupture splatters the guts of your putrefied relations like a guck filled cyst, if you become weak, difficult, selfish, feeble, a quitter, a commitment phobe, an adulterer, a transsexual, bisexual, homosexual or asexual, then certainly you shall be a FAILURE. Isn't that the story line you were fed? Well, it sure is the script you swallowed and puked up. And, being a RESPONSIBLE person, you didn't want to fail, did you? You wanted to learn your lines and act them out. You wanted to be a success. A fucking, rousing success on the trivial stage of life. You wanted to pass, as if life is measured in terms of pass or fail. Who says? Who's doing the marking? Who's been feeding you this crap and why are you gulping it down? Ah, but gulp you did. And the thought of not living up to this task, obligation, responsibility, call it what you will, terrified you! So what did you do? You forged ahead the only way you knew how; you adopted the taboo against knowing who you are, you hid your self from your self, seeking refuge in illusory displays of masculine preening to the roar of approval from fellow animal kingdom fans.

'You fell in line, suppressing individuation (Schopenhauer would have kicked your ass!) in favor of belonging. Oh, shit. Belonging. Yes, yes, we need to belong don't we? We need to identify with a people, a race, a lineage, a gender to know we're not floundering in isolation. This drive to fit in, to be like others, powerful isn't it? Go it alone? Unthinkable! Goodness, man, to be alone, to live your life ALONE, everyone knows, is an ailment, a social disease, a disorder of the highest magnitude. And you didn't want to be sick. But it wasn't only illness you ran from. Despite inclusion in this or that sanctioned membership, you were still lonely, craving another's company. Uncomfortable being by your self, unsatisfied with who you were, ungrateful for what you had, you sought a socially approved mating coalition, you got married! THAT is what happened to you.

'And in this sad state of affairs, you joined forces, giving yourself to a woman who washed your clothes, cooked your meals, cleaned your house and darned your socks. In exchange, she found peace, order and general acceptance in companionship if not love. Grown up (meaning what? legally sanctioned to court conventionally civilized discontentment in the form of marriage, office job and sexual repression), you read the signs

(DO AS YOUR FATHER DID AND HIS FATHER AND HIS FATHER …) and volunteered for the draft. Other men you knew were putting their left foot in and shaking it all about so why shouldn't you? But you were a strong man and strong men don't volunteer, they do it on their terms, they *take* a wife. At least that's what they tell themselves. For you, what kind of wife was suitable? Subconsciously, you sought vulnerable women who marveled at the comparative size of your sex organ, who used two delicate hands, with room to spare for a third, when jerking you off. Thick enough to be snared by a woman who eagerly stroked your vanity, who was the real jerk off? Sure, she may have got lost in the woods of lofty conversation, but she knew that the only fluid *tête-à-tête* that mattered came spurting out your little head. Your big, pointy head never could penetrate feminine guile.

'*What are you thinking*!? Dismayed friends cried out. And for good reason. The woman who chose you (don't for a minute think you chose her) was driven by survival instinct, a vulture's appetite. Sure, she tolerated you, enjoyed your presence at times, indulged your eccentricities, but all that was dependent on you feathering a secure nest, which you did, and then some. You remember what she said, don't you? Partnership. Such a lovely word; conjuring connotations of fairness and cooperation, a relationship between equals, fulfilling and substantive. Yes, yours was a partnership. Ahh, isn't that sweet! A good old-fashioned *quid pro quo*. I do for you; you do for me. That's what she told you. And that's when the eight ball fell into the corner pocket. Game over. She slides on that dazzling ring and, WHAM, possession and eminent domain transfer. From here on in, she was the ticket master; no more banging her caboose on the kitchen table dressed up in corset and lace unless you paid full fare. Now, she fucks on her schedule. This was the bargain you struck, this was the train you were riding and there were no scheduled stops along the way.

'Surprise, surprise. The bargain turned sour, didn't it? Shocking? No, man, not shocking in the least. There you were, prancing around in that cape of yours, protecting your real identity, until the superhero savior gig got grounded and you drifted into a spiritual death spiral. But don't blame her. *Au contraire, mon ami*, I'd say congratulations are in order. A hearty *mazel tov* if you will. Unlike you, she at least didn't subscribe to the taboo against knowing this part of her, the part that thirsted for a protector to walk by her side. Claiming membership in a gender known for its' keen third eye, she knew full well the need to guide protective parts into place sooner rather than later for fear the bloom wilt from her flower ahead of suitor's call. After all, once the corner is rounded past a certain age, once young and beautiful are no more, unhitched women have their mug shot plastered on UNWANTED posters. Publicity was out of the question for this humble gal! Indeed, the shame would be intolerable. Going at it unaccompanied, this matter of life, was not an option. No, once she positioned herself atop the social mantle, once betrothed to an outwardly respectable man, sporting proof thereof on her annular finger, she refused to let go, refused to put her very survival at stake. For without you, who knew what lay in store for her? And what about you? What has become of you?'

One's heart and head care but a hoot about positioning of the feet. Follow the heart, the head remains upright and the feet untangled.

'Round, round we go. Religions depart. Temples vacate. The world cracks. But wait. All is not lost. Into the vacuum rush swamis, shamans and soothsayers hawking paperbacks, pitching e-books, clashing over methods of delivery yet united in dangling the same goal: regurgitating the same mumbo jumbo written way back when.

'In seminars, workshops and celebrity led retreats, rattlesnake swill sends lost tribes and forgone flocks on inspirational benders, infusing followers with ether of a kind hooked up to astral channels floating beyond this planet's four corners, and leading to a special kind of madness. And what's wrong with that? Questions multiply, answers are murky at best, so why not take a pass on tried and untrue religious heavyweights and give the transcendent brown kid on the block a shot at the title? Maybe the kid will teach us how to lead with the heart, block psyche's ill-conceived feints and jabs, reveal the wisdom of being and the folly of seeking and becoming. Give as much energy to contemplation as to action, the kid says, maybe then you will learn to lead an authentic life, be who you are, love who you are and realize that, on your own, you always have been and will be whole.

'But you're still figuring that one out aren't you? That life is wasted unless you live your honorable truth until the day you die. And on that day of departure, your MAKER will ask:

WHY WERE YOU NOT SAM?

You will answer, *BECAUSE I THOUGHT YOU WANTED ME TO BE LIKE YOU.*

And your MAKER will reply, *NO. I WANTED YOU TO BE LIKE SAM, NOBODY ELSE BUT YOU COULD BE SAM.'*

'Intuitively, children understand. Unburdened by learned constructs, reason, logic and stilted education preparing them for THE FUTURE while negating the importance of living today, a child's soul flourishes, miraculously unsullied by one and the next cacophony of distractions scattered in their midst, calling out to BECOME smart, popular, respectable, rich. Until, that is, the temptress of bright lights, big cities and little men deceive youth, steal innocence, shutter purity, and direct their attention to the

MEAT OF THE MATTER. How can you have your pudding if you don't you eat your meat!? Time is meat, time is money, time is to be used, not wasted, not killed; get on with your life, young man! (This is what we do isn't it? Get on with life. As if there is somewhere to go, a place superior to where we are, when the only place we'll ever be is here). Strive, strive, strive! Postscript your name with letters from worthy institutions, append ever larger digits to your asset balance, secure an upright zip code, proudly announce rising status and contribute ten per cent of your salary toward fabricating division by usual means of wallet, race, religion, class and occupation. Persevere and while you're at it, don't forget to raise the drawbridge and batten down the hatches. You know, keep the riff raff out. Let those weak kneed liberals buy the world a coke. You're not sharing what's rightfully yours, the pudding you've worked so hard for. Besides, what with time flying, isn't the job of taking care of yourself difficult enough? If you're to achieve real important things, stick to your agenda, focus on who and what matters, focus on you. Why? Because you're an adult and that's what adults do, it's what we learn to do, it's what we're conditioned to do: accept suppression of autonomy and squashing of free will via guerilla marketing tactics and coercive moralizing meticulously designed by Campbell's soup cream of the crop neuroscientists and copycatted by so-called benevolent democratic ruling governments, block-headed dictatorships and fixed on domination industry lords each functioning to instill impotence of individual expression and thereby reinforcing adherence to custom the byproduct of which is mass cowardice and continuation of a status quo perpetuating delusions of stability and frowning upon change all so artificially anointed crowns do not fall and smash to bits.

'Rebuffing, hairy knuckled hands, the spirited child playfully mocks, 'You should, you should not, you must, you must not. Is this what you're telling me? I say, stick it in your ear!' Alive and kicking, the child stands his ground, fire in his eyes, curiosity and wonder by his side.'

Ω

Imagination interruptus when a Hermes paper bag toting woman hiding behind oversized black and gold Chanel sunglasses screeched, "Excuse me. EXCUSE ME!"

Maybe she was an actress, maybe a princess, maybe born in a leafy enclave where sense of entitlement is commonly propagated. Regardless, her manner, her dress, her dragon breathing aura all supported a bald insistence to be thought of as an important person. Impatiently, she barged past, slithering between me and the front door to the Bank of Montreal building, pushing her way inside with arms so thin my thumb and forefinger could have encircled her bicep, possibly her thigh, though I didn't try.

Wedging a foot in before the door swung shut, I held it in place until the rest of my body followed through. There, on the ground floor, I was met by a fragrant resin of burning frankincense. I looked up to the second floor to discover the source; a shoeless, mustachioed man preaching to passersby near the escalator landing. His pulpit was a makeshift cardboard throne on which illegible handwriting messily summarized immanent evils.

"*ZEITGEIST!* Say it. Say it! This word containing hard consonants, a definitive ending, no ambiguity. This concept ushered in by the Romanticists for use by all. The spirit of the time, yes? And what is the spirit of our time?"

This was good. Harmless entertainment. After the fiasco with Vivian I could use a break. I placed my box on the floor, sat on top, and set up as the sole attentive audience member.

"Ideas! Who among the brethren has an original idea, a thought that hasn't been thought, a whim not stolen, copied, imitated or recycled? Robert Zimmerman. That's who. As the poet foretold, change did come, as it is wont to do, but not the change he imagined. Tides, too strong for one man to hold back, snared all in its wake, the revolution fizzled, Jesus Christ Superstar drowned and the beat generation switched allegiance taking up worship at the altar of green.

"Ladies and Gentlemen, I beseech you! Sift through your thoughts, search your soul, ask yourself, why have you not adopted gratitude as your attitude? Yes you, old man sitting on box, what sayeth YOU? Speak! You who chases money, this is your life, this is your pitiless existence, wanting more, getting more of THINGS THAT DON'T MATTER, digging your soul deeper into poverty, expanding emptiness, unplugging from friends, from sustenance, and all the while doggedly making love to your bulging balance sheet.

"You despicable shit. You and your contemporaries, spineless twits, know nothing cowards daring not to contemplate problems of your *Weltanschauung*. Then again, why would you? Reflecting on the welfare of others only cuts short self-focus, on empire building. You know the word, don't you? 'Others'? It refers to someone who is not you. But what do you care? You're in it for yourself. There is no larger cause. Society exists outside your borders. Only your roof matters, only your dinner table, your opportunities, isn't that right? Fuck the rest of us! But don't think for a gentrified Manhattan minute that you're not paying a price higher than Tribeca real estate for your damned insularity! You know what that price is? Huh, do you? Stagnation. Look at you, rotting, falling further into despair, lingering among misplaced notions of purpose, if you have any at all. Why? Because you're addicted to the running wheel; because you scoff at the rainbow bridge."

The preacher mounted a unicycle, riding it down the escalator to the ground floor, pointing his long, bony fingers at me. Apparently, I had been recruited for the show. Balancing himself directly in front of me, I saw ribs jutting out from underneath a torn flimsy shirt, skinny legs lodged in threadbare harem pants, fungal infected yellowish toenails calling out from dirty bare feet, and poppyseeds stuck between his two front teeth.

"Righteous people form our world's foundation. We, the righteous, prop up pillars extending from sea to sky and heaven to earth. Humanity needs these pillars. Never will there be too many. And for every newly minted righteous person, one more pillar is created, all others strengthened. But for every heathen like you, pillars crumble causing all to suffer. Is this what you want, to be the cause of suffering? I've been watching you for a long time, boxman. Longer than you know. And I know you want to join forces, don't you? You do want to cleanse yourself, begin anew, reinforce the pillars, don't you? How do you get to where you need to go? I will show you. But first I must look into your eyes, to confirm you as a just and worthy candidate."

"Only if I can look into yours. Fair is fair."

Pulling out a pen flashlight, the preacher aimed a dim beam toward my eyes.

"Like too many others, you're blind! Blind to HIM, to HIS sublime nature, his LOVE. But do not be worried. I am HIS messenger. I am your savior. I will cure you. I will show you that you are nothing less than divinity in disguise. I will open you, teach you the true meaning of love. And you will then learn to let humanity flow into your heart, to show compassion, to pray, even for the wicked, depraved and fiendish, that they too may one day wake to the righteous path and shine bright the light of understanding. You will do with others just as I am now doing with you, teach others to connect with the SOURCE of all that is thereby allowing humility to take hold, sweetening judgment's bitterness."

"All that from a mini flashlight? I'm impressed."

"Every body part is represented by a corresponding part of the iris. Detailed examination of location and texture of iris pigment flecks reveals your roadmap. You have honored me in revealing yourself."

"While you're at it, do you mind checking for signs of stones? The kidneys have been acting up. I'm thinking it might have something to do with a recent shawarma feast but it's best to check these things out, be on the safe side if you know what I mean."

"Go ahead, make fun, you with your infantile humor. I know your ignorance. I know you know nothing of the genius of iridology. We owe it all to Ignatz von Peczely, our Father. Bloody genius I say! When he accidentally broke an owl's leg, von Peczely serendipitously discovered a black stripe appearing in the lower part of the owl's eye. He then theorized the eye marking to be directly correlated to, and caused by, the broken leg. To be sure, he broke the owl's other leg. *Voila*! A second horizontal stripe instantly appeared on the owl's iris. The genius had proved himself correct!"

"Good for you; hitching your wagon to a bird mutilator."

"What, you believe the profession has come into disrepute? What have you heard? WHAT? It is lies, all lies! The medical experts are running scared, that's what it is. They're jealous, protecting their domain, keeping out the competition to ensure patients remain in the dark. The smear campaign started with fake data written by American assholes who bribed so-called respectable journals to disseminate bastardized stories concluding that iridology is a hoax. A hoax! I'll tell you what's a hoax. Those stethoscope waving egomaniacs are a hoax! Oh, but we'll show them! They want the glory, jewels and fame all to themselves but they won't get away with it if I have anything to say!"

"Glory and fame are givens but jewels? What's this about jewels?"

"They attack our legitimacy, demonize us, try to destroy us. Why? Because they fear we will spread the truth and then they will be out of business! That's what life is about for those kind, business!"

"Your philosophy is based on breaking bird legs. I'm guessing Mr. Pez didn't endear himself to either rationalists or empiricists."

"Oh boxman, you are so naïve. Or do you stupidly bear the mule's burden of rationality, dismissing all that doesn't measure up to your arbitrary standards of evidence, proof, validity, substantiation, verification, corroboration, authentication and certification? Does your cynical, closed mind question von Peczely's methods? Is that it? Is it better to hold prisoner millions of cats and monkeys in sterile, non-descript warehouses injecting them with chemical carcinogens, dutifully noting varieties of cancer metastasizing throughout the body, blithely recording all manner of torture and standing by as helpless beings die an excruciating death? This is humane? This is the practice of medicine? Respect for God's creations? You people pledging allegiance to the Hippocratic Oath reek of a hypocrisy all too common in the self-proclaimed virtuous. And his name is not Pez! Stop calling him that! Ignatz von Peczely was a humanist! The owl's legs were broken, then its neck. It died a swift and praiseworthy death in service to all nature. So there."

"Hippocrates went the way of the dodo. It's a free for all today. The only rite of passage for medical-folks-to-be involves indenture to a financial institution of their choosing. Collateral's the name of the game now, not unsecured words."

"What do I care about your rites! I am telling you the truth about iridology! Do you wish to know why?"

"Nine sessions of electric shock therapy and your tenth one free?"

"Goad me all you want, boxman. I know you are not well. In your eyes, the windows to your liver and pancreas, I see a storehouse of pain."

"What happened to the soul? I would have bet my last *zloty* the eyes are windows to the soul. Even if the poets ignored facts, it sounds so much prettier than pancreas."

"What are you afraid of? Is it humor that safeguards your shaky belief system?"

"Want one? Goji berry covered in dark chocolate. Otherwise known as a wisdom boosting superfood endowing all who consume it with sprightly brains. Downside is it causes scrotal hair to fall out and engenders frenzied passion for smearing avocado and salt on women's knees."

"Is life one big joke to you? Is it all meant to be laughs?"

"Even if you're not into the avocado and salt thing, you've got to try these gojis."

"Don't treat me like a clown, boxman!"

"But I love clowns!"

To bolster the import of his message, the preacher tried, but failed, to expand his sunken chest before speaking.

"Our meeting here today is no mistake. Oh no, I chose YOU because you need me. Think about it. Did you choose to meet me? In a city of more than five million people, what are the odds that you and I would be having this conversation? There are no coincidences. There is reason for everything and even if we do not know what that reason is, we must nevertheless believe the circumstances of our lives are preordained, we must make that bet because there is everything to gain and nothing to lose when we go on faith. So join me, my friend, a big shift awaits you."

"I feel a shift coming alright. My cheeks are numb; time for me to stand."

"Imbecile!" the preacher cursed. "What's inside the box? No, do not speak! Tell me, is the box getting heavy?"

"You ever read those little strips of paper crinkled inside fortune cookies? I had a few the other day. The first one said that confusion is the beginning of knowledge. Of course, I couldn't resist a second cookie that, I soon learned, was for adults only. It told me I would meet Jenny, a bubbly, Korean woman with a bouffant hairdo who would grant me three wishes one of which would be to trace the outlines of her unusually petite areolas until her nipples stiffened. Naturally, though the written words excited me, I was experienced enough to know better. I guess you could say I didn't believe the message. Lo and behold, when I paid the check and got up to leave the restaurant, a wisp of a woman dressed in a see through top approached me and introduced herself as, you guessed it, Jenny."

Rising up, the preacher dusted his hands three times.

"I have led you to the threshold of your mind according to its dimensions and needs. It is not within me to force you to drink kool aid. If you do, however, mishaps will be few. If you do not, suffering will persist. Goodbye boxman. You are on your own."

I slipped a five-dollar bill to the preacher. He took it straight away then wheeled back to the escalator, elevated to his throne and resumed lecturing.

Ω

The down escalator led to an underground tunnel where posted signs directed me to the North and South subway trains. I carried the box. In it were possessions that didn't matter to me. I could throw it away, maybe toss it on the tracks, let it be ripped apart under the next train. But I didn't want to let go. What would happen if I did? I wasn't sure. Should I try? Maybe I should. Shouldn't I? Maybe the box symbolizes my imagined burdens? If I leave the box behind, my burdens may lessen, even vanish. And unburdened, maybe happiness would return. Happiness. Have I ever known happiness? Would I recognize it? Maybe it has passed; I've had my fill and now it's a fading memory out of reach. Must it be this way? Do I not have any say from here on in? Charles Schulz, speaking in bubbles through an acerbic beagle, said that happiness is a warm puppy. Is it that simple? And what about Henry Miller: no money, no resources, no future, no past, no hope, Miller was the happiest man alive.

'Hope. It's a drug holding top spot on the worst offender's list, prolonging misery and steering you toward death. Give up hope. Instead, become hopeless, see meaninglessness everywhere because it is true that life has no meaning. Yes, absolutely true. And whatever you are doing, whatever you are trying to accomplish or whatever you do accomplish, is entirely useless in the grand scheme. Fact is, you're born, you die. In between, you seek refuge for your suffering. That's what life is, suffering. But it doesn't matter. You don't matter. Because you're going nowhere, wherever you're going. So you see, there is nothing to hope for. Stay away from hope. It is a mask covering reality. Or, is that what you want? Camouflage? Do you prefer delusion over seeing life for what it is? I think this is it. For if you were to look, I mean really LOOK, at this idea of life's meaning, if you did this, then you might stop moving and if you're still in the moment, then you may begin to rediscover and reconnect with your self. Maybe you would even put down your box and find substantive reasons for being. But who am I kidding. That is not for you. Not yet anyway. Motion is what you crave, it's what you must have, to stay in motion. Right? When you're warm, open a window. Cold? Put on a sweater. Turn away from pain, stay comfortable. Isn't that what it's all about, pleasure? And when pleasure dissolves, move forward, find something new, something that displaces discomfort, be it a warm body, a new philosophy or ancient religion; don't bother with this stale notion of faith in your self, that what you're experiencing you're MEANT to experience and LEARN from.'

Fine. I get it. You're saying Miller's right? Toss aside fantasies of how life should be, experience life raw, the good, the bad and the ugly, forego built-in escape routes and big leaved magnolias bloom forever more?

'Miller wasn't happy! We don't know who or what Miller was. Only he knew. The persona you're talking about was myth assembled through stolen literary license issued by and to himself. He didn't live what he wrote never mind believe it. His writing was swashbuckling horseshit. He was a depraved misogynist who dined on other's desperation. Regardless, you're not Miller and you're definitely not built to scope the Provence countryside in search of pliable mother-daughter teams amenable to ingesting warm bottles of Beaujolais before submitting to diddling.'

But you just said … I mean … didn't Miller know … Anais, help me?

'Henri, *oui, oui,* he was terrible! But in a good way, yes? Maybe his head was loose, not screwed on tight as you say. But the ladies, they liked him very much so he indulged his passions. Why not?! Why should he hold back? Henri did not restrict himself with other's morality, he was not controlled from the grave by others who came before. No, Henri lived life according to his own rule-book, according to no rules at all, and in this way, he was free, so free that he ceased to speak of freedom as a goal. And ladies, they are very much attracted to a free man; he is like a wild animal, out of control, very exciting! I loved Henri. I saw Henri as he was, not as I am, not who I wanted him to be. And because I loved him so, I did not judge him. No, judging is a pastime better left to those spilling bitterness from their heart. Me, I am not bitter. No, I am like Henri; a gleeful child for whom every day lasts forever and not long enough.'

Chapter 12
Wide Beam

Better bread with water
than cake with trouble
— Old Russian Proverb

Hello again, Doctor. That's right, another dream. Lie down? No, I prefer to sit. May I proceed? My grandmother, Hannah, I saw her. Is she alive? No, died twenty-five years ago. How old was I when she died? Fourteen. Was I close with her? I don't know, what's close? My mother's mother, she fed me pea soup, corned beef sandwiches, chopped liver on saltine crackers, and brought me trinkets from her annual winter trek to Mexico. Does that make for close? May I continue? Okay, so there I am, in my childhood home. The house is empty. No furniture, no pictures hanging on the wall, no refrigerator humming, nothing, or so I thought until I heard a voice calling to me, calling my name. Whose voice? Hannah. Who's Hannah? What do you mean who's Hannah? Hannah is my grandmother! So this voice is calling out and I'm anxious and excited thinking I'll get to see Nana again, and the voice is getting louder and I'm trying to pinpoint where it's coming from and I'm searching through the house and I know

I'm getting closer and then I come to the laundry room and I see her, at least I think it's her.

Sitting on her haunches, she's decked out in full metal body armor from head to toe strapped in place by steel chains and locked up in an oversized dog kennel big enough to house a St. Bernard. Why is she a St. Bernard? Who said she was a St. Bernard? I didn't say she was a St. Bernard. Still, your question isn't too far off because her head, as I remember it, was intact though it sat on top of the body of a Border Collie. What's with the nodding? I'm nodding, Samuel, because this is good; Hannah would have been cramped in the kennel if she were a St. Bernard. Tell me what happened next. What happened next was she spoke to me. She could speak? Oh, she could talk alright. Once she sees me, she stops calling my name, gets this happy look on her mug and starts lacing into me as if we saw each other only yesterday.

'Didn't I tell you to find yourself a nice girl, a Jewish girl, who will take care of you like I took care of your Zaidy? And you, Mr. Bigshot with the fancy university degrees, what do you do? You waste your life running after dead ends!'

I say to her, Nana, after twenty-five years, this is how you greet me? But she had no interest in carrying on so that was the end of our conversation. Next thing I know she's standing up in the kennel, trying to push her nose through the cage, and it seems to me she wants out so I release the latch, reach inside, untangle the armor and chains and set her free. Gingerly, she lifts her four legs as if to make sure each of them works, shakes her body like a wet dog drying off after a long swim, darts out of the room and bounds out the nearest open window. She's too fast for me but I run out of the house anyway and watch her sprint down the middle of the road chasing after a slow moving convertible. Once close enough, she jumps into the car's back seat where she instantly transmogrifies to full human form and, grinning from ear to ear, basks in the wind caressing her hair. That was the last I saw of her.

'That's it?'

The end.

'It's a short dream.'

Short, long. What does it matter?

'What do you think it means?'

Do we have to play this game? You're the analyst. Analyze.

'Hmm. First off, you did not see Hannah in the kennel nor did you see a St. Bernard.'

A Collie. It was a Border Collie, not a St. Bernard.

'Nevertheless, these apparitions are instructive. They represent a part of you that has been locked up for quite some time, likely ever since your grandmother passed on. Should I repeat what you said about Hannah? You talked of food. Your primary memories are of being fed. Do you understand? Hannah symbolized maternal comfort, a source of nurturing. And when she left this world, you felt exposed and unprotected. How did you respond? Like a child.'

Excuse me. I was a child.

'Nevertheless. You did not know that love nourishes growth but also prunes; that it knows peace, pleasure AND broken dreams, pain. This lack of comprehension led to shutting down your heart, hiding it. Where was your heart hidden? Chained up in a kennel, an enclosure speaking to your illusory sanctuary. Sure, the Keep Out sign may have saved you from emotional harm being done unto you, but what else was barred entry? Love. You deprived yourself of giving and receiving love. An unsustainable state of being if ever there was one. So your subconscious rebels, pressing you to release yourself, to bring forth illumination, to welcome warm breezes brushing against your skin.'

But that's my subconscious talking. How do I break free when I'm awake?

'You asked that I analyze. I analyzed. Now you're asking me for solutions too?'

Ω

It was one of those daydreams that I could direct; move in any direction. And I wanted it to go on but it ended when my attention turned to an overhead New York Times Square size billboard that followed me like Mona Lisa's gaze. Shilling for a home improvement store was an intense looking man on the other side of middle age dressed in forest green overalls splattered with multi-colored paint drops. He was arranged against a white background, holding a broad paintbrush in front of a spotless easel. Behind him were eleven open paint cans, all different colors. The caption underneath read, *I've got to paint.* Manly in a gentrified backcountry Lee jeans Chevy truck kind of way, the pitchman projected a smooth, but not oily, manner. Baring synthetic white teeth and buckets of manufactured confidence, he was there to persuade the impulsive, fickle and unsure. Be like me, he beckoned, pursue purpose free from tangible reward or recognition, and contentment will be yours.

Be like me? This is what's happening, isn't it? Our proliferating global village championing homogeneity, wrestling individuality to the ground, standardizing not only the external world but our individual wishes too. May we not find our self without others telling us what to dream? And what happens to those pursuing dreams lolling on the fringe? PENALTY in the form of DISAPPROVAL, dished out by normal people like the professor who struck up conversation with me at a dinner party I attended a few months back.

'Nice to meet you, Sam. What do you do?' he asked. Extending his hand in greeting, I shook it as forcefully as I could causing him to wince. Bored by excessive niceness among acquaintances, I wanted to play with a new persona.

"I bench press twice my weight, run in melting snow through fields of wild crocuses in the Bernese Alps foothills, am a card carrying member of the Toy Train Collectors Association, play lead triangle for the New York Philharmonic and skip to my lou."

"I meant what do you do for a living?"

"Out with it, man! You're chomping at the bit to know how I fill my pockets, to pigeon hole me by occupation!"

"I was merely asking you …"

"Gigolo."

"Gigolo?"

"Echo?"

"Come on, Sam. You're pulling my leg, right?"

"If you pay for it, I'll pull legs and most any other body part."

"You're not joking?! Have you no self-respect?"

"Kind sir, I respect no one more than myself. For I am what is known in the trade as a compassionate companion, one who puts others needs ahead of his own. Hey, I like that, it would make a good tagline. Think I'll put it on my business card. Would that be proof enough for you? Business cards don't lie."

You call this an act of compassion? You're taking advantage of people's loneliness. This leaves you with a clear conscience?"

"You asked of me what it is I do. This is what I do; it is not who I am. As for my patrons, it is not I but they who hold the advantage. Given my lengthy resume and inspired imagination, I'm the best bargain in town. And as far as a clear conscience goes, ha ha, to that inquiry rest assured I sleep well, very well! What man doesn't after satisfactory ejaculation?"

"You disgust me."

"Good for you, professor; spinning voluntary social pleasantries into a morality play. Tsk tsk. Must say I am surprised, coming from a learned man like yourself. But what do you say we cut the bullshit and I'll tell you what it's all about. I'm a seller. My patrons are buyers. Seller and buyer, private individuals, free of coercion, consensually execute commercial transaction. Temple and government are sidelined though they have been known to spy and surreptitiously participate when lights are low. Buyer derives fleeting sexual/psychological satisfaction. In exchange, seller acquires money. Buyer and seller both get what they want. Everybody's happy. Even Conservatives and Libertarians, esteemed guardians of free market enterprise when it suits their purpose. There you have it. Happiness is my game. What's your annual take? Eighty? One hundred thousand? Working what, ten or twelve hour days, six, seven days a week, lecturing, researching, writing, battling bureaucratic and administrative dweebs protecting their fiefdoms and you struggling to shield yours? I run my own show, work my own hours, and fill my pockets with a quarter million a year, cash. I'm not fleecing anyone, professor. I'm filling a need in the marketplace of human behavior. Isn't that the beauty of our system; whatever need arises, someone is there to plug the hole? And for my troubles, I rest like a pampered infant, stretched out in a custom made seven-foot long redwood crib in my multi-million dollar Yorkville condo. And I always have a fucking partner. As in, a partner I can fuck. How often do you fuck?"

"That's none of your concern."

"From what I gather, I'm guessing once a month, if that. Gaunt, sallow skin, unsightly paunch resting on those stilts for legs. Professor, the bees don't come a buzzing to bitter pollen. But hey, don't get me wrong; I'm not critiquing, only calling it like I see it and I see a guy who toes the line to other's expectations, who cultivates ulcers, chokes off sensual instincts, shrinks desire and DENIES that the economics of satisfaction demands appeasing the entire human condition, the physical, psychological and spiritual. And you, professor, have ignored the physical for too long leaving you severely out of whack. Tell you what, I'm generous, I'd be delighted to share pointers. Let's start with this: when you and your wife are making, well, for want of a better term, let's call it love, what happens right before you ejaculate? Do you get a tingling sensation running up and down your spine?"

"I don't know. I've never thought about it. Look, I'm not talking about this. Goodness, man, you're a gigolo! And I don't buy your act, seeming so pleased with yourself, even proud. Surely, it's a façade. What could be more meaningless than a life devoted to pursuit of base sexual encounters? Moreso than the women who retain your services, it is you who suffer from loneliness and clamor for relief from a miserable existence. I pity you. A man of minimal substance fooling yourself into believing you're imparting happiness, even joy, to yourself and the people you call patrons. What do you know about joy? Joy is not ejaculation. Joy is a harmonious state of being carried over from one moment to the next, persisting regardless of circumstances."

"Hah! Another poster boy for sexual sublimation. You say you teach at the University of Toronto? Economics, right? What's economics? Predictions, the science of guessing the future based on extrapolations from the past. This is meaningful work? Isn't all 'meaning' subjective, professor? Don't we all myopically differentiate meaningful from meaningless? Nothing means everything. Everything means nothing. Take your pick. So what does an economist contribute to society? I say you're the worst kind of shaman is what you are, one who doesn't dance, partake in ritual smoke or sacrifice virgins. And this is what you devote your life to, this brings you joy? Heaving limited energy into generating big research dollars, attracting star students, solidifying your position atop the professorial heap, contributing quotable snippets to popular media, this feeds your sense of worth, honors you with collegial and societal respect, and justifies an enduring limp dick? This trade off is satisfying? What about your wife; is she satisfied with a paltry cheese string hanging between your legs?

"What my limited intellect doesn't get is how you're not blowing your wad every day, what with twenty year old undergraduate girls, excuse me, young women, eyeballing your crotch, patently signaling willingness to dirty up elbows and knees and get all sloppy in exchange for a grade bump. Fair trade off wouldn't you say? Everyone leaves happy? Even joyous? How the fuck do you do it, professor? Maybe I'm not asking the right question. The better question is WHY don't you do it? Loyalty to the wife? Poor sense of self? Think you're too old?

"Do you understand your power? The sexual charisma attributed by women to men strutting on stage, crooning into a phallic microphone, or lending their image to cameras broadcasting on big screens? Power professor! As long as you hold the reins, there will be females of all shapes, sizes and dispositions begging to be balled. So what do you do? Instead of using your god given penis as intended, day in and out all those sweet pussies stay parched as you mechanically lecture on about fiscal policy, gross domestic product, interest rates and inflationary pressures. How about pumping up your own inflationary pressure? Cut yourself some slack, reduce your workload, and the next time one of those barely legal honeypots mind melds with you while poking her pink, hold her back after class for a private session. Know what I'm saying, professor? You're a man. I'm a man. We're the same. You've got to be true to your self. Denial doesn't eliminate desire, only stuffs it in a closet. Why do you do that? Stop redirecting all that pent up sexual energy into your work. Is that what you think you want, more work, fewer orgasms? Stop listening to your thoughts and take a closer look at your self, professor. You love to learn, right? Then learn to be you, stop with trying to please others, block out the clamoring for conformity, the pathetic craving to be accepted by bubbleheads proclaiming ownership to life's instruction manual, recruiting and petitioning saps into this membership or that group; get away from phony salesmen pitching self-serving policies, drafting the dejected by promising a risk-free, detestable life rejoicing in worship of mythical characters, dead people and faceless institutions. Theirs is the dirty business of obeying and honoring uniforms, names, lineage, degrees, titles, and exulting in asinine affinity to folklore. Accept, reject, do or do not what is best for YOU! Others' expectations, specious disappointments and demands for consistency? Screw 'em. No explanation, no justification, no apology for who you are, for walking the path that isn't a straight line, that crisses and crosses, zigs and zags. So here you are, stuck in a zag. They come, they go. So what? Deal with it!'

Ring Ring. Once again, I'm interrupted.

"Hello?"

"Hello, who's this"?

"You don't know who you're calling? How about we start with you telling me who you are."

"Is this Mr. Shackleton?"

"No, it's Mr. Rogers. Goodbye."

"No, wait! Mr. Shackleton, it's me, Vivian. I'm sorry. I'm nervous, that's all. I thought it was you because this is the number I found in the office directory and it sounds like you but, um, can I speak with you?"

"Lady Aberlin, you are speaking with me."

"Mr. Shackleton?"

"I'm on my way to an early lunch, Vivian. The scent of garlic laden hummus hangs heavy in the air and a Roman bugle is sounding the call of Jerusalem; the restaurant that is, not the holiest of holy cities."

"What a coincidence! I'm around the corner from you! Would it be okay if I meet you there? I'm crazy for their grilled eggplant."

"I don't know Vivian. It's probably not a good ..."

"Pleeease, Mr. Shackleton. It's important to me. I'll be there right away, okay?"

"Okay, why not."

Did I really say that, why not. The question is why. Why should I do something, anything without first having a reason, without being somewhat sure I know what I'm doing, why I'm doing it and what will be the likely consequences. Then again, am I fooling myself thinking I could rationalize my words, my actions, as if reason could win a game of tug o' war against lust? I mean, I'm still carrying her bra in my box!

"Mr. Shackleton! Hi!" There she was, so soon, and I questioned the coincidence of her being so close by. We entered the restaurant and sat down at a table for two.

"I'm famished! Are you hungry? I already know what I want: the beet root frappe and a warrior bowl on brown rice. Soba noodles don't sit well with me. I ate the noodles last time I was here, it was during a weekday, a Tuesday I think, yes it was a Tuesday, I remember now because I wear my pink pashmina every second Tuesday, which also happens to be payday, and I recall being excited about receiving my paycheck that day because there was a big sale at Winners, their once a year sale. About half an hour after returning to the office, my stomach was in an awful state and I had to ask one of the other girls to cover for me as I ran to the washroom where I stayed for some time, I don't even know how long, and when I came back to my desk the girls asked me where I had been because it had been so long since they'd seen me that they thought I had gone home but I reminded them I was in the washroom and was feeling a bit under and as I'm talking my stomach starts doing the whirly bird again so I ran off and I almost bumped into a paralegal carrying a tower of papers and did she ever give me a nasty look but I couldn't stop to apologize because I really, really, needed the toilet and when I surfaced the second time the girls told me to go home because I was pale as a sheet but the worst happened after I went home and I fell asleep on the living room sofa because I was so exhausted and I didn't set my alarm or anything and it was after seven o'clock before I woke all panicked because Winners closes at nine o'clock and it's at least a twenty minute subway ride and then a ten minute walk so, at best, I thought, I would have an hour to shop and this was so disappointing to me because how could I possibly get all my shopping done within an hour and what if the subway broke down on my way there and I didn't arrive until after the store closed then I'd have to wait until next year. I was so upset that I went back to sleep."

Mercifully, a waitress arrived and took our order.

"Vivian, about what happened earlier ..."

"Oh no, Mr. Shackleton, don't apologize, please, you have nothing to apologize for. I'm the one who feels terrible. I was like a schoolgirl throwing myself at you like that so I'm the one who should be apologizing. I want you to know that I'm grateful for what we shared even though you probably don't think of me in a, you know, intimate way, or do you? Oh, there I go again! Always wanting more; that's what gets me in trouble and it's probably why I'm not in a relationship. Just like you're not in a relationship either, right?"

Vivian spoke with one eyebrow raised and a fist wrapped tightly around a knife. Whatever passion was in my pants was fast succumbing to fear for my safety. Redirecting the glare, I said, "Vivian, you're a smart, attractive woman; you'll find someone."

"You really think so?! Then why do all the men I meet leave me? They're so nice in the beginning, you know, when they're courting me, and I fall hard for a gentleman who's sweet and funny and treats me well, someone who likes to laugh and have fun and dance and there was even one who would take me dancing and he won my heart faster than anyone until, that is, he turned on me, as if I did something wrong but I don't know what I did to make him change and be mean to me. I used to think it was my fault but I don't anymore. I guess men are just like that."

"Post and beam fissure."

"What?"

"The male animal traipses across a figurative balance beam, challenging himself to merge strength with understanding, consciousness with energy, potency with tenderness. But it's too much. He wavers, energy conduits seize up and he falls, piercing bloated pride, leading him to hunker down in the valley, alone with woe, spewing misplaced aggression or some other maladaptive behavior. See, the cause of a man's fury is not you; the cause of a man's fury is the man. If he exists unaware of constructive outlets through which to channel wrath, leave him be."

Once the applause settled, I swallowed a forkful of roasted eggplant.

"Do you like to dance, Mr. Shackleton? Do you think we could go dancing one night? If you're not a dancer then we could do something else, if you wanted to that is."

The eggplant wriggled down my duodenum, plummeting first class toward my toes, singeing my throat along the way and then, thud. There I was, face down on a plain white plate greased in olive oil.

"Mr. Shackleton? Mr. Shackleton!"

Vivian gasped. She crossed the table's divide to touch me, to pinch me, to see if I'd respond. I didn't. I couldn't. But I was conscious and remained attentive to her raving. Vivian rushed to my side of the booth, her hot onion and garlic scented breath dripping in my ear, drifting down external auditory and acoustic meatus, beseeching me to rise from Jerusalem's tupperware. Struggling to push me upright, to hold me still and keep my head from involuntarily jerking forward and falling again, she swung her legs around my waist and sat on my lap, the better to steady a lolling head and dab oil from my face.

The commotion, and the uninformed observer's perception of a lap dance, soon caught the waitress's attention. She sauntered over to inquire as to whether things in the mirror were as they appeared. Vivian waved her away, telling her it was a fainting spell and I would be fine. Indifferent, the waitress nodded and resumed delivering food.

While the waitress may have been assured, I wasn't. At least not until Vivian's pelvis commenced grinding against mine. Trying to rouse me from slumber, her gross motor ministrations did indeed turn up the temperature, expand blood vessels, inflate a flapjack ball sac and extract me from stupor. Yet, I feigned unresponsiveness, wanting to see how far Vivian would go to raise me from the near dead. Reaching into her reliable bag of tricks, she leaned forward, pressing my face between her Middle Eastern spiced bosom. Reflexively, I tongued cleavage. The jig was up.

"Oh my god, Mr. Shackleton, you're alive! What happened? I didn't know what to do. I thought maybe you had a stroke. You weren't moving and I thought, well, I thought the worst and I was scared and didn't want to lose you so I almost called an ambulance but I thought first I should hold you because deep down I knew that our holding each other would make it all better and it did, oh my god, it did! Here, drink some water. What can I do? What can I get for you?"

Still ensconced inside her blouse, her nipples stared me down, practically begging me to nibble. Imagining that chewables would allay the agony brought forth by her presence, my tongue again stretched forward only to be intercepted by Vivian who, suddenly aware of our proximity, disembarked.

"I'm okay, Vivian. I, uh, just blacked out there for a minute. The heat in this place got to me; guess I was dehydrated. Thank you. I'm fine now."

Drifting, the oxymoronically named Organization of Scientific Sages came to mind. The OSS recognizes *jumbled chemistry* as an honest to goodness spiritual disorder of universal magnitude in which sufferers are afflicted by scoundrel molecules splitting into hostile groups of atoms separating into rogue electron charged ions wreaking havoc through random, uncoordinated, diffuse eruptions zipping across bodily terrain in a scattered, unsynchronized manner impairing the pre-frontal cortex. Fundamental, elemental, rudimental cranial structures scream for support, electrolyte gangs pour through gaping dikes in swiss cheese holed cognitive functions alarming sensations, disquieting thoughts, roiling emotions, overwhelming any semblance of psychic order and effectively shutting down the human unit. Hmm, seems the Sages have provided me with a plausible diagnosis. Now, where do I find the elixir?

"Vivian, why did you want to meet with me?"

"I just, I just had this feeling, Mr. Shackleton, that, I had this feeling that you, that you should be with me. This may sound strange to you, a lot of people think I'm peculiar, but I get these visions about the future and, after our encounter, after you ran away from me on the street, and that's okay, I understand what I did wrong and why you had to leave, I thought about what happened and I realized that, to act the way you did, as if you don't care, well, you must not be ready for me. I want you to know that

I didn't take it personally, your rejection I mean, because really, I see how you look at me Mr. Shackleton and I've lived long enough to be able to read what's on a man's mind by the way he looks at me, not to mention how excited you were when we were doing, you know, in the office, so I figured that you want me as much as I want you but now is not the time and I should be patient and respect that you're not ready yet even though I know I could help you get to the point where you'd be able to express your true feelings for me. Mr. Shackleton, I could help you overcome whatever barriers are standing in our way. Will you let me help you? I want to help and I know I can because even though you may see me only as a receptionist, I'm more than that and I want to show you everything that I am. For one, I have a special talent for making people see that most things we call problems aren't problems at all. It's more that our energy is sucked away from harmony and into darkness. So, if you'll let me, I want to bring harmony back to you because I know for sure that once you're feeling better, you'll see how deep our love is for each other. Believe me, I never would have behaved as I did if I didn't absolutely know that our love is the real deal. And even though I want you so bad, I've accepted that we're not meant to be lovers yet. But I also have to get you to understand how much you care for me and this is why I had to see you again, Mr. Shackleton, and why I have to ask you to accept my help to lead you out of darkness because it's for your own good."

Not that I needed more evidence but her soliloquy was more than enough to substantiate a finding of erotomania induced delusions.

"I could use a change of scenery; how about we go for a stroll?"

Like an excited child waiting to blow out candles at her birthday party, Vivian escorted me through the doors of Jerusalem and into the outside world where I began concocting a plan to flee.

"You look pale, Mr. Shackleton. Why don't you come home with me and rest. Don't worry, I won't bother you; I only want to care for you. We don't have to tell anyone about us yet if that's what you're worried about. We can keep our love a secret until you're ready. You could lay down in my bed; you'll love my bed, it's so comfortable! If I could, I would live most of my life in bed! Wouldn't you too?"

Every word she spoke compounded my nausea and quickened my heartbeat in a frantic, run for the hills sort of way.

"We're very much alike, Mr. Shackleton, you and me. I'll bet you didn't know that we even share the same cultural background. Did you know that in a past life I lived as a Jewish child during the 1859 pogroms in Odessa? It's true. I have one strong memory of when I was a child living in Odessa and my mother would prepare our meals and before we would sit down at the dinner table she would insist that our whole family gather together and feed our animals first. Do you know why? My mother said that animals are pure, their intention always true, and the more pure a being, the closer they are to God. She was so right! I know because I would watch people talk to them or pet them and whenever people did that they would light up and the more they lit up, the brighter the animal would shine. I remember when I first met you, how bright you used to shine but, and I don't say this to be mean, you don't give off the same glow that you used to. I think it's because you've worked so hard all these years solving other people's problems and not caring enough for yourself or, more likely, not having someone show you the love you deserve. Have you thought about that Mr. Shackleton? You deserve someone who loves you unconditionally just like I loved our animals. Oh, can I tell you something super exciting?!"

"No."

"Hah, hah, you're so funny Mr. Shackleton! But you have to promise not to tell anyone, not yet. I rented a recording studio last week and recorded three songs. It was amazing! I've always wanted to be a singer. I don't sing loudly; I'm a quiet person, you know that. I sing hymns, beautiful melodic hymns, and the recordings were pitch perfect! Even the owner of the recording studio told me that I have an exhilarating voice; that was his exact word, exhilarating. And he invited me to come back to the studio anytime to record more songs but I'm not sure when I'll do that because it is awfully expensive to rent the studio but I'm hoping that my first recordings will sell well and with the money I earn from these songs I'll be able to record more and, here's my big dream, are you ready, become a full time singer! Can you imagine?! I can't describe to you how excited I was, being in a recording studio, wearing headphones and singing into the microphone while the sound engineer made sure that all systems were go; that's the lingo. I thought I was Celine Dion. She's so beautiful, don't you think? Speaking of whom, I have a friend, his name is Howard, and he works at Tiffanys on Bloor Street, that really expensive jewelry store where all the stars shop, and he says that Celine Dion visits the store with her husband twice a year, once on Valentine's Day and again during the Christmas season. Howard says that Celine and him have become close and he personally helps her choose jewelry and that he could arrange for me to meet with Celine. Wow! Can you imagine, meeting Celine Dion?! I'll be so nervous! Should I call her Celine or Ms. Dion or maybe she's old fashioned and likes to be called Mrs? When I meet her, I'll give her copies of my songs and my hope is that once she listens to me singing, she'll want to sing a duet with me.

OMG, what a dream that would be! I'll bet she even has her own recording studio, don't you think? I'm sure it's going to happen. I mean, why else would I have met Howard? The universe doesn't act randomly, you know."

Morphine! Morphine! When would she stop talking? Would she stop talking? Suppose it's my own doing. First, I went poking in the bush and now the eggplant face flop. But I couldn't get away yet. I had to bide my time until my legs were more solid than rubber.

"I knew this would happen. I just knew it! Imagine that. Me cutting a record, I think they call it 'cutting', with a superstar! I can't wait! Maybe I'll be a superstar one day too! Don't worry Mr. Shackleton, I won't forget about you, I could never do that. I'll invite you to the studio recording, I mean, if it's okay with Celine because I'm guessing, since we'll be partners, that I'll have to discuss it with her first but I'm sure it will be okay. Why wouldn't it be?"

Hope is imagination's fire; delusions fan the flames. I was on the lookout for a water hose.

"Here we are, Mr. Shackleton."

"What?"

"We're home. You're coming in, right?"

I felt ill, my head hot and sweaty. Gumby legs or not, I had to get away from this nut job.

"Vivian, I'm leaving. I'm not well."

"Oh, Mr. Shackleton, that's why I brought you home. My home is your home too. You know that. Please, I told you that I'll take care of you, that I have to take care of you. It's meant to be; don't you know that by now? Why not lay down? Mr. Shackleton, I'm asking you nicely. Please, lay down in my bed. You'll feel better in my bed. I promise. It's a lovely bed and it's mine and it smells like me and soon it will smell like you too.

And I'll join you. We can resume where we left off in the office. Wouldn't you like that? Oh, I know you would. Let's start by undressing you. Or would you like a sample of me first? Would you like to lick my nipple like you were trying to do in the restaurant? Here, I'll take out my breast. Here you go, lick it. Go on, lick my nipple! Don't be shy. Lick it and you'll get hard and then you can be inside me where you belong. You do want to be inside me, don't you? That's where I want you, to climb in as deep as you can.

What do you think of that? What do you think of me talking like this? I've never talked like this before. Do you like it? I'm getting excited. Oh yes, I am! Wait a second, okay now, guess where my fingers just went. Go on, put my fingers in your mouth, then you'll know how excited I am. Do you have an erection? I want it, Mr. Shackleton. I can't wait any longer. I want to see your erection! Lets go to my bedroom, Mr. Shackleton, where you can pull it out and give me it to me. Did you hear me? Give it to me! Now!"

One large breast hanging out the blouse of a demented woman demanding I lick her nipple was all the proof needed to wake me from the anesthesia of good manners. Letting loose guttural screams that drove Vivian back and brought out firearm toting neighbors, I grabbed for my throat and robotically lurched away, not stopping until she was out of sight.

Chapter 13
Destination Calls

*We only become what we are
by the radical and deep-seated refusal
of that which others have made of us*
— Jean-Paul Sartre

Malak shops for 1970s style clothes at second hand consignment stores, borrows books and magazines from public libraries, listens to long play records on a garage sale sourced Technics turntable, spends afternoons befriending docile nursing home residents, dishes out warm cereal to the hungry and homeless at local food banks, cares for injured squirrels at a wild animal refuge an hour out of town, clips grocery coupons, reads Braille, walks her neighbor's Chinchilla rabbit, bounces on an original Hansburg patented pogo stick in winter snow and, in contravention of rules and regulations promulgated by the Canadian Liberated Urban Chicken Klub, steals warm eggs from backyard residential chickens.

The neighborhood in which she lives, located in a hip, non-gentrified, ethnically diverse, historical setting preferred by creative types and immigrants, has as many chickens as New Delhi has cows; chickens being something of a present day craze among a particular subculture of middle class, mostly white, women feeling one or another kind of metaphysical void. Studies have been commissioned, and results are pending, to get to the bottom of this fowl phenomena. In the meantime, pilfered eggs are a mainstay of Sunday morning breakfast for Malak and a chocolate Labrador retriever named Sadie, the only other red blooded animal residing at her modest brick town home.

Malak's not married. She doesn't have or want children despite being at the tail end of childbearing age. Although, once upon a time, in days gone by, Malak did endure pregnancy. After giving birth, she forsook motherhood, skipping out on an immature donor and his slack jawed parents who saw fit to raise the child as one of their own on a mid-sized pig farm in Turtleford, Saskatchewan.

It happened like this: being all of seventeen, wooed by a snippety boy with bulging biceps pledging his love upon daily renewal of his vaginal access pass, Malak gave love back the only way young lost girls know how: through tender loins, bartering her vagina in hopes of securing love. Her cherry coarsely picked, her belly blossomed and her teenage mind, prone to Prince Charming daydreams, fantasized about life happily ever after with the outwardly handsome boy and their darling offspring.

However, on the seventh day after conception, her gastro intestinal tract revolted. That day, and every day thereafter for nine successive weeks, she was altogether pooped from tossing too many cookies. The boy, frustrated by access pass denial and Malak's diminished enthusiasm for flexing arms, buckled up his vows and demanded she abort. Malak, not knowing which way to turn, called on her spirit guide for advice. Answering deep in the heart of the night, the gassy guide held Malak's hand, foretold that the pregnancy must be seen through to fruition and, once the child is delivered, she must then take leave. Her lifelong motto being, In Spirit Guides I Trust, Malak accepted her role as a vessel, a mere carrier, and welcomed her responsibility to the child for forty weeks, but no more. And so, not a moment too soon after the mature fetus chunneled down and through her slippery elastic canal, Malak washed, dressed, handed child to the boy's parents, said farewell, and set out to find half a dozen old fashioned glazed donuts because those were her favorite and she was really hungry.

And she's been on her own ever since, learning along the way not to build a stairway to heaven but to embrace life head on, not shying away from anything or anyone, especially loud, small folks; those populating the square majority who savagely critique disrespect for ordinary social niceties. 'Do you think you're better than us? Do you?!' they say, their fragile sense of self undermined by visible signs of DIFFERENCE, their message thrown into doubt by an independent thinker, a rebel, a damn mutineer. Simulating insight, together they nod and concoct plans to bring her down a notch or two, to bring her onto their side, where she belongs, where everyone belongs, in the company of their opinions.

Unflinchingly, Malak dismisses them. Brimming with the river of life, sagaciously she courses past sisterhood and brotherhood preferring the company of selfhood. Here, she answers to no one except her self. Here, she need not compromise autonomy. Even when it comes to supporting herself, Malak does so on her own terms. In the conventional sense, she doesn't work, hawk goods, sell services or spend money like a good patriot. As a matter of conscious choice, not necessity, she lives a materially simple lifestyle conducive to peaceful existence, a state of being high on her priority list. Still, she has to pay for groceries, other than eggs, somehow. To do so, she employs her mathematical talent and a dash of *chutzpah*. Every summer and winter solstice, Malak buys a

Greyhound bus return ticket to Las Vegas where she makes use of her aptitude for numbers to earn, if you can call it that, more than enough money to support herself and Sadie. To minimize risk of recognition or being found out to possess a mental calculator of genius proficiency, she doesn't visit the same casino more than once every five years, limits her winnings to a reasonable sum, and dolls up and dumbs down in body hugging apparel accentuating cleavage, thighs and painted toes before parking herself at a busy blackjack table, putting on her game face (replete with broad ditzy smiles and high-pitched hiccupped squeals of delight let loose after each win), ordering up chips, sucking diet coke through a straw, and getting down to the business of counting cards on her way to beating the house.

$$\Omega$$

Cloud cover snuffed out moonlight as dusk settled in. Not knowing where else to go, I walked until Malak's address came into view under haze of towering street lamps. In staccato bursts, I pounded on the front door. No answer. I knocked again using both fists. The inside lights were on, I was sure she was home. MALAK! I hollered.

The sound of heavy, brazen footsteps approached. The door crept open. I looked up at a giant of a man upon whose body was perched an ostrich egg sized head.

"Who are you?" the giant pleasantly inquired.

Under ordinary circumstances, close up encounters with shaggy throwbacks to 30*th* century B.C.E. who shelter both eyes under one eyebrow and adorn their neck with band-aids as if they were a fashion statement would empty my bladder on the spot. Presently, however, I was too consumed with myself to let ogre inspired terror activate incontinence.

Like a kid, I asked, "Is Malak home?" stopping before following up with whether Malak could come out and play.

Flashing a smile that would make a python turn tail, Big John invited me into the front hall then softly called for Malak, who soon appeared. Standing by the man's side, she measured no taller than his midsection.

"Sam? What's going on? It's late. Why are you here?"

Why was I here? Because I was in the neighborhood? Because I wanted to be with a friend? Because something inside me was breaking? All of the above?

'It's time to take stock,' said Psyche, steering me.

Take stock. Of what?

'Your escape plan.'

I'm escaping? From what? From whom?

'No more games. Let's bring it out in the open. You've been running from your self for years, chasing excitement to block anxieties.'

So I run a little, I'm anxious now and then. Who isn't? Life's good. I'm happy.

'Wrong. You're intoxicated then you crash. Whether work or women, you seek excitement. You equate excitement with happiness. Doesn't happen that way. You know that, man, I know you do. And by now you also know what's waiting for you whenever excitement dwindles or recedes, don't you? That's right. Misery. Despite best efforts, covering it up with a veil doesn't make it go away. Oh, you've tried, how you've tried, to make it go away. With love. You thought love would do the trick. So you looked for it. And more than once, you thought you had it. But you didn't. Sure, you had a woman but not love. You had pleasure and you got all wonky, still, that's not love either. Love isn't thrills. Love isn't tingling sensations. Love is patient. Love arrives on the scene after passion fades, not before. You, however, can't wait. You don't know how. Excitement fizzles and you call it off. Then you leave the comfortable hideaway that is someone else's bed and, no surprise, misery pipes up. Did it ever leave? No. But now you take notice. And you don't like it so you try to reason your way out of misery, back to a place of happiness. Man, reasoning may have served you well with the suit and tie crowd but it doesn't understand the heart, nor the heart reason. Look at you. You're worn down, exhausted. You need rest.'

Feeling weak, I braced myself against the wall. On an unspoken gesture from Malak, her hyper pituitary gland stricken friend helped me to the living room sofa. After the two of them spoke out of earshot, the lumbering giant hugged Malak then coolly grabbed his coat and bowler hat, the only kind that suited his shrunken head, and offered a non-menacing goodnight to all.

Quietly, Malak gathered a heavy blanket around my shivering body, kissed me on the forehead, and turned out the lights without saying a word. Silently, she sat with me. She shared space with me. She comforted me. Being with me was enough. Being with me was everything. Malak understood there was nothing more to say or do. She understood friendship.

$$\Omega$$

Early morning the next day, undressed windows illuminated beams of bright light radiating from morning sun. Squinting through fatigue, I spied a barefoot Malak wearing green colored boxers and a man's pastel yellow button up collared shirt.

"Oh, good, you're up."

"Kind of."

My mouth was pasty dry; tongue clumsy. I lurched toward the coffee table reaching for a miniature ceramic cup filled with steaming green tea. The slight caffeine jolt cleared cobwebs, stimulating my on switch.

"Okay, out with it. What was that all about last night?"

"You're asking me? What do I know? My life script has been torn into Lilliputian pieces; certainty sabotaged by ongoing turbulence. The crazy thing is, it's all my own doing. What's crazier is I don't know why I do what I do. My latest? Pushed Nina off a cliff. Or maybe I jumped. Now I'm not saying I shouldn't have done either but why am I wasting my time like this? Others my age are settled, working to build career, family and social circle, nurture what they have, stir the mortar binding the bricks of society. Me? Where am I? What am I doing? You know what I am? A wayward brick."

"So you're a brick. A wayward one. What's wrong with that? Absolutely nothing. For someone like you, being an outsider is what makes you feel more at home. Sam, the life you're living is the life you're meant to live. Stop with the struggling, the looking back, stop apologizing for the past, making it into an obstacle. Past is dead. Don't hang on. And as far as your life script is concerned, dear, you didn't arrive in this world with a template. You're crafting your self as you go along. Personally, I think you're doing just fine. Better than fine. Better than most. How many others would be willing to abandon the comfortable life you led because of a vague notion that it didn't feel right? You're to be applauded for acknowledging this tireless drive to overhaul your life, to putting an end to living in conflict with yourself."

Malak was sitting in full lotus posture on a sheep's wool rug. Done talking, she lowered her eyelids, stretched out her arms and opened her palms face up. The tips of each index finger on each hand touched thumb to form a circle. Each foot was set against the opposite upper thigh. She was an Albertan rocky mountain firmly earthed to the ground, a personified mountain, mind you, exhibiting fully exposed reproductive parts.

"You do know you're bare under your boxers?"

"Is today's lesson on prudishness, Ms. Martin?"

"Dear highness, call it what you will but the fact remains that southern exposure obligates stirring of primordial urges."

"Close your eyes, dear."

"Too late. Your image has been processed and stored."

"Then do what you have to do but please do it in the toilet. I need thirty minutes for my morning meditation."

"Would you like a blanket to cover up?"

"This is my house. This is my ritual. This is what I do. You're disturbing me. If you're bothered, that's your issue."

"Yes, I'm bothered. In the bare presence of exalted vagina, I'm pleasantly bothered."

"I'm not moving. You're not a boy, Sam. Admire my anatomy as you like. Just be quiet, please, or leave the room."

"Maybe I could join you?"

"You're welcome to meditate."

"I'm thinking about joining in another way."

"Sam."

"It's morning. I can't help myself."

"Even if I wanted to you couldn't handle me, Sammy. You haven't been with someone like me, someone who likes being on top, who enjoys knowing that men feel emasculated when they're with me."

"Oh, divine Lakshmi, I love it when you talk nasty!"

"You won't let me be? Fine. The sooner we get it over with, the sooner I get to meditate. And, Samuel, don't say I didn't warn you."

Malak untangled her crossed legs, slipped out of her shorts, pounced onto the sofa, mounted my chest, clasped her hands about the back of my head and thrust her pelvis into my face, her wrinkled vaginal lips suctioning against my mouth and nostrils, forcefully grinding forward until I started panicking for lack of oxygen. Cleverly, I tongued open her fleshy pink cavity, averting imminent brain damage by frantically inhaling whiskers of air swirling about down there. Barely able to breathe, I contemplated tomorrow morning's headlines: 'Man Snuffed Out by Asphyxiating Pussy'. Desperate to avoid media attention, dwindling energy was channeled into my upper body and I pushed off against her sturdy legs, rejoicing in the plop slop, poppysmic sound jolting forth upon suction release. Rolling out from under Malak, falling to the floor, I gasped for air while holding a triangular pillow in front for protection.

"Finished so soon?" she chirped.

"This is the secret of your attraction?" I wheezed, wide-eyed.

"There are parts of me that you don't know, dear."

"And now there are parts of you I know all too well. What do you say we pretend this never happened?"

"Sure, we could pretend. After all, imagination is one concept distinguishing us from other animals; it's the underpinning of growth; an indispensable block integral to climbing the self-actualization pyramid. And often, wouldn't you agree, imagination is more gratifying than reality?"

"Reality would have outshined fantasy if someone would have played along."

"Sammy didn't get what he wanted?"

"To be the muffled victim in Attack of the Killer Pussy has been a masturbatory dream of mine since I was nine. Whoever said dreams don't come true? The lummox who was here last night, this is what you do with him?"

"The man to whom you derisively refer has a name. Cory. Our activities are none of your concern, dear. Don't pass judgment based on your alpha male competitive disposition. You should know by now that true beauty is within. Cory's formidable physical presence belies a gentle, sweet manner that flowered only after he stopped working as a cop for the Toronto Police Department. Six years ago, he was riding shotgun with his partner, chasing a stoned drug dealer at high speed down Yonge Street at four o'clock in the morning. A drunk pedestrian crosses the street. Cory's partner, focused on catching the dealer, doesn't see the pedestrian until Cory shouts at which point their car swerves to avoid hitting the man and slams into a telephone pole. Cory's airbag doesn't deploy and the force of impact propels him forward through the front windshield. He lands on a concrete sidewalk, head first, and suffers irreversible brain damage and extensive facial scarring requiring reconstructive surgery. The Police Department gives Cory a disability pension, discharges him and claims he no longer has the mental or emotional aptitude to perform his job, his wife leaves alleging she omitted the vows about loving in sickness, and he falls into depression. Today, he's not who he used to be, for better or worse. He spends his days counseling other brain-injured victims, motivating and supporting people to appreciate the life they have, encouraging them to welcome their second chance. Cory is so warm, open and sincere that people quickly overcome intimidation based on his appearance. His injury was a gift to himself and to people he has since met. His refreshing attitude? If he's not six feet under, everything else is gravy. I'm going to shower. You staying a while, dear?"

"No, no, I have to, um, meet someone."

"There are clean linens in the washroom if you'd like to clean up. Help yourself to breakfast."

Malak kissed me on the cheek and skipped off to shower.

"Hey, Sammy," she called out, wrapped in a towel, "they ain't worth a dime unless you play 'em."

"Riddles aren't my strong suit."

"Play your cards, Sammy. That's what they're there for. Get in the game and play your cards."

Play my cards. What cards? I have cards to play? I don't even know where the deck is never mind port, starboard, aft or stern. Should have learned to read a compass but my own haywire magnetosphere keeps interrupting pole signals.

Chapter 14
Orb

*The struggle itself toward the heights is enough to fill a man's heart.
One must imagine Sisyphus happy*
— Albert Camus

Her lair was housed in a neighborhood unmarked by uniform zoning. A mixed-use quarter, in the lingo of commercial property developers, populated by an array of merchants offering giant exercise balls, recalled toys, lederhosen, bikini waxing, raw food, nail care, permanent tattoos, long play records, men's hats, designer kites, Hungarian candy, and matchmaking services advertising confidentiality between matchmaker and overbearing parents seeking a mate for their son or daughter.

The neon sign said no appointment necessary. I walked in. There she was, sitting gracefully, hands upon the table, acting as if she expected me. Lying about the small space were the usual accoutrements including a copy of the Bhagavad Gita, healing crystals, spirit boards, betel leaves, imitation gems, pendulums and a neon crystal ball balanced on a sliver of red velvet cloth. She motioned for me to sit across from her then pressed a button and a time clock started.

"Why did you come? What do you want? Do you know? Don't answer. Don't even try. You don't know. I know you don't. But I'll tell you. Are you listening? Listen and stay quiet. You suffer. Of course you suffer. Who doesn't suffer? Everyone suffers. But you persist. Why? Why do you persist in prolonging your pain? Is it necessary? No. It's optional. Do you understand? Pain is optional. And this is the option you choose? Give it up already. Let it go. There's nothing to fear. You'll be okay. Everything is okay. Just the way it is."

"Your standard spiel?"

"Why do you do this, burying yourself alive?"

"We'll get to that. First, tell me how much you charge for helping me dig my way out?"

"What, you're looking for a deal? There is no deal. I don't deal. This is your life. It isn't to be played with. Whatever I charge to help you avoid lasting ruin is worth triple what you'll pay."

"Ahh, you're no stranger to bargaining. Okay, you won't give me a price yet. Will you at least let me peer into the crystal ball to see whether my coming here was a good idea?"

"Oh, I've already peered, Samuel. And I know you've come to the right place."

Incense smoke filled the cluttered room, dimly lit by a forty-watt incandescent buzzing bulb attached to an overhead string. The psychic was a woman of medium height, her contoured feet fitted on simple leather sandals; plump pear shape immodestly exhibited underneath a black smock dress; unruly tangerine hair partially hiding a neck ringed by multi-colored beads strung along a gold chain; and a patrician nose that, on first glance, didn't belong. Mounted on the wall directly behind the round, antique cherry wood table where we sat was a photo of six women bearing striking, though not identical, physical resemblance despite an age span among them of significant years. Each wore an expression suggestive of harboring a shared secret.

"How do you know my name? I never told you my name."

"You think I'm a fraud? A hack who doesn't deliver the goods? I wish you well, Samuel. You may go now."

"Look, I was drawn here. I don't know why. I admit you're a novelty act for me. No offense. If I'm coming off as contemptuous, I apologize. How about we start over? You haven't introduced yourself."

"Seja."

"That photo on the wall; are those your sisters?"

"No. It is only me. I have my photograph taken once every seven years. It is in the seventh year that we complete our cycle, shed our skin and renew. I like to be reminded every now and then of my changes, of the fact that tomorrow I will be someone new. But we are here to talk about you, not me."

"I'm all ears."

"You are heavy."

"Heavy? I've been called a lot of names but, really, with my frame, heavy hasn't made the list."

"No more words from you."

I had been warned. Inserting a dramatic pause long enough to make me fidget, long enough for me to wonder what kind of parent would hire a matchmaker for their child on the sly, long enough to consider whether Seja's powers exceeded those of mere mortals or whether I'd stepped into an imitation Coney Island funhouse, she then proceeded to speak in a voice so deep I could've sworn she was channeling Barry White.

"This is a Tarot card. Do you know Tarot cards? Every day at sunrise I lay these cards on the table, this table at which we sit, and one card jumps out. Today, it was the card of Judgment so I knew that someone who had lost hope would visit. Let me explain.

Drawing the card of Judgment does not mean you will be judged. No, it has nothing to do with that. Instead, this card determines whether actions, values and behaviors are right or wrong for you. In other words, the card evaluates honesty and reveals truth. Not truth as you or I see it, tinged with our own biases, but non-judgmental truth according to the laws of the universe.

"Looking into the card of Judgment, I see you are frozen at a crossroad. I'm told you will remain there until such time that YOU judge what action is to be taken, YOU decide what challenges are to be accepted and YOU figure out your new mission in life. This is what must be done and will be done as long as you are patient, reflective, and trust that a higher presence has been set in motion supportive of your resurrection."

"Resurrection, huh? I don't know. Jesus imagery brings me round to prim Janet, otherwise known as SHE who evoked holy desire of a sort not publicly sermonized by the pied piper carpenter. An old girlfriend with a predilection for panty liners and polka dot bonnets, Janet had a fondness for moonlight mass. We were young, I was pheremonically inclined to her virtuous vapors, so I tagged along. How could I not? It was like exploring a new species, being among the observant. Besides, majoring in cultural anthropology at the time, and wanting to be published in the Anthology of Heathens, I assumed that assimilating with Janet and her kind would provide unparalleled perspective and knowledge beneficial for thesis writing. That and the potential thrill of defiling a fair-haired maiden left me no choice but to mingle with the minister and his bland flock.

"Eagerly anticipating her manual ministrations, there I was, kneeling on a dusty, termite infested floor in front of a nineteenth century pew surveying a benediction seeking congregation.

I had waited all day. I had summoned heretofore unheard of self-control to save myself and avert spewing before the clock struck midnight; not a light undertaking for a teenage boy. But as chimes rang past twelve, and hope of the stroke of delicate hands grew and grew, control came undone. Once blind communion got under way, I rushed to make my move, scooted over on the bench, rubbed hips up against Janet and unbuckled my pants intending to place within her grip not the symbolic wafer like body of Christ but the Hardened Genitals of Sam. No sooner had I popped a button than pious Janet landed a forearm whack to my midsection followed by mutterings of sacred unmentionables and a hoarse insistence that I beg for Almighty forgiveness. Beset by visions of carnal steam rising from Janet's smoldering offering and a concrete erection scrambling to rip through heavy denim, I reluctantly agreed to her terms on the express condition that begging take place after her hand became one with Sam. Miffed, she turned away, resuming recitation of pleadings skyward.

"To the disappointment of anxious Anthology of Heathens editors, my opportunity to subvert Janet went unfulfilled and, to this day, my assignment remains incomplete. This is why when you mention resurrection, into my head pops the prodigal son stuck on a big stick together with thoughts of good girl Janet and my foiled attempt to become privy to her golden triangle."

"I asked you not to speak. Didn't I tell you no more words? As I was saying, you are at a crossroad and though the dawn may be dark, you will find what you are looking for if, and only if, you believe the light will show itself."

"If I understand correctly, I'm to stand on the spot marked *x*, wait for the anointed time, waters will part, and that's my sign to gallantly ride on through to the other side? This tale sounds familiar."

"I am a messenger, Samuel. Minimize the import of my message at your peril."

The timer rang. Seja held out her hand. I paid, the session was over, but Janet fueled fantasies still coursed through my head as I passed through the rusted door on my way out. Then Jack called.

"Elise asked me to call, see how you're doing."

"Gee, Jack, you care."

"Look Sam, I'm busy okay? This fucking project has morphed into a nightmare. A bunch of lousy Mexican illegals up and left me with no warning 'cause some asshole is paying them two more bucks an hour and now I'm running behind schedule because my crew is short. On top of that, the architect has a log up his ass and is shifting blame to me for cost overruns; what the hell can I do about skyrocketing material prices? You wanna blame someone, blame the investment bankers playing their commodity speculation games, driving prices to the brink before dumping their positions ahead of market collapse. The numbers were off from the start. Same old game of under quoting total cost to pry financing from nervous bankers to get the project off the ground then go knocking on their door when the money well runs dry knowing full well the pinstripes have to open the vault if they're gonna recoup principal any time soon and the kicker is that, to save face, the fucking architect and his moneyed henchmen scapegoat some sap as the unpredictable source of excess spending. I'm that sap? No fucking way! Without warning, three blue suited geeks appear on site, grilling me about delays, worker efficiency, product quality. I don't stand for that bullshit. I told 'em if they didn't like my work they could fuckin' fire me. That's when they start massaging my balls saying I misunderstood and they have no intention of firing me. What the hell do these *foie gras* fuckers know about my job? Their only concern is numbers, strategizing to maximize the building's value once completed, then finding a buyer willing to pay more than they did. That's not my job. My job is to put up the best damn building I can and I can't do my job right if I can't rely on my workers showing up the next day!"

"So quit."

"Quit?! Who do you think you're talking to? I don't quit. That's your response? Man, no wonder you're such a goddamn mess. You don't just throw up your hands when it doesn't go your way. You work harder. You fuckin' work harder! I made a commitment to other people and to myself; that means I see it through to completion. Come work for me, Sam. I could use the help and you'll find out what real work is. When was the last time you worked with your hands? It'll be good for you. Anyway, why'd you call me? I've got my own problems not to mention Elise can't get it through her thick head that after working fourteen hour days, I'm tired. You know? It's not like I'm twenty-two anymore and can fuck all night long. When I get home, I gotta rest. All I want is for her to make me dinner and let me relax in peace, let me recharge. Is that so much to ask? Huh, is it? Elise says I don't fuck her enough anymore and wails on about how I no longer find her attractive. What am I supposed to say to her, huh? Should I kiss her ass before bed and tell her she's beautiful? That's bullshit. She knows I love her. I'm not gonna say it every day. Next thing you know she'll want me to hug her every morning before I leave for work. I can't handle that needy crap. If she's not getting enough, I told her, go find a young stud to ride. Then she gets all pissed, telling me I don't understand her. You show me one woman who says her man understands her, go on, just one, I tell her. I don't know what the hell she wants!"

"You called me, Jack."

"I don't know who called who! You think I'm keeping a scorecard? Did you hear anything I said? I need a drink. What's going on with you?"

"I'm leaving a psychic's den."

"What are you doing to me, Sam! As if my blood pressure isn't high enough, now you're telling me you're pals with a psychic? What the fuck?! You're letting some mystic moron nail her claptrap into your head? Are you banging her too or just screwing her spirit? You go that route and the next thing you know you'll be slip sliding away to the bottom of Mount Loser flashing peace signs and passing communal paper plates filled with ant infested rice and beans back and forth with the scum and socialists. Is that what you want? To tie up your hair in lice infested dreadlocks and perform sun salutations three times a day along with hordes of other half-baked imbeciles? You stupid prick! Meet me at the site and I'll give you a job. Get your hands dirty. Nothing's better for a moaning schnook than a hard day's work."

"I'll see."

"You'll see? Don't give me you'll see! What else do you have to do? Who are you meeting with next? Merlin? Ask him to break his fucking wand over your head 'cause nothing else seems able to break the spell of idiocy you're under. I've got all the gear here at the site; you show up and let hard work talk sense into you."

"Maybe."

"No maybes. Be here within the hour!"

"Jack, I can't even hammer a nail without pounding my thumb."

Is this the sign Seja was talking about? Is Jack the one to lead me beyond the crossroad? Maybe all I need do is show up, use my hands, get out of my head, the spell will be broken and after that one thing will lead to another and then I'll have a plan to move forward, new dreams to dream.

'Go on then, what are you waiting for?'

Something's holding me back.

'Well, at least you recognize it.'

You mean you know? What is it?

'*Vasana.*'

What?

'You're still consumed by *vasana*, habit energy, that which winks us down familiar rabbit holes simply because these are the holes we know: familiarity, ease, convenience. Shimmying on up to the dark side of the moon, gripping us, keeping us in place, hustling us to the seeming safety of a KNOWN world and KNOWN behavior, *vasana* thrives on states of discordance, its fumes feeding embedded tentacles of fear fastening us tight and stiff to the sidelines, deceiving us into believing we're traveling the RIGHT path when the truth of the matter is we're lost on the side of the road, cowed into choking on a trail chock full of familiar ruts. Why take a chance, why go see Jack when you don't know what will happen next? Best to prolong your state of suspension, no? At least here you believe you're safe, yes? And if you believe it, then it is so, is it not?'

What are you saying? I won't take chances anymore? That's not me. I don't shy from risk. How do you think I achieved so much?

'Hah! Time to rip out the rear view mirror, my friend. You want an accurate portrayal of your condition? Let's start by reviewing self-proclaimed authoritative texts presenting varying definitions of the word 'stasis' including, stoppage of bodily fluid flow, slowing of circulating blood current, and, my favorite, a period of stability during which restrictive harnesses rigidly affix thus preventing both evolutionary advancement and customary self-flagellation. Regardless the particular definition, each infers stagnation, washed out, a waking coma. Sound familiar?'

It's true. A pod of my own making, here I sit in the amphitheatre's dark back row clad in overcoat, gloves and toque. Sheepishly, I raise my hand acknowledging it was I who snared myself from myself, suspending growth until further notice. And what is a pod to do but pray to thee Soter, begging for thy spirit to be liberated from self induced afflictions, to be delivered off the fence of dormancy.

And on hearing my prayers, Soter thunders, 'I DO NOT LISTEN TO THOSE WHO NEGLECT TO INSPECT THEIR PANTS! Deflated balls of yesteryear shall stay splayed upon pyramid's bottom, not to ascend until you venture forth.'

Crossing onto Bloor Street West, welcomed by a smog fouled ventilating breeze, I had my choice of saviors among countless temples smartly designed to mollify modern anxiety exacerbated by spiritual destitution. It was here where I could comfortably shoehorn into an assemblage of my choosing, one amenable to my credit card limit. The golden road offered *Prada, Gucci, Burberry, MAC Cosmetics, Hugo Boss, Chanel, Hermès, Louis Vuitton, Holt Renfrew, Tiffany & Co., Escada, Ermenegildo Zegna, Cartier SA, Rolex Harry Rosen, Calvin Klein, Cole Haan, Vera Wang, Lacoste, Ferrari, Maserati, Rolls-Royce Motor Cars,* Pottery Barn, *Williams-Sonoma, Bang and Olufsen, Max Mara, Montblanc, Bulgari, Birks, Coach, Guerlain, Swarovski, Puma AG, Aldo, Aritzia, Club Monaco, Banana Republic, American Apparel,* Roots, *Guess, Nike, Zara, Lululemon, Sephora, Gap, H&M.* Choose one, sung jolly saints, anyone will do. I wanted to choose; I really did. But, since none offered testicle resuscitation services, the plastic card didn't budge from my pocket.

Along comes Dandy.

'*Au contraire monsieur*! Let me introduce you to our exquisite merchandise, an extensive array of unique clothing, accessories and accents that, rest assured, confers social inclusion, steadfastness and a most satisfying redemption. Our apparel bestows instant affinity, it will transform your, how do you say, *boules*, to granite, the texture of which will be smoother than a baby's bottom, and you will look, oh, you will look so *debonair*! Join us, *monsieur*, shelter yourself in our offerings, and you will stand above your audience and be delivered.'

My audience? What audience? Who's looking at me?

'*Oui, mon ami, les audience*. Fashionably dressed, you are on display, *non*? Upon donning new attire, they will look, stop, stare, covet, hunger, lust for you; they will want to know who you are, whether you eat green or pink peppercorns, who is your favorite grunge artist, and how big is your house. This is what you want, *monsieur*, for people to notice you? Yes, it is what everybody wants! First they notice, then they listen. Ahh, but what better medicine than to be listened to! We listen to IMPORTANT people do we not? But let's not get ahead of ourselves. Look at you; the emperor wears only his under garment. Tsk tsk. Our kind covers our self, feeds blemish free illusions, makes our self attractive and desirable from the outside, yes? The women, they want a well-dressed man, one outfitted in uniform projecting confidence, poise, clout and influence, a man who will dominate them and others. The men too, will show respect, even deference on sensing your power. I promise you, *monsieur*, in our clothing virility will become you, you will become virility, and never again will you feel excluded from your community, from the collective, from us.'

Looking outside, I saw a sixty-odd year old bald woman wearing wrap around sunglasses, a bikini top and bottom riding a skull decorated skateboard in the middle of the road, stubbornly oblivious to traffic; middle-aged heterosexual couple of sufficient height and attraction holding hands, strolling, taking turns licking one double scoop ice cream cone and smiling; gang of surly white teenage frat boys in muscle shirts and hi tops prowling the sidewalk five abreast daring red rover to cross over; Rubenesque hottie gliding in four inch heeled silver shoes, translucent miniskirt and satin bra showcasing pensive nipples; and African

American man in navy power suit, solid pink tie and fine Italian leather brief case complete with padded shoulder strap, striding stridently, purpose and destination known.

I think I am on display therefore my audience awaits? I need my audience, they need me and together we climb and conquer? Is this the way it's done? Will my spirit rise only if I transform, if I become one of them, join up, sign in, toss my hat into a ring, any ring will do?

Oy. How did I get here? Round, round I go, no nearer to circle's end, to returning to my self, moving into my self, imperfections and all. Unless I am close and don't know it? Maybe I'm already there, here, or wherever it is I am. Although ... what if there's nowhere else to go, no one else to become, and this search of mine has been futile from the start? Sure, I could go with that, why not give it a try? If I do, I have a feeling answers will come and I'll find, yes, I'll find ... damn, thought I had it. What is it I will find?

A croissant. Forget fortune cookies; truth is to be found in croissants. Standing in front of Future Bakery off Brunswick Avenue, a lone table on the outdoor patio gestured. I accepted. An unhurried waitress, mid-twenties, east Asian/Caucasian hybrid soon approached. She wore a wrinkle free short sleeve t-shirt, long shorts, and bounds of enthusiasm known principally to youth, puppies and, oxymoronically named, television personalities.

"Jane Austen," I said.

"My name's Roxy. Jane won't be in today."

"So you know the author?"

"I'd love to chat but I don't get paid to socialize. Would you like to order?"

"There is no charm equal to tenderness of heart."

"You're enlisting Jane to flirt with me?"

"So you do know of her!"
"What woman doesn't?"
"What man does?"
"Why do you say that?"
"She's the stuff that Hallmark cards are made of. Classic nineteenth century British sleepers, obvious, overdone plots and rambling commentary about social hierarchy, failed relationships and dreary minutia of blue blood conversation."

"I don't read her that way. Jane's ideas are full of witticisms and warmth. She explores the depths of human emotions, thoughts and feelings. She champions the potential of the human spirit, finds humor in everyday life. As a woman living in the late eighteenth and early nineteenth century who never married, wrote her first novel at age fourteen, major work at age twenty, never published under her own name because of inferior status conferred upon woman, I think she was truly remarkable."

"Simply because she had a vagina?"

"The obstacles she faced and surmounted because she had a vagina were enormous! Do I recognize her genius based exclusively on gender membership? No. I admire Ms. Austen for her strength of character, literary contribution to society and the voice and sense of empowerment she bequeathed to women."

"What about her obsession with pomegranates? You don't find it odd?"

"I don't recall her use of pomegranates."

"Oh, sure, littered throughout her works. The righteous fruit, pomegranates are. Six Hundred and Thirteen seeds buried in the pulp and juice of each and every one of these juicy marvels. Coincidentally, same number of commandments handed down from Mount Sinai, which begs the question, the pomegranate or the Torah, which came first? Cynics, of whom I've been known to count myself, claim that the rabbinical council responsible for commandment crafting picked the venerable *punica granatum* because of its visible resemblance to the human vagina; rationality taking a back seat to three randy rabbis. Brazen as they may have been, those black hats beautified the pious pomegranate by placing it front and center during the Jewish New Year holy days. Though never publicly acknowledged, after being primed with a bottle or two of aged Manischewitz, the exalted men of lore were known for wondering aloud why the chosen deciduous shrub not only resembled the look and feel, if not taste, of the female vagina but also stored copious seeds symbolizing man's sperm."

"What are you saying? Austen planted the pomegranate in her stories as some kind of coded message about what, hermaphrodites?"

"Did I say that? Oh no, Lady Austen was much too English, too proper, too aware of her place, and, to be fair, the times that she lived in barely tolerated outing a female author never mind revelation of the true meaning of the pomegranate. To chance being tarred with a reputation as a purveyor of smut would have been literary suicide. Janey sought cover by subtly inserting the wholesome fruit in the shadows of her stories, in the corners of frames telling lovers tales. She knew very well that, metaphorically, the fruit symbolized union between one man and one woman or, possibly, one man or woman alone who happens to be gifted with dual genitalia. That said, anyone who's given it any thought recognizes the overt sexuality inherent in all fruits and vegetables. The peach, cucumber, nectarine, zucchini, coconuts, bananas, beets, pears; do you know their origin? Flowering plants. You see, run of the mill blossoms contain an ovary and inside the cell of each ovary resides soft, oval shaped ovules that store the flowering plants female sex germs. Once fertilized by male sex germs, these mature into seeds. Eventually, the blossom's ovary, bearing ovules, enlarges and develops into the fruit that we eat.

So, you see, even flowers have sex. Except for the asexual ones, like blue violets."

"What do violets do for fun?"

"They fulfill their purpose, dry up and wither away. Utilitarian sad sacks. Spinsters. You do see the connection don't you?"

"Between?"

"You, me, zucchinis, figs, even blue violets. I mean, how different are we? We live, we reproduce, we die, all sharing the same genetic commandment ordained by nature, all connected, all conscious (who's to say figs don't have consciousness?) except that human consciousness is infused with a degree of self-awareness that makes believe we are worthy, that we matter more than other life forms when, in fact, we don't and this is precisely why the only ancient law worth abiding by is that which commands thee to love, every which way, the zucchini."

"Of course! How could I have missed the connection between zucchinis and pomegranates? But, you know, it sometimes happens that an unusually large pomegranate results in the zucchini feeling small and lost and the pomegranate, being a kind fruit, experiences remorse when knowingly contributing to another's feelings of inadequacy."

"When you're not filling stretched gullets of the depraved and lonely, what do you do?"

"I'd love to continue our fascinating discussion but I've already spent too much time talking. I need to work. Tuition isn't free."

"What are you studying?"

"English. Ph.D program at University of Toronto."

"When will your handlers pass you?"

"I'm defending my dissertation in June."

"And after the cap and gown ceremony and trying on for size the title, 'Dr. Roxy', what then?"

"Same old. The 'Dr.' prefix isn't legal tender and won't pay my rent. While a doctorate in English impresses my parents, the world outside of family and ivory towers doesn't have much practical use for rote recitation of Shakespearean sonnets or a well-turned phrase. It's discouraging but I'll keep at it. I have to. It's me. It's what I'm made for. Since I began reading for myself at age four, I fell in love with stories, fairy tales and poetry, all brought to life by ink on a page taking me away to an enchanted land. When I first learned that I could earn a living by reading, writing and talking about literature, I was beside myself! I would actually be paid to engage in my one true, unadulterated love. Of course, that happened before our society started dumbing down; the English language as we know it being eviscerated a little bit more every day by twitter and texting; acronyms and symbols having supplanted what was once known as words; accurate spelling no longer a prerequisite for literacy; and, owing to proliferation of the keyboard, schools don't teach cursive writing and that most beautiful art form called calligraphy will soon be extinct. I imagine signatures too will one day be an historical footnote, to be replaced by digital thumbprints, or maybe a grunting sound, in the not too distant future. Less writing, less spelling, less need for the ABCs and guess what happens to the English subject? Next up on the rapidly expanding endangered civilization list is reading as the wide, wide, world of video spreads to all four corners and digital devices do the reading for you; all you have to do is stay passive and listen. How convenient is that; we won't have to bother teaching kids to read anymore! It's so sad it makes me want to cry. The reality is that previously hallowed English departments are downsizing if not being shuttered altogether. That, together with no more mandatory retirement age, means tenured professors haunt arched hallways until both feet rest horizontally, leaving me with an ornamental piece of paper and a waitress job until the day I spy a familiar face in Sunday's obituaries. Unfortunately, my erudite peers tend to remain upright and arguably lucid well into old, old age, so, by the time a position opens, one or more younger generations will have lettered themselves, possibly leaving me out of the running because I'll then be in the midst of my advanced years, not to mention my current career doesn't exactly provide a credentials boost. Oh well. I'll just wait until the stars line up for me. Until then, I'll be filling the trough for a never ending parade of hungry people."

"This doesn't bother you, devoting ten years of your life to study and research, to obeying adults intent on keeping one foot on your neck knowing you would be up and coming competition, that you're vaunted piece of paper cost you well over six figures and future years of shoveling out of debt, and now your daily existence is reduced to scribbling prose on a notepad taking food orders from spoiled leches like me?"

"We all make up timetables, plans and agendas but the fact is no one has much of a say about if, when or how life's variables line up. Sometimes, the best we can do is stand still. You, me, that blade of grass, each of us is helpless in the face of nature's random whims and vagaries. I've done all I can do for myself and now, if I want to get to where I want to go, I have to be patient. Then again, maybe I won't *go* anywhere. Maybe I'm meant to be a waitress. I'll have to wait and see. I can exert all my energy into making my dreams come true but, in the end, with so many factors at play, who knows what will happen next?"

"Selfless. Admirable. Still, not even a smidgen of disappointment that the next rung may be out of reach?"

"I'll share a secret with you: there is no value in naked ambition. Thomas Merton said that when ambition ends, happiness begins."

"Intelligence without ambition is like a bird without wings. Dali."

"You're quoting Dali? Salvador Dali was a certifiable crackpot terrified of grasshoppers! Do you want to order something?"

"Not yet. I'm enjoying our banter."

"Uh huh, and some of us have responsibilities. I don't get paid to banter."

"I'll pay you."

"Excuse me?"

"I'll give you money. How much do you want? What do I care? Money is a token, an artificial, arbitrary medium of exchange. Its value based on nothing more than our belief that it has value. We devote an inordinate amount of energy to thinking, dreaming and scheming of ways to earn money. It greases the collective game of social economic regulation. Money is our master and we are its' slave. It creates stability and instability, creation and destruction, unity and strife, partners and rivals. Does it bring us freedom or dependence, despondency, suicide and murder?"

"So you're a rich oddball? Only people who have piles of money have the luxury to wax philosophical about it. However dreamy my notions about money may be, the reality is I don't want to go without the basic necessities. I'll be back in a few minutes to take your order."

My gaze fell beyond the string cordoned patio. I saw life forms melting together, people converging as part of an infinite whole connected not only to each other but also to leaves on trees, alert birds, sober earthworms, pretty butterflies, flea ridden rats, thirsty maggots, hungry mosquitoes and dung enriched soil; each form forsaking individuality, abstaining from imposed nomenclature, such that not one of them existed on its own, each depending on the other.

Was I dreaming? Rubbing my eyes with two fists in the manner of a weary infant, I looked upon my reflection in a large glass window on the café's building side. There, I saw myself surrounded, better yet, joined to all that I observed. Liberated from the delusion of me, myself and I, freed from the separation, I saw in terms of wholes. The line between subject and object, observer and observee, was no longer, it had dissolved. And here, in the company of others, in the companionship of life, haze cleared to be replaced by a perspective laying bare *our* struggle, not only mine alone, but all nature of life and I saw that whatever lives, whatever grows, endures struggle, at one time or another, most often somewhere in the middle, between bold lines of heroism and despair. It's part and parcel of the process, I thought. Instead of trying to bend it my way, welcome the process.

Roxy returned. "How much?" she wanted to know.

Snap! Just like that, Roxy's lingering bouquet pierced my bubble of unity, out from which sprang horns of confusion resting atop pulsating temples. And there, I imagined, was the rub and with it, Genie, she of billowy satin pants, womanly belly and vampish veil, indifferent to trite earthly concerns, yet subservient to out of bottle duty, who had delivered Roxy to me. A blessing or curse, I did not yet know. Regardless, my thoughts had turned inward, to a fast rising appetite for perfumed pudenda.

"Am I selling something?" I replied.

"How much will you give me? You said if I leave with you now you'll give me money."

"What's the going rate for an unfulfilled Ph.D serving aged nuts?"

"I have a sweet spot for older cashews. Ask me out for dinner and we'll go from there."

"Older? Oh, Brutus, how ungallantly thou bruises thy ego! Experienced, ripened, seasoned, all preferable adjectives."

"I'm being kind in not mentioning lonely, melancholic, lost."

"Ack! How dare you bare my soul! Exposed, vulnerable, stripped of defenses, but not as yet of Jockeys, I am reduced to quivering marmalade at the utterance of your offer. It is settled then: we shall dine!"

"Alright. Give me your number and I'll call you in an hour with restaurant details. Let's plan to meet about six-thirty. My shift doesn't end until five o'clock. I need some down time before we go out."

"Six-thirty?! Hmm, I was hoping you'd be amenable to a pre-dinner orientation among and between ourselves."

Seated, I spun my chair round so Roxy's waist was eye level, my hands landing on rotund hips.

"THAT is not on the menu," declared Roxy, backing away. As she did so, competing parts of Psyche spoke up.

'Sir. Sir? May I speak? I've been quiet all along. But after hearing you attribute cause of this young woman's presence to a fictional cartoonish character, it's just that, you've given me pause, and cause, for concern. I know, believe me I do, that you want answers. We all want answers. Moreso as we get older, as we look up from our perch, as we witness friends and family struck by troubles, broken hearts, disease, loss and death, as we find it more difficult to deny our ephemeral journey, and realize the ultimate uselessness of our everyday projects. Yet, it is also true that many answers are hidden and are not to be found through machinations of the coconut swiveling atop our shoulders nor by seeking higher ground. Sir, what concerns me is not your search for answers. No, stepping back, expressing doubts, questioning meaning, is healthy, even corroboration of your evolution. But you seem to have concluded that nothing means anything; rather than by design or metaphysical purpose, our world, our lives, are accidental and, ultimately, irrelevant. Maybe you are correct. We really do not know all the whats and whys, the wheres and hows. Still, though I have no qualms with your persistent thinking in terms of meaninglessness, may I suggest that your ride will be that much more tolerable, even enjoyable, if you were to lighten up, carry comic irony by your side?'

'Humor? You think it's funny, him popping into this dreck filled café, trying to charm his way into the bloomers of a down and out waitress? Has he thought ahead? What happens after the conquest when she interprets his interest for interest!? This is how he starts with all of his flame outs, confusing testosterone tsunamis for love. If he wants to get to know the waitress, and she for whatever ludicrous reason consents, okay, let him get to know her, go for a stroll, have dinner, kiss her good night. But that's it! No depleting her with deception, shenanigans, pledges and false promises, making her believe he cares when his only aim is temporary reprieve from his baffled brain. The roadside distractions must end! The waitress, that's what she is, a distraction from his course, and now is certainly not the time for distractions, not when he's so close to learning the journey's purpose.'

Roxy sat. We were side by side but she made sure to keep ample space between our chairs.

"What's your story, Sam? Your clothes and poise shout Bay Street financier, big house in a leafy neighborhood, divorced, too much time on your hands so you spend your days trolling for women on sunny weekday afternoons because how else is a perplexed guy like you to fill the void? Of course, there's also the possibility that you're a gardener tending to backyard fields of money trees planted on your finely groomed estate."

"The money trees were ripped out. Rotten to the core. Replaced with giving trees."

"Oh, that is one of my all time favorite books, The Giving Tree! I cry every time I get to the last page. But back to you.

Before we go anywhere, tell me why the long face hiding behind smiles and charm? Tell me more about Sam, the guy in there," Roxy said, lightly tapping my chest.

$$\Omega$$

Thomas: What's on the docket?

Frankfurter: Whether Mr. Samuel Shackleton should ball Ms. Roxy Wu.

Thomas: Him again? How many times will he ask us for help before getting it straight? Every time he's here, we end up running over the same old ground, finding the same old fears. We're judges not psychiatrists. Let him see a shrink.

Holmes: It is our duty to help. Let us approach the issues differently this time. First, we must deal with the underlying concern of resetting Mr. Shackleton's compass. Once the compass is reset, he may then determine where it is he wishes to go.

Frankfurter: The kid's focus is on resetting the girl's spine, not his compass.

Thomas: Enough of this! Once a *schmuck* always a *schmuck*. If the kid doesn't want any of Ms. Wu, I'm gonna get myself some.

Frankfurter: Keep dreaming.

Thomas: You don't think I could?

Frankfurter: I doubt you remember how anymore.

Thomas: Don't insult my manhood, Frankie!

Frankfurter: Manhood? What does that mean, anyway?

Thomas: You want me to show you? Huh? I'll show you what it means!

Holmes: Gentlemen!

Bang, bang goes the gavel.

Holmes: Let us proceed in a civil manner, shall we? Good. Now, we all know that what lies behind us and what lies before us are small matters compared to what lies within. As this concerns Mr. Shackleton ...

Thomas: Shackleton's a lost cause! Now if you'll excuse me, I've got something that needs tending.

Frankfurter: Get your hands above the table, Tommy. If I don't see your hands out from under your robe in three seconds, I'm calling a mistrial. One ...

Thomas: Do what you want. I didn't ask to be here. For that matter, I don't know why I'm here. Nothing ever gets resolved with this character. Know why? Because he doesn't want resolution. Without difficulties, he'd be choked by boredom.

Holmes: Gentlemen, you have no option but to persist for union of a man's soul lays in the balance.

Thomas: Revoke it! Revoke his soul. Thirty-nine years later and he doesn't know what to do with it so what good is his soul? There, it's settled; the scales are rightly weighted.

Holmes: We are his appointed shepherds and, as such, we are obligated to deliberate on the task at hand.

Frankfurter: Let the record show that despite knowledge of an adult lifetime of honorable service to society evidenced by home ownership, responsible employment, dependable consumer behavior, paying taxes, more or less satisfactory commitment to monogamous relationships as befits a man, Mr. Shackleton concludes that his existence has been empty, perhaps meaningless, and questions any future value to be realized from continued existence.

Thomas: From what source, exactly, does this man derive his conclusions!? I've been sitting high up on this bench for twenty-one years listening to fools from all walks of life argue in their own self-interest. You think this is fun? You think I enjoy participating in selfish acrimony, bitterness, hostility and rancor wrapped in the stench and mock decorum of civil debate? But so what? What does it matter if I judge my life to be enjoyable or not?

Frankfurter: I submit that Mr. Shackleton is searching for fulfillment.

Thomas: Bah! Fulfillment he's had. His expectations are out of whack. Fulfillment comes and goes; he's got to stop whining and enjoy while it lasts. Are we done? We've had our say; let the clerks write up the judgment and let me take a run at Ms. Wu.

Frankfurter: Hold your horses, Caligula. The sight of you without that robe will be sure to take that girl's breath away, permanently. So, unless you warm to dead bodies, sit tight and shriveled.

Holmes: Let's stay on topic, shall we gentlemen? In response to your comments, Justice Thomas, I beg to disagree. Fulfillment may be a daily occurrence and, with effort, it may indeed last a lifetime. Certainly, fulfillment is a transitory state if, and I stress *if*, it be dependent on extraneous factors such as triumph or award. Those prone to such dependency surely remain forever moored to intrinsic thirst of desire; one who cannot slake desire, whatever that desire may be, remains ill at ease in the present moment believing that only future accomplishment ushers in peace and satisfaction. And though such beings may realize their aspirations, this realization fuels bottomless wanting of more. It is indeed a vicious cycle. Insatiable desire to fulfill the next goal lends ongoing strength to a grip of dissatisfaction which, in turn, blurs our need to live for today. For what is the future but a figment of dissatisfied imagination where one sidetracks to an underworld of dreams and fantasy, removed from the present and thus from reality. Sadly, one who is removed from reality suffers a futile search for fulfillment.

Thomas: Haven't I been saying exactly that all along? Will you look at that ass! How could that kid not want to plug her tank?

Frankfurter: Tommy, at your age, you should know by now that having is never as pleasing as wanting.

Ω

'Your move, Samuel.'
I know.
'Well then?'
Not sure.
'Harumph! The time is now. You've put this off long enough.'
Still.
'No. No more still. You're done with the still!
Well then, what should I do?
'Tap into your pineal gland.'
Why?
'That's where the seat of the soul resides.'
And?
'Once connected, your soul will guide you.'
Connected to what?
'To yourself, to life, and away from deceptive thoughts advocating false sensations of separateness. You do not stand apart. No one and no thing stands apart from life. This is not possible. For though you are an individual, it is only through the uniqueness of your relations to the physical world and all living beings that you may learn who you are and know what it means to live.'
Sigh. I don't understand.
'Understanding will come when you stop trying to outwit the forces of nature.'

That's it? That's the answer?

'Man, there are no answers. Only choices.'

Okay, let's say we do it your way. What am I supposed to do while waiting for my soul to come knocking?

'Continue doing what you're doing.'

What am I doing?

'Wandering.'

Where has wandering got me? All this questioning, this searching and I still don't know where to go, what to do or who to be. I'm looking for something, that much I know, but I haven't found what I'm looking for.

'Well, that's it, man! There is nothing to search *for* ... searching *is* the purpose.'

The End

CPSIA information can be obtained at www.ICGtesting.com
Printed in the USA
LVOW13s1747060913

351348LV00001B/6/P